T0208439

ETHEREAL

ETHEREAL

Al Price

Library of Congress Control Number:		2019918048
ISBN:	Hardcover	978-1-7960-7000-2
	Softcover	978-1-7960-6998-3
	eBook	978-1-7960-6999-0

This is a work of fiction. All of the characters, names, incidents, organizations, and dialogue in this novel are either the products of the author's imagination or are used fictitiously.

Scripture quotations marked NASB are taken from the New American Standard Bible®, Copyright © 1960, 1962, 1963, 1968, 1971, 1972, 1973, 1975, 1977, 1995 by The Lockman Foundation. Used by permission.

Scripture quotations marked NLT are taken from the Holy Bible, New Living Translation, copyright © 1996, 2004, 2007. Used by permission of Tyndale House Publishers, Inc. Carol Stream, Illinois 60188. All rights reserved. Website

Scripture quotations marked KJV are from the Holy Bible, King James Version (Authorized Version). First published in 1611. Quoted from the KJV Classic Reference Bible, Copyright © 1983 by The Zondervan Corporation.

Any people depicted in stock imagery provided by Getty Images are models, and such images are being used for illustrative purposes only.
Certain stock imagery © Getty Images.

Print information available on the last page.

Rev. date: 12/16/2019

To order additional copies of this book, contact:
Xlibris
1-888-795-4274
www.Xlibris.com
Orders@Xlibris.com
803240

DEDICATION

In honor of all college walk-on football
players who courageously pursued
their noble quest

Some things you must always be unable to bear. Some things you must never stop refusing to bear. Injustice and outrage and dishonor and shame. No matter how young you are . . . . just refuse to bear it.

—William Faulkner, *Intruder in the Dust*

ETHEREAL DEFINED

The quality of being able to place oneself on levels of invincibility and seeming to belong to another world created through poetic imagination with notions of justice and fairness.

CONTENTS

PROLOGUE

The University of Mississippi
AUGUST 1983

Head football coach Marvin Wortham walked into the athletic office at Ole Miss to see the three walk-on players who had been chosen for possible athletic scholarships. Coach Underwood, the quarterback coach, had notified two of the three to meet with the head coach at 11:00 a.m. Only two players were there, so Coach Wortham asked, "Where is Mistral?"

There was silence for a moment, and then one of the boys said, "Coach, he thought he was not going to be offered a scholarship. Coach Underwood looked everywhere for him and couldn't find him. I heard he went back to the dorm and started packing for home. He wouldn't talk to anyone, and he left."

Coach Wortham was furious to learn that Aeamon Lee had not received word of the meeting and asked, "Well, where the devil is he now?"

The player told him he guessed Aeamon Lee had gone to the Oxford bus station to go home the same way he had arrived. Coach rushed out to his car through the hot August sun and hurriedly drove to the bus station on Van Buren Avenue, arriving as the bus was about to pull away. As it started leaving the station, the bus abruptly stopped as Coach Wortham stood in the middle of the street. The bus door opened, and the coach walked in. Seeing Aeamon Lee, he beckoned Aeamon Lee to come with him. Coach explained that all Aeamon Lee's hard work, daring, and skills had earned him a spot on the roster. He would see if there was a scholarship lying around someplace if Aeamon Lee qualified. These two stalwarts of football athletics left the bus and walked toward the car to return to campus.

The emotion of the moment was overwhelming. Aeamon Lee had gone from the greatest disappointment in his life to the greatest opportunity, all in a matter of minutes. He couldn't say much at the moment, just "I won't disappoint you." All sorts of things were rushing through his mind. It took a while for the realization of what had just happened to sink in. As he put his suitcase in the coach's car, he couldn't help but gradually realize that he had made the team after all. He would have an opportunity to play football and, at the same time, get a university education.

As they drove back to campus, Aeamon Lee's mind carried him back to Goshen Wells, Mississippi, and some of the amazing events that led to this moment. The past several years had been such a tumultuous time in his life. But this was his time, his chance, and the events of the past few years flowed through his memories. The coach talked about what his plans were for the coming season, but Aeamon Lee's mind traveled back in time to put it all in perspective.

He couldn't help but think of those times when his life seemed to be at a dead end. Those times when he was fighting and brawling on Sorghum Hill and that beer joint in Louisiana just to stay alive. The night he had to jump into the Mississippi River to save Jo-Nathan, his best friend. The day he went to town to avenge the beating of his crippled father, or when he wandered the streets of Memphis trying to find ways to make some money to spend on his senior trip. Every desperate moment, every word of encouragement, and every word of doubt all passed through his mind at the same time he was contemplating what lay ahead.

CHAPTER 1

Walking on the Ethereal Plane
1978–1983

Martha Elizabeth and Pleadis Lee Mistral moved from a little community in Northwestern Louisiana called Union Mills to Goshen Wells in Scuna County, Mississippi, in 1969. They bought a farm of eighty acres called the Old Scott Place. Aeamon Lee, their son, was three years old at the time. The Mistrals were small-time farmers who planted mostly corn, soybeans, and some cotton. They had continued farming even though most small-scale farmers had given it up.

Plea, as what most people called him, had asked an acquaintance earlier if he knew any place for sale in Mississippi that offered more opportunity. One day, when a man was passing through Union Mills, he told the Mistrals about this farm that was for sale near the town of Leapwood, northeast of Jackson, Mississippi. In time, Plea was able to contact the owner and buy the place, paying the down payment with savings he had from the sale of his crops. He could pay off the balance on the entire farm in ten years. The bank in Leapwood would hold the note. And so began an unforgettable adventure into a new life in another place with their young son.

They came to Mississippi with very little. There were two houses on the place as well as a barn, some wooded areas, and fields for cultivation. The Mistrals notified an African American family back in Union Mills, the Markums, about the other available house. They could move there and help with the crops or do anything else they wanted. They had five children, and the Mistrals had developed a close friendship with them.

The Mistrals and the Markums both had relatives in Mississippi. The Markum's oldest son was Jo-Nathan. His mother—Mama Kate, as she was affectionately called—wanted to make sure nobody called him Jonathan, so she put the hyphen in so it would sound like two names, Jo-Nathan. The Markums had worked together with the Mistrals for years, and they were just like family. So the Markums decided to move into that second house on the Old Scott Place near Goshen Wells to live next to the Mistrals.

* * *

Martha Mistral named their only son Aeamon Lee (aim-mon). First, the Mistral name is French, common in Louisiana with its diverse ethnic history. Plea also claimed that his ancestors came from a town in the South of France. Martha thought her ancestral background was Scots-Irish, so she named him Aeamon. This was the way she wanted it spelled. The middle name Lee was common in the South, and since he was a son of the South, she thought it would be appropriate to give him this name. Putting all three names together gave it a personal and special meaning. Thus, he was Aeamon Lee Mistral, a child she always regarded as a special gift (ALM) to the world.

*   *   *

When Aeamon Lee started school, the Mistrals had a problem because the family never received a birth certificate for Aeamon Lee from Louisiana. Their request for one was denied because there was no formal record of his birth. They attempted to convince the Louisiana Vital Records Office that the midwife had failed to turn in the information and, subsequently, could not be located. This did not persuade the state to give the family a normal birth certificate. They issued a No Record of Birth certificate form that simply contained the family's stated claim—that Aeamon Lee Mistral was born on October 12, 1965, in Union Mills, Louisiana.

Actually, his birth had been a rather strange and unusual event. About one month before he was due, a lady wearing a long dark dress with a shawl and a scarf over her head walked up to their house. She appeared to be someone from a much earlier European century. She announced that she had been sent to care for Martha until her baby came and that she was a capable midwife. Martha and Plea didn't know what to make of this, but he agreed that she could help because of her obvious kindness and gentle spirit. She visited Martha every few days, never saying where she was from. They had the impression that she was from New Orleans, but they were not sure.

* * *

When the delivery date came, she brought two other women with her dressed in the same fashion. They appeared experienced in the process by preparing all necessary items and sent Plea to sit on the front porch. With great skill, they went about their duties in silence. The midwife told Martha that she knew a form of delivery that would ensure her baby would have great intelligence and strength. After the son was born, there was the usual admiration for such a beautiful baby by both Martha and Plea. Before leaving, and after she had given instructions to Martha, the midwife leaned over to whisper in Martha's ear. "There is something you must always treasure in your heart. Your son will have a special mission in life. I cannot tell you what it is. At the proper time, you may tell him about his need to find that mission." And with this said, the three women disappeared down the road from their house.

* * *

Aeamon Lee was a good son in most every way. Academically, he excelled but thought that sometimes his teachers stereotyped him because he didn't have what the other students had materially. Their low expectations affected the way they evaluated him. By working hard and helping his strong father, he learned respect and independence. Possessing a strong sense of what was right, any experience of injustice infuriated him. Aeamon Lee fiercely defended school friends who were bullied. This led to trouble at school and on the school bus because everyone involved got the same punishment.

By reading extensively, Aeamon Lee developed a remarkable ability to retain the material, especially subjects that students his age were not reading: literature, philosophy, religion, politics, and poetry. Growing older, he often quoted sayings, writings, or verses. Most of the time, others did not know what he meant, so he patiently explained the meaning of the quotation to those who asked. Every time he found a quotation that had special meaning to him, he wrote it down on a three-by-five index card. Over the years, he accumulated several stacks of these cards. He kept them close by, and in moments of free time, he would read them over and over, finally memorizing most of them. Much inspiration and insight about life and living were learned from these varied sources. To others, he sounded older and more mature than he was.

* * *

Aeamon Lee's father had always been an active and strong man, able to plant and harvest crops. The family had lived off of what he was able to make from his farming. Most of these farmers had disappeared. Plea had plans to give it up in time and take a public job. They were considered working class because they paid their bills and just got by financially. Each year was a new beginning for them, however. Their life was similar to that of sharecroppers under the system of peonage in the Old South. He had an old tractor and some plows, and he kept them all in good condition. His '68 Chevrolet pickup ran most of the time. These were their essentials in making a living.

Martha always worked at home and was an excellent seamstress. She also made some money herself by doing other people's ironing and some housecleaning. She even sold chickens and eggs from time to time.

The house they lived in was not the house Plea wanted. When they moved into it, Plea assured Martha that, one day, they would have enough saved up to make the repairs and remodel parts of the house. Martha never complained.

In some ways, Martha was always the primary emotional strength in the family. She had an optimism the family needed, a faith that was strong in the face of adversity, and she could cause people to feel better even in the worst of times. People told her that she was just like Melanie in the movie *Gone with the Wind*. When she and the others were out in the garden working on a hot day, a cool breeze occasionally came along and blew in their faces. Martha would say, "That is God's way of telling us that he sure is smiling on us today."

*   *   *

At age twelve, something tragic and spiritual happened to Aeamon Lee; it would be the first of several defining moments in his life.

Aeamon Lee's father, Plea, was sawing down a red oak tree to split for firewood, and the tree fell the wrong way. Before he could dodge it, the trunk of the tree hit him on his side and knocked him down, pinning him. Though there had been times when he had cut wood by himself, luckily Amos Markum, Jo-Nathan's father, was with him this time; but Amos couldn't move the tree off Plea. Amos ran to the house, yelling for help. He had a unique distress holler that was recognized. Aeamon Lee and Jo-Nathan ran toward the woods and found Plea. Aeamon Lee cranked the chainsaw and sawed the tree in two above where his father lay. The tree was still attached to the stump, and he and Jo-Nathan amazingly lifted the tree off enough so that Amos could pull Plea from under it. Plea was hurting bad as they carried him to the house. They hollered for a neighbor to come take him to the doctor. Neighbors always responded to other neighbors' calls for help when it was needed. Hollering was still an art form, especially where there were few telephones or cars.

The doctor in town x-rayed Plea and found that he had broken his hip. He would not be able to walk much or be able to do anything unless he had expensive hip surgery in which a pin could be inserted. Plea never did receive adequate treatment primarily because they had no medical insurance and not enough money to pay for medical services. Doctors didn't seem interested when they found out these things. Plea was a proud man who had always provided for himself and his family. Reluctantly, he submitted a disability claim because of his inability to walk without experiencing great pain. In five weeks, the denial of his claim came in the mail. Evidently, the doctors had not stated the magic words on the claim forms needed for him to draw his disability. Because of the doctor's stated belief that he could recover with proper treatment, Plea was denied again on his appeal.

In the meantime, Martha and Aeamon Lee spent much of their time taking care of Plea. It was extremely hard for him to get around by himself. Having this amount of attention and to be this helpless hurt Plea profoundly. He eventually developed a deep depression for which he received no treatment. He was given some anxiety pills, but they didn't help much. All they could hope for was that the hip would grow back eventually, and he could be well someday.

Late one evening, soon after Plea had his accident, after Aeamon Lee had gone to the side room where his bed was, he overheard Martha and Plea in the front room say something that frightened him to the bones.

"I don't know what we are going to do," Plea said to Martha. "Amos is not well, and they have their own things to do, and it's time to start plowing and getting the ground ready to plant."

"But, Plea, you can't do any of that."

"I know, and I've been trying to figure things out. I've thought about leasing out the land."

"But that wouldn't be enough for us to live on. We don't have that much to lease," Martha reminded.

Aeamon Lee had already started developing a strong mind and body. He had determination to do well against any odds. But this sound of hopelessness from his parents was overwhelming for a twelve-year-old to hear. Martha and Plea would not have said these things if they had known he was listening behind the door. There was heaviness in his chest and tears of fright in his eyes. It was hard for him to go to sleep that night, but one thing was for sure: he wouldn't let his mama and daddy go without. He also knew that if the crop that year was successful, the family could make the last payment on the farm to the bank. He mustered up all the strength and determination a kid his age could find to make it happen.

It was 5:00 a.m. the next morning, and the sound of the old tractor starting up woke Martha and Plea. Aeamon Lee had cranked it up after putting grease in all the right places on the tractor and the plows. He had made all the checks: the tires, the oil, the water, and the filter. He had driven the tractor before, but Plea was always with him and taught him the dangers.

Martha ran out of the house and stopped him as he was driving toward the field and told him they could not let him do that. He looked straight into his mother's eyes and said, "I've got to be about the business and work of my daddy. I know how to do it."

Martha pleaded, "We can't let you do it, son."

"Well, I'll tell you what. Put Daddy in a chair under the shade tree. After I've finished a row, he can motion me if I'm doing something wrong."

Martha just stood there for a while and didn't say anything, so he repeated his proposition. Finally, she turned around toward the house and said, "I'll talk to Plea about it."

When Aeamon Lee came back from plowing one row, Plea was sitting in a chair under the shade. He said, "Now remember, son, don't stand up while it is running. You could hit something, and it would throw you off."

When the Amos Markum children saw what Aeamon Lee was doing, three of the oldest came to help. They were Latoya, Kenya, and of course, Jo-Nathan, who was the same age as Aeamon Lee. Together they plowed, planted, and harvested a crop of corn and beans. They had a neighbor combine the beans and pick the corn.

The one glorious moment came when Martha went to the bank and made the final payment on the farm. Aeamon Lee insisted on going with Martha. He never took his eyes off the banker during the whole transaction. It appeared that the bank was surprised, given their knowledge of what had happened to Plea. Martha carefully received the deed and the receipt and thanked the banker for carrying the note for all those years. Of course, both Martha and Aeamon Lee knew that by paying off the bank, they did not have enough to make it through the winter and until the next fall. But that didn't seem to matter at the moment. When they gave the deed to Plea, he didn't say anything, just looked at it for a long time. No one knew how he really felt.

Their earnings that year were not quite as good as it had been after paying off the bills, the note at the bank, and the Markums for their help. But it was enough for most of the next year. And Martha began to bring in a little with her sewing and ironing for wealthier folks around in the community. There were mothers who wanted their young daughters to be in beauty pageants, and they got Martha make their evening gowns. Many families were buying more cotton clothes that had to be ironed. So every year after that, Aeamon Lee put out the crop, and the family made it fairly well financially each year.

It was around this time that the sheriff came driving up the road to the house one day. He got out of the car and stated he had something to say and wanted the Mistrals to get somebody from the Markum family to come up there. After Amos arrived, he said, "Well, I've noticed you all living here for several years. I just want to remind you that I don't want to hear of any trouble out here." Amos said "Yes, sir" frequently to everything the Sheriff said. Plea wasn't saying anything because he knew what this visit was all about. The sheriff gave him a book to read titled

Race and Reason by Carleton Putman. After he left, Aeamon Lee started reading the book and discovered that the author was trying to argue that black folks were biologically inferior to white people. With his adrenalin flowing freely, he took the book to the back of the barn and buried it.

* * *

Jo-Nathan and Aeamon Lee spent the early fall of that year sawing down red oak trees and splitting them into firewood. After getting enough for both families, Aeamon Lee loaded the old truck with kindling and split wood. Amos drove the truck, and Aeamon Lee sold firewood to the neighbors. He was thirteen-years-old now and felt proud that he was bringing in a little more money with his hard work, which the family desperately needed.

However, that first winter following Plea's accident was harder on the Mistral family than ever before. Even though they had been fortunate to even produce a crop, mainly by their thirteen-year-old son, they would have to do without a lot of things. Plea's medicine took much of their money, and projections indicated that the family would run short of funds before the longest and poorest winter of their lives ended. Sacrifices had to be made. Vegetables came from the usual amount of garden produce Martha had put up. Their meat, however, had to come from the smokehouse after hog killing. Other meat had to come from squirrels, rabbits, fish, and young chickens they had on the place. Aeamon Lee had already gotten plenty of experience hunting for food that could be eaten. He refused to eat possum, though, after finding three eating the inside of the carcass of a cow one time while he was squirrel hunting. Plea said that winter reminded him of some he had back in the late 1940s and early 1950s growing up in Louisiana.

The Mistral's real salvation that winter came from getting five gallons of sorghum molasses made at Odell Newsome's sorghum mill, which had been in operation for many years. In the early years, he was known throughout Scuna County for his skills at making moonshine and sorghum molasses. In fact, this was how Sorghum Hill got its name, because that was where the Newsomes and some of their kin lived and where they met every Saturday night to make music. He also ran a country store at the top of the hill across from his house.

For years, most of the neighbors grew cane sorghum so they could get it cooked, skimmed, and canned at his old mill. The Markum family always raised a lot of cane sorghum. That fall, they offered the Mistrals five gallons of theirs. Mr. Newsome said that Aeamon Lee could help earn the molasses by doing some of the work it took to get it all processed and put in gallon cans. All the neighbors participated in the whole affair by making sure all the families had enough. There was an elaborate division of labor based on skill and experience. Several people had tried to buy the old mill from Mr. Newsome because no more sorghum mills were being made.

The sorghum was usually planted in June, and the cane had to be harvested before the first frost. The seed heads and leaves had to be stripped before the cane could be cut. The cane was run through two or three cylinders arranged something like an old-fashioned clothes wringer. The needed power came from Mr. Newsome's old mule that pulled the attached shaft around the mill in constant motion. The filtered juice was poured into a large vat, which was placed on a burning pit. The pit was dug out of the ground, and fire was built in it to boil the sorghum juice. The juice was cooked over a low fire until the syrup was thick. It had to be stirred constantly with a long-handled paddle. Workers used a long stick to skim the hot juice as it began to boil to remove the impurities. At first the juice was bright green, but as it boiled, it darkened and turned brown. The aroma of gingerbread would drift through the breeze as the sorghum cooked. It took forty-nine gallons of juice to make seven gallons of molasses.

There were two important steps in making good sorghum: you needed someone good at skimming the boiling syrup, and you needed to know when to stop cooking. Only Mr. Newsome made that decision. After he made the decision that it had cooked enough, the molasses was poured in one-gallon tin cans.

All these steps usually took just about the whole day. It took a lot of workers once the process started. They swapped doing the various jobs. Aeamon Lee got to experience the whole process because he worked hard the whole day knowing that he would carry home five gallons of the molasses for their winter fest. The family could make out a meal with the molasses, or it could serve as a condiment to whatever else they had to eat.

Every year, the workers related the story of how one of Mr. Newsome's sons was nicknamed Sticky. It seemed that many years before, according to the embellished story, when they were getting ready to pour the molasses into the gallon cans, several boys got to scuffling, and one of them fell into the sticky molasses vat. He not only got scalded, but they said it took over a month for him to get all the sticky molasses off him. Some said he smelled like molasses for three months. Thus, he was forever called Sticky by everyone who knew him.

Aeamon Lee never knew all the ways sorghum molasses could be prepared as food. Martha made sorghum cookies, oatmeal drop cookies, spiced cookies, gingerbread cookies, sorghum pie, and molasses popcorn balls. The most common meal was to eat the molasses with hot biscuits and butter. Some people liked to stir the butter up with the molasses. When eating biscuits with molasses got old, cornbread could be substituted.

* * *

Plea, it seemed, had lost almost all interest in things he formerly enjoyed, even his appetite. An overwhelming sense of helplessness and hopelessness seemed to dominate his outlook. Plea often sat on the porch or out under the shade tree and just stared out into space. He was no longer the man he once was, and although everyone reassured him, it didn't seem to help. They had tried to interest him in little sitting activities and games that would occupy his mind, but he found no pleasure in any of them. But Aeamon Lee was determined he would find something to make his daddy happy again.

There were times when Aeamon Lee went off into the woods by himself to think about his family and what had happened to them. Would they get through the winter with less than they had before? Would his dad ever get any better? How was he doing being the man of the family now? What would be his future? He fantasized as one being successful enough that he could build his parents a new house, get Plea the medical treatment he needed, and make their life more comfortable. These were things needed now, but there didn't seem to be a way. He cried at times, but no one ever knew of his fright, not even Jo-Nathan. He learned that anger could be a source of strength to help him work more diligently on the hardships that fate had brought him.

* * *

One day, when Aeamon Lee was fifteen, he went by a flea market in town. The marketers were thinking about making it bigger by having a monthly trade day like a lot of other places across the South. These trade days began in 1869, after the Civil War, when there was little paper money with which to use in buying needed items. The first one was in Scottsboro, Alabama. So the system of bartering developed where people brought these things, including animals, to town, usually on the first Monday of the month, and traded with others for things they needed. Nowadays, there are many First Mondays across the South.

Aeamon Lee was looking at all the displays and booths while walking through the crowd. One booth caught his attention. He went over to it, and there were several men sitting behind the tables, talking. They were selling wood-carving sets, and they had on display some of their work. There were carved animals, canes, objects, scenery, and bowls. They had all been carved by hand. They had carving sets for woodworking, wood burning, wood painting, and gourd carving. Aeamon Lee thought that maybe his daddy needed this to bring him out of his depression and despair. He had seen him use his pocketknife many times whittling on sticks.

He found one complete set of long-handled wood-carving instruments that included a straight chisel, skew chisel, wide round gouge, narrow round gouge, and a V-chisel. They even had pattern books to go along with the carving sets. He picked out the set and a pattern book by L. S. Irish and asked for their lowest price. They quoted some price that sounded too high, so he told them the story of his father and how he needed this wood-carving set. They offered the whole set and pattern book to him for thirty dollars. He asked them to set it aside because he would be back later for it. When they wanted to know why, he told them he had to go and make thirty dollars someplace!

Aeamon Lee found the man in charge of the entire flea market, and he asked him what he could do to make thirty dollars. He was willing do anything that needed to be done. The man finally agreed to let Aeamon Lee help patrons park their cars out in a field, pick up garbage, help load and unload items for sale, and keep the booths for people for short breaks. Finally, after three and a half hours of work, he had the thirty dollars, including tips. He went back and got his carving set to take home. But first, the men showed him how each knife worked and why it was needed for certain cuts.

Aeamon Lee often did this type of work to buy things the family needed. He just worked it off some way. Swapping work was not beneath his dignity. He found that there were a lot of people who needed workers for small jobs around a business or at their homes, and much money could be made operating this way. It seemed there were always people looking for someone to help them do odd jobs. And he wasn't ashamed to ask them for work to do.

He proudly presented the wood-carving set to his father at home after supper and carefully explained to him what the men had taught him about each knife. He told him he would get him some wood, any kind needed to use for carving. He reassured his father that he could do some creative things with this carving set. Plea listened, smiled, thanked him, and laid it aside.

Aeamon Lee said, "I'm going to go ahead and gather up some wood and put it on the porch. I'll get some pine, cedar, poplar, and some walnut. I've seen some things carved out of walnut, and it really makes some pretty pieces. And if you need anything else, just let me know."

In the three years to follow, Aeamon Lee noticed the carving set on a shelf in the front room, unused.

*   *   *

The Markums had family scattered throughout the country, and often relatives came in from St. Louis, Gary, and Chicago. Aeamon Lee enjoyed seeing their Uncle Jerome from Chicago more than the others because he spent time with him and Jo-Nathan. He told them about going to see the White Sox play baseball and how people in the stands made bets on the next pitch or the next play, or what the batter or pitcher would do.

What interested Aeamon Lee the most was Uncle Jerome's stories about his poker games, played sometimes on the streets or sometimes in the back rooms of clubs. He had experienced several fights and told how dangerous it was to play poker using real money. Uncle Jerome always carried a deck of cards with him, so Aeamon Lee talked his uncle into showing him how to play poker and how to win. Uncle Jerome said most people in the South played five-card draw and Black Jack. He taught him how to win at both games.

It was amazing how much Uncle Jerome knew about poker, and it impressed Aeamon Lee to discover all the different ways one could cheat. Uncle Jerome taught him how one could mark the cards in various ways. Cards having a recognizable mark on them would come in handy later on in the game. Using a sharp part of his thumbnail, for example, made it easy for him to mark the corner of a card. He would mark sevens, eights, and nines a certain way; and high cards had another marking at a different spot. Uncle Jerome taught him how to palm a card a different way than how it was usually done and how to use a partner. A player may have daubed the card with some substance in his hair. This person was known as a dauber. The player did this by rubbing his hair as if he was thinking and putting the substance on the card, thus marking it. However, the substance could only be seen with special glasses worn by the partner. The partner signaled the player what the next card would be by spotting the mark. These special glasses magnified things three and a half feet away. For example, if it was a high card, the partner played with high chips, or high dollars; and if it was a low card, he played with low chips, or change. If the partner didn't know what the next card would be, he crossed his fingers together.

After several visits to Goshen Wells from Chicago, Uncle Jerome had taught Aeamon Lee everything he knew. With this knowledge, coupled with his remarkable intuitive accuracy, Aeamon Lee became unbeatable at poker. He and Jo-Nathan played a lot when no one else was around. This knowledge and skill would pay off for him later in life.

*   *   *

When Aeamon Lee was a freshman in high school, he thought that maybe he could make the football team, or at least he would go out and see what he could do. He had never played sports at school because of time constraints and living a long way from school. In the first meetings, he discovered that the school provided every part of the uniforms except the shoes, which he couldn't buy. The first day he wore his tennis shoes, and the coaches told him he would have to go to Jackson and get some shoes. He knew that was pretty much out of the question but thought he was doing well. He could outrun the other players in the sprints.

While getting undressed in the locker room after the third day of practice, he noticed a pair of football shoes under a bench. He asked the football manager about them and was told they had been there for a long time, and they didn't know who they belonged to—probably nobody. So Aeamon Lee picked them up when no one was looking and tried them on. They fitted well enough. He put them with his things and, the next day, wore them to practice. He was showing some promise as a running back and was even pushing for some playing time in his freshman year, at least on the special teams.

The other team members had played together for several years and were not too cordial to Aeamon Lee. Also, they knew that he had never played before at the school. In fact, one of them heard about the shoes and went to the coach and accused Aeamon Lee of stealing the shoes. When asked about it, Aeamon Lee told the truth about the old pair of football shoes and how no one was using them.

The coach said, "Nevertheless, you should have come and talked with me about it instead of just taking them. I can't tolerate stealing on my team. You can come back next year when you have bought your own pair of football shoes."

Aeamon Lee had mixed emotions about this turn of events and didn't feel badly about taking the shoes because he knew they were not going to be used. He did feel badly about not getting the chance to play football because he felt like he could have played well. Aeamon Lee didn't try again to make the team mainly because it appeared to him that it was a closed society and he wasn't welcome. This exclusive club didn't want a nobody like Acamon Lee Mistral to come in and share the glory of this glamorous sport.

These jocks ruled campus life and had all the girlfriends. They sometimes bullied other students. After Aeamon Lee broke up a fight between a jock and a new boy at school, he and the jocks were at cross-purposes with each other for the rest of the time he was in school. He rationalized his nonparticipation as not wanting to play on a team with such idiots and of having more important things to do. He consciously chose not to compete and win.

* * *

When he was almost sixteen, Aeamon Lee overheard some men talking about how, years ago, houses were sometimes built with nothing more than a chain saw. His daddy had a pretty good old chain saw. His vocational class at school taught students how to build a foundation, frame a house, and do some finish work. He made a list of all the building materials needed to build a better house for Martha and Plea. He had known for a long time that their house was not repairable.

Aeamon Lee didn't tell anyone his plans. He found a spot not far from their present house, measured it off, and drew the dimensions of the house showing where the rooms would be located. It would be similar to the present house: a straight-lined roof with a porch all the way across the front. It would be bigger, and there certainly would be a better floor—the old house had only bare planks that let in the cold air in the wintertime.

Down along a spring branch, there were many tall pine trees, and he thought he could saw them down, pull them to the road with the tractor so that someone from the sawmill could pick them up. He knew he could get the two-bys, studs, and even some one-bys from these logs to be used for the subfloor.

Aeamon Lee decided that he could get this house built. He needed at least one more person to help him. He told Jo-Nathan about what he was doing first, and Jo-Nathan would help him if they could get the materials. They would start when the crops were laid by.

Aeamon Lee had talked with the men who owned the lumber shed and the concrete company. They told him of some work he could do for them in exchange for building materials. He knew some old builders that had just about retired and could learn enough from them about plumbing and electrical wiring.

For example, he found a pile of concrete blocks that had a bad side to them. The concrete company told him that they all had a good side, which meant you could put the bad side inside of the house's foundation, and it wouldn't show. He would also have to work at the sawmill in order to get his pines sawed into rough lumber.

By this time, Aeamon Lee was big for his age, strong, and with a dark complexion. He was already six feet and one inch tall and weighed around 190 pounds and still growing. His size helped him with the heavy building materials necessary for his task.

So Aeamon Lee started his building, working all day and into the night. It took him all summer to get the pine trees sawed and cut into lumber and delivered back to the house. When school started, he worked from late afternoon until around 11:00 p.m. to midnight. There were times when he went to sleep at school, and his teachers noticed that he appeared to be extremely tired. He slept every chance he got at school and on the school bus.

He laid the concrete blocks on a foundation of concrete while making sure that everything was square. Once this was done, the framing went up in a hurry. Then things began to slow down. Luckily, the sawmill had given him pretty true cuts. He'd rather have bought studs for the walls to ensure that they were level and straight, but he just couldn't get it all done, having to work at the concrete company and at the lumberyard to be able to pay for the materials. By late autumn, shingles were on the roof, which was quite a relief because this would protect the rest of the house from the rain now that it was in the dry.

As the house took shape, he could see the end of a long project. It would take him twice as long to build the house since he had to work sometimes all day on Saturdays at the lumber shed. He worked all day on the house on Sundays, which Martha didn't like him doing. The hardest part of the house to complete was the fireplace. Brick seconds from a brick company near Jackson had to be hauled in to get it built. At times he had money to buy some of the materials, but most of the time, he had to work off the debt. This meant it would take double the time.

What Aeamon Lee was doing for his parents began to spread throughout the community. They knew about Plea and his disability and how the family was just getting by on the small crops he was producing. So people came by and offered to help with some of the carpentry work or to donate some materials. Most of the people just marveled at how a young man would do that for his parents, especially someone at his age. And they talked about how unfortunate it was for the family, for the father to be in the shape he was in. Their sentiment was to go and be warmed and be filled.[1] He didn't talk a lot about what he was doing, even though a lot of people came up to him to ask about it.

He decided to put some twelve-inch Masonite siding on the house. It was not hard to put up and nail against the studs. By this time, a neighbor had loaned him a power saw, though the blade was dull. Finishing the inside of the house would take him the longest period of time.

He was busy continuously until April of the next year when he had completed enough of the house that the family could move in. One of Aeamon Lee's proudest additions to the house was an outside ramp his daddy could use in getting in and out of the house easier. He wanted badly to be able to get his mother some new appliances and furniture, but it would have to wait to another day. When he had finished enough of the house for the family to move into, it was time to start plowing again.

*　　*　　*

It was October 1982, on a Saturday night, and there was the usual crowd at Odell Newsome's Store on Sorghum Hill. Actually, the crowd was gathered in the old school building, which had been converted into a large gathering place. The inside walls had been removed, and a stage was built at the back. It had been a community schoolhouse for African American children for many years until the school was consolidated with the one in town. The building was fairly sturdy because when it was built, it was intended to be adequate for school activities for many years. This prevented complaints that might have increased the demands for racial integration in those early days. The county had abandoned it knowing that it had become a community-gathering place for various events. There had been revivals, church fellowships, family reunions, fish fries, the showing of some old black-and-white movies Mr. Newsome had gotten from time to time, and meetings to discuss community affairs.

Mr. Newsome had a large family and several other kin living on Sorghum Hill. Being a religious fellow, he didn't allow "drinking, drugging, or stealing." This had not always been the case. In his early days, he sold moonshine, which was common knowledge. His regular customers would drive up, and he would get it out of sinkholes around the place. On Monday mornings, the county sheriff's wife would drive up to collect their share. This went on for years, but now all had changed since Mr. Newsome had gotten religion and also because some of his whiskey had gotten bad. Some people called it rotgut whiskey. A fellow nearly died from drinking it. He often said, "That scared the devil out of me, literally."

On Saturday nights, the musicians in the community gathered to make music. The crowd would socialize, jive, listen to the music, or dance a little. People of all ages came to enjoy the entertainment. The smaller children stayed in the houses until they got tired and went to sleep. Sorghum Hill was located about two miles from Aeamon Lee's house and about a mile off the main road. It was fairly well isolated, and many people didn't even know about the place.

People throughout that area looked forward to going to Sorghum Hill on Saturday nights. It was an escape that helped them get through a week of hard work and troubles. It was like being in another world, a world filled with fellowship, laughter, and music. Often, Aeamon Lee quoted the line "Music hath charms to soothe the savage breast, to soften rocks, or bend the knotted oak."[2] This kind of atmosphere allowed people to be themselves with a happier, softer, gentler touch.

Even though Mr. Newsome had a rule about drinking, there probably were some going on outside, away from the crowds and usually in cars. They had to be careful not to make any trouble however.

There was always a bigger crowd when Willie Rivers and the Willie Rivers Band came to play. They got their pay from a collection basket that was passed around at the dance. Possessing a pretty good mix of instruments, they played traditional rhythm and blues along with some more current music. In fact, their repertoire of songs was quite large. They came from around Huntersville where they played throughout middle Mississippi and some in the Delta, where the blues was so popular.

Mr. Newsome's store included a drink machine and a refrigerator. Workhands in the fields walked miles in the summertime to get something cold to drink there. Mr. Newsome would always make a bologna or ham sandwich for workers nearby who came to eat a bite for dinner. A favorite item was his Payday candy bars that he kept in the refrigerator, which made them taste a lot better. He sold a little gas and groceries also, making Sorghum Hill a social gathering place for local African Americans.

Occasionally, some white people stopped by during the week, maybe some hungry hunters from time to time. Aeamon Lee, now age seventeen, was known by all the black people in the area and who liked for him to sing and play with the band. They said he had soul, but more than that, he was trusted and respected. Some white people nearby had suspicions about the Mistral family. The Mistrals were closer to the Markum family than to some white families. This was considered curious among some people.

On that Saturday night, Aeamon Lee was singing "Midnight Special," which was a crowd favorite:

> Let the midnight special,
> Shine the light on me.[3]

His favorite artists were Jim Croce, Creedence Clearwater Revival, and Little Richard. Occasionally, he included a message song or two that he liked.

> Go ahead and hate your neighbor
> Go ahead and cheat a friend[4]

The song was nearly over when the crowd got quiet because Caster Nuckolls and two of his brothers, along with two friends, had walked up. He had a reputation for causing trouble and dealing in drugs. Castor had spent some time in Parchman Penitentiary. Now he was out doing the same thing, but this time, he was more careful. It was just this type of people that ole man Newsome wanted to keep away from Sorghum Hill.

The band stopped playing, and Caster stood in the middle of the floor and said, "Now don't stop the music because of us. We're here to have a little fun ourselves. We don't mean no harm to nobody. We just want to come over from time to time and enjoy the evening with the rest of you fine folks." His brothers were checking out the young females standing around. "I have lots of friends who would like to come with me, and the next time Mr. Willie Rivers is going to play, we'll come back. He is absolutely the best, and we'll all have us a fine party."

Mr. Newsome's blood pressure got all worked up and finally said out loud, "You're not welcome here. We don't want you to come back. Stay away. We know what you're up to."

This made Caster real mad; and he pointed his finger at Mr. Newsome, smiled, and said, "Now, you listen here. This is a public place, and we'll come if we want to, and you or nobody else can't stop us. So in two weeks, we'll be back, and believe me, we'll all get down and have a good time." He then left with his brothers, and they drove off in their late-model car.

The rest of the evening was rather subdued, and the music-making stopped early. The men were talking among themselves as the women gathered up all the children to get ready to go home. Aeamon Lee went up to the men and assured them that everything would be fine two weeks from that night when Willie Rivers and the Willie Rivers Band would be back. He told them he would get some of the boys together and decide on something to do. His first thought was to get a man he had heard about who would burn a house or barn down for fifty dollars. Only very few people knew about this man, and no one ever talked about him. But the better angels of his nature[5] would not allow him to burn down Caster's house.

Aeamon Lee picked out some brave and strong friends—Early Edwards, Spunky Walls, Terrence Taylor, Jerrell Jenkins, Jo-Nathan Markum, and Maleah Marcelles. Maleah stated that her sister and brother would help out if they were needed. Together that night, the fearless defenders of right developed a plan of action to take should Caster Nuckolls and his friends return. Caster always had brothers and friends to stand with him or nearby when he went anyplace. They expected him to do the same thing when he returned.

After two weeks, Willie Rivers and the Willie Rivers Band returned to play. Aeamon Lee was present, playing and singing with the band. The food was almost gone, and the smaller kids had all gone to sleep in the surrounding houses.

Things were winding down when Caster Nuckolls and his friends drove up. They got out, but one stayed in the car, one stayed outside the car, and one stayed at the door while one went inside with Caster. Aeamon Lee slipped out the back door and came around to the front, and they started with the guy standing by the car. Spunky, Early, and Aeamon Lee took him down, put duct tape over his mouth, tied him up with ropes, and threw him onto the back bed of a truck. The one in the car heard the commotion although the music had gotten louder as planned, while Caster was "welcomed" inside. Terrence and Jerrell knocked him over the head with a plank, and while he was trying to regain consciousness, he was tied up and thrown in the truck also. They got the attention of the one at the door, and before he knew anything, he was wrestled to the ground. He was also tied up and thrown into the truck.

Maleah Marcelles was a neighbor of the Markums and Mistrals and was often referred to as a woman who was a tower of strength. Her parents had died some years before; and because her sister, Marleece, was about ten years older than she was, she and her brother, Landon, were allowed to continue to live on their own. They had inherited their parents' place and their resources, which meant they enjoyed a more comfortable life than most of their neighbors. She was part of the community in Goshen Wells who loved the music and the friendship on Sorghum Hill. She was an attractive young woman with olive complexion and long, silky hair.

She volunteered to entertain Caster while the others were outside, keeping him distracted. With his attention now directed toward Maleah, Caster forgot about the boys that had come with him. His brother was called outside and ambushed like the others. Now there was a large stack of bodies in the back of the truck all tied up. Some of the other men came over to the truck to make sure these fellows stayed tied up.

The question arose, Who was going to go in to get Caster? Aeamon Lee wouldn't let anybody else even think about doing it. He would do it himself. You see, he had this thing about fighting, brawling, and winning. He was good at it! He'd had several fights before, and when he sensed he was fighting over some kind of injustice, he was unstoppable and unbeatable. It didn't make any difference what the situation was or how many people he had to subdue; he prevailed one way or another.

He went inside, went up to Caster, who had been carrying on with Maleah, and said to him, "I think it's time for you to learn a lesson."

Caster turned Maleah loose and said, "What lesson are you talking about?"

"That no slimeball devil like yourself is going to disrupt our music and fun."

"And no smart-aleck white boy is going to tell me what to do!"

Aeamon Lee grabbed Caster by the shirt and threw him into a stack of chairs in the corner. Caster got up, breathing hard, and looked around for his friends. "Where's my brother?"

"I'm afraid he's all tied up and can't come in right now," Aeamon Lee said.

"That don't matter, I'll teach you a lesson," Caster responded.

He drew out a switchblade, opened it up, and started toward Aeamon Lee. Witnesses told Aeamon Lee to look out. He knew he had to keep his eyes on the knife and be quick to grab Caster's arm. He moved to the middle of the floor where Caster lunged toward him with the knife. Aeamon Lee grabbed the arm with both hands and thrust it down on his raised thigh, breaking Caster's arm. At the same time, Maleah Marcelles took the chair leg she had picked up and used it to knock the knife out of Caster's hand. Now the two fighters started punching, and Caster was definitely at a disadvantage with only one arm worth using. Aeamon Lee's long arms, big hands and agility were definitely in his favor because Caster was overweight and out of shape. Besides, he usually let his entourage do his dirty work, but they were all tied up at the time.

Aeamon Lee hollered for all the others to go outside. Maleah Marcelles, with chair leg in hand, said she was staying. The other women, the young children, and most of the men did leave. Aeamon Lee beat Caster up pretty bad, including busting his head open against the walls. Finally, when it was obvious that Caster had no more fight in him, Jo-Nathan reminded Aeamon Lee it was time to stop. Spunky, Terrence, Jerrell, Early, and Maleah tied Caster up, dragged him outside, and threw him into the truck also.

About five miles away was a holiday gathering place called Legion's Lake, which was built by the Civilian Conservation Corps (CCC) boys. It had several gathering halls and cabins there, and at the bottom of the hill was a fairly large lake with a levee running out across the middle. The boys got the keys to Caster's car and drove it down to Legion's Lake, following the truck full of tied-up bullies. They drove Caster's fine car into the water, and the boys threw the gang of bodies one by one into the water where it was not deep enough for them to drown. Caster and his gang were told to never return to Sorghum Hill. Aeamon Lee and his fighting buddies drove back to Sorghum Hill, leaving Caster and his buddies to get out the best way they could.

Ole man Newsome told the boys he would call the sheriff to report that Caster Nuckolls had tried to disrupt their dance. He would ask the sheriff to tell them not to come back. Mr. Newsome would not press any charges against them. The whole community respected Mr. Newsome, and the law knew the history of Caster Nuckolls. They were more than willing to oblige Mr. Newsome. He and the boys knew that Caster wasn't about to tell the sheriff what had actually happened to them.

* * *

It was after midnight by now, and Jo-Nathan and Aeamon Lee caught a ride home. Looking closer, Jo-Nathan noticed that his friend kept holding his arm below the elbow. Aeamon Lee knew that Caster's knife had cut him on the arm, but it was not serious, just bleeding a lot. "I'm not worried about the cut. I just don't know how I will explain this to Mama." They took a clean rag and wrapped the wound up. The houses were about two hundred yards from the road and were only about fifty yards from each other, with Aeamon Lee's being the middle house. The old house was now used for storage.

Walking in the darkness toward the house, these two seventeen-year-olds talked a little about the bigger picture of their lives. They were in their senior year at Leapwood High School. In fact, both of them had talked about their future a lot lately since everybody else at school, it seemed, had started making their plans. They had to keep in mind that neither family had any extra money. All they did was just get by.

Out of the blue, Jo-Nathan said, "I want to ask you something. For the longest time, I've noticed that when you are faced with threats and competition, you always seem to come out on top. You don't live, act, or talk like the other kids in school, and it doesn't bother you. Like tonight, there was no way Caster Nuckolls was going to get the best of you. How do you do it? What is the reason?"

Aeamon Lee paused for a while and then said, "Jo-Nathan, remember this: 'If a man does not keep pace with his companions, perhaps it is because he hears a different drummer.'[6] For me, there are times when I live life on the ethereal plane."

Jo-Nathan replied, "Whoa, wait a minute. Don't throw those big words out at me like that. We've known each other for most of our lives. Make it plain and simple."

Aeamon Lee explained, "There are all these levels or spheres above the earth, like the atmosphere, troposphere, stratosphere, and mesosphere. The ethereal plane is above all the other realms. It is opposite of anything earthly. It is almost like it is something heavenly. So the way I see it, no matter what it is that you are facing, there is a level above it that can help you overcome it. When you live your life on the ethereal plane, there is always a way to succeed or win. You put yourself on this higher plane, and then it becomes easy to find a way to get over it or through it till you win. I don't accept many human limitations. These are not options. It doesn't mean that there are no consequences to your actions and decisions when the devils of the world try to cross you. I got hurt tonight, but there is always an angel to take care of you, like Mama."

Jo-Nathan said, "I think I understand. I sure wish I had it, whatever it is that you just described. So you never even thought about losing that fight with Caster Nuckolls?"

"You got it right. There are some Bible stories where people lived on the ethereal plane. My favorite is about David and the Philistine giant, Goliath. Back then, when war was about to break out between nations, two of their soldiers would duel first in a fight to the death. This battle set the tone for the entire war. When David volunteered after no one else would, the people said, 'You're just a boy, and he has been a warrior all his life.' But David had some credentials. He told them about killing a bear and a lion, and he didn't see any difference. David refused all their heavy armament and only took his slingshot, a peasant's weapon. Goliath looked no doubt like a Sherman tank. Just his armament weighed 125 pounds, and he laughed, 'Am I a dog, that you come to me with sticks?' When Goliath looked into David's eyes, he couldn't move. And David felled that fearsome giant with a single stone.[7] On that day, he lived on the ethereal plane. That was sort of how I faced Caster Nuckolls."

Aeamon Lee continued, "I don't know why preachers don't talk much about Jesus running those moneychangers out of the Temple court. The scribes and Pharisees were selling animals for sacrifices to the poor people who couldn't bring them from their homelands. They were being exploited because of greed and fraud. That Temple tax had to be paid with a Phoenician silver half shekel. So they had to exchange their Greek and Roman money for this. The moneychangers collected about fifteen percent for this transaction. It was a dirty business. Jesus physically drove them out because of their injustice. I would like to have helped him turn those four-legged tables and chairs over and drive those crooks out with that whip.[8]

You know, I wonder if he didn't do a lot of this when he was seventeen years old. Preachers talk too much about themes of weakness and not enough about taking on those who exploit and defraud others for profit. This description of Jesus in the Bible doesn't fit their image of a gentle Jesus, meek and mild.

"I also like Elijah the prophet and John the Baptist. Man, they stood their ground. They were their own men and couldn't be bought off."

Jo-Nathan said, "I have one more question. For years I've wanted to ask you about this. I want to know what that is in the palm of your hand. I can't read it, and I know it says something." Finding some light, Aeamon Lee showed it to Jo-Nathan, who got down really close to his hand. The writing was "Rev. 14:14."[9] "That's the last book in the Bible, isn't it? I'm going to look that up."

Aeamon Lee explained, "A long time ago, they would put an image in the palm of your hand to identify you. It's sort of like a tattoo."[10]

Aeamon Lee told his mother that he had an accident and got this cut. She cleaned it and pressed the flesh together with some tape. She fixed it so that he could have the wrapping off most of the time to enhance the healing. It quickly healed but left a scar on his arm, a scar among several he had already accumulated. He never told his mama and daddy what really happened at Sorghum Hill.

*   *   *

In those growing up years, from age twelve to seventeen, Aeamon Lee had to become a man too early in life. He didn't get to hang out with the other kids his age much, didn't date the girls much, and couldn't go to many of the community and school activities. Most girls thought he was uncultured only because he just didn't have much money. Besides that, his family was not numbered among the somebodies in the community, so it was not socially popular to be seen with Aeamon Lee Mistral. "He stole football shoes and likes to fight," people said.

There were times when the classes selected representatives for Boys State, class officers, or class royalty. He was never nominated, but with his level of self-assuredness, he shared his interest and asked why he never was considered. He never got straight answers. Another kid pulled him aside and explained, "I've heard that you've got to be somebody before you can be chosen. They call it pedigree, credentials, and stuff like that." Soon, Aeamon Lee realized that it was not based on inherent worth but rather on inherited status and wealth.

He was a quick learner, however, and he never had academic problems other than the fact that some of his teachers just couldn't accept that someone with his background and living circumstances could be as smart as he was. He was a victim of stereotyping and suspicion. People thought he was older than he was. But underneath the exterior was the deep sense of longing for a mission in life. Often, there was disappointment, but he always remembered to live above these earthly spheres, and at times, he had to live on the ethereal plane. One day, he would leave Goshen Wells to make his life and find his opportunities. He often wondered what he would find and where his hopes would lead him.

It seems that when the life story of most kids is told, there is one teacher that has believed in them and has encouraged them to do well in life. For Aeamon Lee, one such teacher was Ms. Babe Markle (no one called her Babe), who saw potential in him. She talked with him about his plans and his other studies now that he was a senior. She reminded him of all the various ways a student could get a college degree. She didn't want him stuck in a place of few life chances like Goshen Wells. He never forgot that teacher and the inspiration she was to him.

* * *

It wasn't long after the Sorghum Hill fight that another incident occurred that increased Aeamon Lee's reputation of being a hot-tempered kid who wouldn't allow what he saw as injustice.

Across the hill from where they lived, there had been a vacant house that was now rented by a Hispanic family named Ramirez. Hosea and Rita were the parents, and Alex and Joel were their two boys, ages fourteen and eleven. Hosea helped work on a natural gas pipeline going through this area of the state. They had moved a lot in recent years and were reluctant to get acquainted with neighbors. People around Goshen Wells referred to them as dagos, and in the South, this usually referred to anybody with darker skin but was not black. Dagos supposedly were to be avoided because they "had no morals."

The Mistral's found them to be a close-knit family who wished no harm to anyone. They worked hard and enrolled their two boys in the local school. Because they looked different—or peculiar, as locals said—they were generally avoided. The two sons became the object of bullying by some kids in town. Bogus Swisher's two boys and some of their friends beat on the Ramirez kids every time they saw them. The Ramirez family admitted their concerns about this behavior to the Mistrals because the sons had gotten to the point where they did not want to go to school.

One day, the Swisher boys wanted to engage in some mischief, so they decided to go out to the Ramirez house to beat up the boys. Their excuse was that they thought the two boys had not shown them enough respect at school. They were driving Bogus Swisher's new truck and wanted some excitement. They drove in front of the Ramirez's house where they found the two boys. They started pushing, hitting, and yelling at them. The mother, Rita, told the Swisher boys to leave them alone, but the boys kept on anyway. Rita then ran out the back door and hollered across the bottom for help.

It happened that Aeamon Lee and Jo-Nathan had gone to the woods to try to determine the severity of the approaching winter. While exploring these signs, they heard Rita. Aeamon Lee ran across the field as fast as he could. He figured out what was happening when he saw the truck. This was the behavior that infuriated him.

He ran directly to the brand-new truck, cranked it up, and drove it down the hill, off into a spring branch that ran across the road and down through the bottom. He threw the keys as far away as he could. He then ran up to the house after the Swisher boys, Kyle and Bradley, who, by this time, had seen Aeamon Lee and had quit beating on the boys. They yelled at him that their daddy would get him for taking his truck. He didn't listen to any talk. He was in no mood for talk. These boys were also seventeen, and he didn't mind roughing them up. It was time to teach them some needed lessons. He didn't beat them up with his fists as much as he rubbed their faces in chicken manure. He threw them to the ground several times inside the chicken fence where there were mud piles.

Aeamon Lee's aim was to teach them a lesson to the point that they never would come back out there. After tearing off their shirts and getting them filthy, he made each one apologize to the boys and to Rita.

He made them repeat after him everything he could think of that made them appear sorry and weak. "I am sorry . . . because I don't like people like you . . . but really you are people too . . . people loved by God [this was the hardest thing for them to say] . . . and do not deserve . . . to have smart alecks and bullies like us bothering you . . . We are cowards . . . and we will not retaliate or harm these boys or this family ever again at any place." These words were all things that embarrassed them and hard for them to say. He then sent them walking back toward town.

Aeamon Lee set up a system whereby Rita or Hosea could get in touch with the Mistrals should these boys ever come back to their home. Alex and Joel were to report to him if the Swisher boys ever attempted to hurt them at school. Rita and Hosea regretted having to call for Aeamon Lee's help. They said, "You are so young that it is unfair to ask or expect you to help us with this problem."

Aeamon Lee simply replied, "'Some things you must always be unable to bear. Some things you must never stop refusing to bear. Injustice and outrage and dishonor and shame. No matter how young you are.'"[11]

Joel Ramirez was special to Aeamon Lee because he was always so expressive of his gratefulness. A few months earlier, he had gotten deathly ill. He had a high fever, and the family didn't know what to do. They didn't want to take him to see the doctor in town if they could prevent it. They called the Mistrals over to help them. They washed his face and body with cold cloths. Aeamon Lee could feel so much energy inside himself, and he faced all problems with determination of fixing them somehow. He asked everyone in the room to leave. He took his big hands and, starting at the top of Joel's head, gripped and rubbed his hands all over Joel's weak body all the way to his toes. He called the family in and asked them to continue washing Joel's body with the wet cloths.

Joel broke out in sweat that dampened all the bed linens. He rose up in bed and told his mother that he was thirsty and hungry. His fever had broken, and soon his strength returned.

The Ramirez family was so grateful and amazed at Aeamon Lee's courage and willingness to protect them that they gave Aeamon Lee a nickname, Santo Tomas. They always referred to him with this Spanish name. It seemed that they got the name from a legend about a man who came to a Mexican village hundreds of years ago, bringing blessings and healings. In his presence, the people felt secure. He brought life and religion back to the town.

Hosea Ramirez said to Aeamon Lee, "You have those powers. You do not understand that fully now, but gradually, you will discover that you have them. And you will always use them for the good of the people." Aeamon Lee was flattered but didn't respond to his descriptions and predictions.

*   *   *

Aeamon Lee had the highest level of self-confidence, tenacity, and special skills that anyone around had ever seen. Those who didn't know him well were afraid of him. They knew him only by a faulty reputation. Some people didn't try to figure him out because there appeared to be so many paradoxes. There were some things they admired, such as his building a house for his parents and the way he did it. Other times they heard distorted things about his fighting and brawling. But really, he was not much different from kids who wanted the best life possible for his family and saw a need to protect the innocent against injustice.

Aeamon Lee had many unusual skills, including playing a guitar. On many evenings, he sat on the front porch with Martha, Plea, and Jo-Nathan to play and sing. Jo-Nathan sang harmony to a lot of his songs.

Knowing how religious his mother was, Aeamon Lee wrote a song that reflected how he felt about himself spiritually. He knew many thought of him as being really bad. Yet he knew in his heart that he was doing right, and he sang this for his mother:

When my spirit is overwhelmed within me,

I think back and remember the days of old.

And when my spirit fails, I long for thee;

Answer me quickly, for to you I lift up my soul.

O Lord, hear now the prayer of your servant

And answer me in your love and faithfulness;

Enter not your servant into judgment,

For no one in your sight has righteousness.

Chorus: For, O Lord, I know I am your servant;

I lift up my hands to the God I've found.

Let me hear of your love in the morning,

And let your good spirit lead me on level ground.

For my enemies have persecuted my soul;

They have crushed my life to the ground

And have made me dwell in dark places,

Where I lost my way and was cast down.

O Lord, hide not your face from your servant,

Lest I become like those who go down to the pit;

O Lord, bring now my soul out of trouble

And deliver me so that I may never quit.

Chorus: For, O Lord, I know I am your servant;

I lift up my hands to the God I've found.

Let me hear of your love in the morning

And let your good spirit lead me on level ground.[12]

Martha was obviously very pleased that Aeamon Lee wrote such a stirring song. She wanted him to sing it at church. He said he would tell them that he had a song,[13] and he would sing it and see what would happen. The preacher, Bro. Weldon Watson, complimented him for his willingness to get up and sing this song. But he said, "I get concerned sometimes about your aggressive behavior." He also reminded Aeamon Lee that he prayed for him often that he would someday overcome his propensity for fighting.

Aeamon Lee assured him, "I only do it when someone deserves it."

He got to playing and singing more with Willie Rivers and the Willie Rivers Band at Sorghum Hill. He loved this time on Saturday nights as much as anything he did in his life. Many white people just couldn't understand how he could have so much fun and satisfaction by this association. His singing and playing were more of an amusement at school functions. Ms. Markle saw his talent and always encouraged him to continue to develop his skills, but she saw him succeeding by using his intellectual skills.

There were times when even Aeamon Lee marveled at how easily he could learn complex skills. He gradually learned that he had a keen insight into all sorts of things that were happening around him and in the world, but he didn't speak of this ability much and just kept it to himself.

* * *

Plea had become another personality. There were times when his emotions were overwhelming, causing him to do some spur-of-the-moment gesture to assert strength he no longer had. One rainy day, Martha asked Aeamon Lee where Plea was. After looking out toward the barn, they saw Plea trying to get there with a walking cane. While running toward the barn, his daddy fell in the mud. Aeamon Lee picked him up in his strong arms and carried him back to the house. They didn't say anything to Plea. They just dried him off and changed his clothes. Aeamon Lee went out onto the porch to think for a while, feeling helpless. He went back in and told his dad that he would find a way somehow, someway, sometime soon, to get him walking again—whatever it took!

That was not the only time when Plea's self-esteem and what pride he had left would be shattered. Amos and Plea once took the pickup truck to town. Amos drove the truck when needed, loading up Plea and taking him with him even though it put Plea in some amount of discomfort. They had several stops to make to get a list of things needed by both families. Amos and Plea went into Hollis Clanton's hardware store. Plea decided to look at the tools. He couldn't move around much, so he stood pretty much in one place. Clanton had some other customers in the store. Knowing that Plea was not there to spend any money, he thought Plea was in the way of the other customers. He told him to move aside and pushed Plea, who fell on his hip. Clanton didn't even apologize for his actions. Amos got him out of the store and back to the truck. Amos drove straight home and stopped in front of the house.

Aeamon Lee and Jo-Nathan were down in the lower field gathering some black-eyed Susans, daylilies, and Indian paintbrushes for Mama Kate and Martha to put in various flowerbeds around the house. They saw Amos and Plea drive up to the house. Aeamon Lee looked a second time and saw Amos and Martha trying to get Plea onto the porch. Knowing that something had happened, he ran toward the house with Jo-Nathan right behind him.

It was one of the lowest points for Plea. There had been a time in his life when nothing like this could have ever happened to him. He had been as strong as a Knight Templar. He didn't want his wife and son to see him this way, and this hurt him more than his hip. Together, all of them got Plea inside and on the bed where Martha tried to get him some ease. Aeamon Lee got Amos back on the porch to ask him what had happened. Amos didn't want to tell him because he knew Aeamon Lee wouldn't allow things like this to happen. Amos was afraid of how Aeamon Lee might react. Amos apologized for taking him to town and not looking out for him better. Aeamon Lee insisted that Amos tell him what happened. Amos reluctantly told him how Hollis Clanton had pushed him down on the floor in his store.

Jo-Nathan, who immediately knew what Aeamon Lee would do, was the first to speak. He started begging Aeamon Lee to let it go and not retaliate.

"One of these days, you're going to get hurt bad or shot, and you'll be no good to nobody," Jo-Nathan warned.

Aeamon Lee looked at him and said, "'A man does what he must—in spite of personal consequences, in spite of obstacles and dangers and pressures—and that is the basis of all human morality.'"[14]

He proceeded to get into the truck and wouldn't let Jo-Nathan go with him. He drove to town, thinking all the way, *It's going to rain thunder and lightning on a sunny day.* Just recently, he had sung these lines from the Creedence Clearwater Revival (CCR) song:

> Have you ever seen the rain
> Coming down on a sunny day?[15]

On that day, it was an angry thought. He was mad at the town anyway for allowing the abuse of the Ramirez children. If the whole town got in his way, they would seriously regret it. The words of one of their other songs kept coming into his mind:

> As long as I can remember,
> The rain been coming down.[16]

He went first into Clanton's store and said, "You knocked my crippled daddy to the floor of your store for no good reason."

"Go on and get out of my store before you say something you'll regret," Clanton yelled.

"You'll regret this day for a long time," Aeamon Lee responded.

"Don't you threaten me, you uppity piece of white trash, and get out of my store."

Aeamon Lee said, "I may not have your family pedigree, Mr. Clanton, but to me, injustice is intolerable no matter what female dogs you hang with."

Aeamon Lee swung the backside of his hand and hit Clanton in the face. He stumbled across his checkout counter onto the floor. He got up, but Aeamon Lee caught him again, this time with his fist straight into his jaw. This time, Clanton was bloody all over his face and wouldn't get up.

"I'm calling the law on you." But Clanton wasn't getting up to do it right away.

Aeamon Lee asked, "By the way, you know anybody else in this town who wants the devil beat out of them today? Because I'm ready."

He left the store and started looking around, kicking anything in his way. Some men saw Aeamon Lee and tried to calm him down, but he was not ready to be calmed. He started pushing them out of his way, and that situation ended up in a fight. He whipped all three of these men to the point that they just walked off eventually. A crowd formed, and people were running to get close to see the fight.

He asked anybody in the crowd if they wanted to fight. "All I know is, I sure do, and I'll take on any or all of you." There were no takers.

It was like he was letting out all his anger built up for many years even on people who had nothing to do with his misfortune. He wanted to find Bogus Swisher, whose sons had beat up the Ramirez kids. He asked where he was, and somebody said he was in the barbershop. He went in and got him by his coat and slung him out the front door. Outside, he shouted, "Children are not born to hate. They are raised to hate."[17] He roughed Swisher up pretty bad. By this time, someone had called for the sawmill boys to come into town to help corral this boy who was fighting everybody in sight. The sawmill was less than a mile out of town, and four of their men drove into town. The sawmill always had the toughest, strongest men in the county working for them. Now the fighting would really get ugly.

Aeamon Lee went out into the middle of the parking area in the street where there was a lot of room. It was an old-fashioned brawl. He wouldn't let any of them get a hold of him, and he picked up whatever he could find and did damage to every one of them. They fought all the way down the street to the other end. He was backing up, but still not a single one of them had been able to grab him. He had hit every one of them solidly.

While the fighting was going on, the deputy sheriff, Coy Buckler, drove up. The fighting stopped. He didn't even ask what was going on. He paid all his attention to Aeamon Lee. He didn't ask these grown men what they were doing in town fighting with this boy.

"Now, I'm going to have to put you in the car, and we're going to the sheriff's office." What he meant was that he was taking him to jail. "You'll have to let me put these cuffs on you."

"Mr. Buckler, I'll go with you to the sheriff's office, but I can't let you cuff me."

Aeamon Lee did not trust any of them and was fairly sure that once he was cuffed, the men would attack him. The deputy's presence would not stop them.

Aeamon Lee again reassured the deputy as nicely as he could. He stated that he would get into his car, cause no trouble, and allow him to take him to the sheriff's office. In fact, he went over to the squad car, opened the back door, and got in. The deputy reluctantly agreed to take him in this way but made him get in the front seat. He didn't have anyone else to ride in the car with him.

At the jail, Aeamon Lee was locked up with adult prisoners. Nobody knew how old he was because everybody assumed he was more than eighteen. Later, the sheriff came by to check on him. This was Friday afternoon, and they said they would get word to the family that he was in jail. There would be no visiting hours until Sunday afternoon. He was informed of possible charges against him, including disorderly conduct, and he would be arraigned on Monday morning in court.

*   *   *

On Sunday afternoon, Martha was there to see him when visiting hours started. She had brought him something to eat, and after examining it, the jailer let him have it.

She said to the sheriff, "You know, he is only seventeen years old."

The sheriff, Buster Toole, was startled when he heard this and asked, "Ma'am, did you say he is only seventeen?"

The sheriff, like so many of the others, had thought that Aeamon Lee was surely older than that. Now, he had a juvenile locked up in his jail with adult prisoners. He was supposed to have called the juvenile officer, who would have taken him to the juvenile detention center in Jackson, where other juveniles who got into trouble with the law were taken. This episode looked bad on the sheriff, so he decided to let him out to go home with his mother. The sheriff called Hollis Clanton and Bogus Swisher. Clanton had decided not to press charges, especially after what he had done to Plea. The sheriff had to persuade Swisher not to press charges, because he sure wanted to after what had been done to his new truck. But again, he was reminded of the circumstances that led Aeamon Lee to drive his truck off into the branch.

Martha gave assurances to the sheriff that they would not file a complaint about him being locked up with adult prisoners. Then Amos Markum, Martha, and Aeamon Lee went home in the old truck with no charges filed. Aeamon Lee never did tell Martha and Plea the whole story about what happened in town, just the part about Hollis Clanton. He also felt afterward that maybe he could show more discernment when he was angry.

*   *   *

Jo-Nathan and Aeamon Lee were like brothers. They had grown up together, worked and played together, and trusted each other. They looked out for each other. Aeamon Lee treated Amos and Mama Kate with respect, and they thought of him as one of their own. He had eaten many meals at their house. He was never ashamed to take Jo-Nathan anyplace with him.

They had a lot of discussions together, usually while they were working and sometimes at night on the porches. At the end of one night's discussion about life and living, Aeamon Lee summed up what they had all said. "The truth is that life is difficult, rarely reasonable, sometimes unfair, sometimes complex, and sometimes it is good." That bit of philosophy seemed to be consistent with their common experiences.

Aeamon Lee's independence and unique thinking was shown in several ways. He asked Martha if she could make him some shirts, and she said she thought she could if she had all the measurements.

"But why do you want me to make your shirts?"

"Because I don't like store-bought shirts. Actually, I have drawn up a shirt design that I really like, and this is the way I would like for you to sew them. I've made the cuffs simpler. The main difference is that I would like only a three-quarter-length sleeve with a little V-cut underneath. I've got big wrists, and sometimes sleeves coming all the way down to my hands get in my way."

Aeamon Lee showed her how to sew the collar. Some shirts were button-down, and some were not. He liked some solid color shirts and some with large colorful designs that were made of cotton and had been starched and ironed and clothesline dried. In fact, he liked everything to be clothesline dried, especially the sheets and pillowcases. They had a cleaner and fresher smell to them. Martha proceeded to make him a stock of these nice shirts. He didn't care much how his jeans looked, but shirts were important, and he would wear these shirts made by his mother for many years.

Other students at school stared at the odd design of his shirts, and some even asked where he bought them. He always told them he ordered them from a place called Mama's Sewing.

*   *   *

Martha and Plea were churchgoers and were members of a small church in the community called Pilgrim's Rest. After Plea's accident and disability, he didn't get to attend very often. He couldn't sit on the hard pews, and even with pillows he was terribly uncomfortable. Aeamon Lee was taken to church all his life. As he grew older, he thought the church was more interested in form rather than substance. It seemed to him that the church wanted most of all to make sure they had done all the right acts of worship. Actually, they called these actions *items*. The people, however, were generally cordial, and Martha and Plea had developed most of their friendships through this little church.

On some occasions, Aeamon Lee went to church with Jo-Nathan at Zion's Grove, where there seemed to be more spirit. They were not nearly as formal and ostentatious in the demonstration of their faith.

Aeamon Lee sometimes sneaked out of Pilgrim's Rest and went over to the Zion's Grove church, where Jo-Nathan sang in the choir, to enjoy the services. On one Sunday when he walked in, the church was singing several of his favorites—"Stand by Me," "Were You There?" "Just a Little Talk with Jesus," and "Every Time I Feel the Spirit."

Aeamon Lee developed a set of core beliefs and sought to make these a part of his faith. He carried this faith wherever he went. Going to church services became an automatic part of his life on most Sundays. Primarily, he felt that the performance of good works was a sign of his faith. Aeamon Lee always felt his need for personal redemption because so much of his conflicted life was filled with his physical and verbal reactions to injustice. There were times when he couldn't discern the difference between right and wrong regarding the things he did on various occasions. His perspective was that he would always do what he thought was right, pursue it with all his might, and then leave the consequences to God.

CHAPTER 2

The Summer of Adventure
MAY 1983

School was winding down, and there were the usual senior-year class activities. He attended those he could afford. The class didn't have much leadership, and by the end of the year, there was no money for a class trip. As an alternative, the class spent a day at Ross Barnett Reservoir with a picnic lunch and some games on the beach at the swimming area. However, most of the class planned on some kind of special trip with other members of the class when school was out. There were three such groups, and all of them were going down to Destin or Panama City, Florida, for their high school graduation trip. Cost per person was somewhere around $400, and neither Aeamon Lee nor Jo-Nathan had money like that. However, they did have enough money saved up to get to Memphis by bus.

It was still a big deal to get to go to Memphis. He and Jo-Nathan had planned on this trip for months. Even though their parents were not too sure, they finally gave in knowing Aeamon Lee and Jo-Nathan needed to do something special for their graduation.

So Jo-Nathan and Aeamon Lee were taken to Jackson where they caught a Trailways bus to Memphis early in the morning. It went straight up Interstate Highway 55 to Memphis. The bus station in Memphis was downtown, and this was where they wanted to be. All the way to Memphis, Jo-Nathan said he wanted to see Beale Street, if nothing else. This was where many blues singers from the Mississippi Delta and Highway 61 had gone to perform. The city of Memphis had begun renovation of the street, making it into a tourist attraction.

Jo-Nathan reminded Aeamon Lee several times that he could only be gone for few days. But the main problem they had was that they simply didn't have much money to spend. So Aeamon Lee decided on a possible way he could make some money—using his poker skills. He thought they might be able to get into some street poker games. He had heard Uncle Jerome talk about street poker in Chicago. They walked from the bus station over to Beale and were generally disappointed that not many stores and clubs had opened. However, there seemed to be a lot of construction going on.

They walked up and down the street and saw one club but didn't go in because they didn't have any ID that indicated they were old enough. Aeamon Lee spotted some men talking and asked them if they knew where they might find a street poker game. Their response was negative, and the boys got some advice that they had better watch out trying to play poker in public. But they didn't know where any games were going on inside either. Finally, Aeamon Lee found two guys near W. C. Handy Park who said they would play with him if they could find a safe spot. He rounded up one more fellow who agreed to play in one of the off streets. They found a spot between a parking lot and a building. Jo-Nathan was the lookout to watch for the police.

Aeamon Lee had a deck of cards, and another man also had some cards. They had to have a draw of the cards to determine which deck they would use. They played five-card draw, which was the particular poker game most played on the streets, besides Black Jack. Aeamon Lee won sixty dollars before the other men decided they had had enough and left. But sixty dollars would not get them very far in Memphis, so the boys decided they had to find some other way to make some money.

They had seen an advertisement for the Regional Macho Man Boxing contest on one of the store windows on Beale Street. It was going to be held at the Mid-South Coliseum, starting that night. There would be $2,500 in prize money, with the winner in the heavyweight division getting $1,000. They didn't know too much about it and began asking some of the people with whom they had struck up conversations. They all said, "Stay away from that thing." One fellow said, "There are three reasons why people enter: on a dare or bet, to earn a little respect, or because they just love to fight. That last bunch is the ones you better watch."

Another fellow said it was more like a brawl than anything else. He had been to several events. When Aeamon Lee heard the word *brawl*, he got more interested.

Based on the little information he had, Aeamon Lee decided to go out to the Coliseum and check it out. One of their new friends drove him and Jo-Nathan out there. All the way there, Jo-Nathan was saying, "Haven't you had enough brawling already? No telling what this is all about, though we sure could use the money, provided you win." Supposedly, it was for amateurs and not professionals.

Upon arriving at the Coliseum, Aeamon Lee found out that they were still looking for participants because they liked to have around twenty to thirty fighters per show. They were still lacking a few, and it was getting close to the deadline for signing up. They weren't too careful about who volunteered. They just wanted to have enough fights for all the people who had bought tickets. Aeamon Lee told them he was eighteen, the legal limit, and that he lived in Tupelo, Mississippi.

He had heard of another fighter who said he was from Arkansas, and he figured they'd let someone from Elvis's birthplace enter the contest.

Aeamon Lee measured out to be six feet four inches tall and 210 pounds. They took his blood pressure and pulse. A young doctor was there asking questions in an accent hardly anyone could understand. At any rate, it didn't appear that anyone was disqualified. Most of the fighters were in the lower weight division.

Most of the other participants appeared to be overweight and out of shape. You had to use sixteen-ounce gloves, and after about thirty seconds, somebody said it was a matter of endurance. After that, exhaustion was the main thing to deal with. A few years earlier, the sponsors had to change the rules because some fighters had gotten seriously hurt. So now it was pretty much pure boxing, although there was still a lot of slapping and pushing and head butting. In addition to the sixteen-ounce padded gloves, you were required to wear headgear, groin protectors, and mouthpieces; and they had shortened the rounds. There would be three seventy-five-second rounds with two weight classes: 160 to 184 pounds and 185 to 300 pounds.

Aeamon Lee found out there was a fifty-dollar entry fee, which was taken out of the sixty dollars he had won in the street poker game. He and Jo-Nathan stayed around the Coliseum. There appeared to be camaraderie among the guys, but after the fighting started in the ring, you had to watch out. It was serious business then.

Every fighter had to have a nickname, or they would give you one for the program. There was Psycho Man, Monster Man, One Punch, Jawbreaker, and Doomsday, among others. Aeamon Lee chose Blues Man, because that's where they had spent most of their time in Memphis, on Beale Street. He also could sing the blues, except now he wanted to give it to someone else. Besides, he didn't want to sound too intimidating by choice and antagonize more than he needed to.

Two nights of fighting were scheduled. Winners on Friday night fought on Saturday night for the prize money. On Saturday night, you had to win at least two fights to win the championship. There was a second in each corner to give advice before the fight and after each round.

On Friday night, it appeared that each fighter had his own supporters—both men and women—who had a portion of seats down on the floor next to the ring. They usually came in together with their leather jackets, tattoos, and long hair. The competitors' supporters and the other fighters' supporters sometimes fought below the ring. Some even tried to get into the ring.

Some with seats on the front row would sell their seats when they found out that blood and snot sometimes reached the front row. The crowd could have easily been mistaken for an Outlaw Country Music concert, except this crowd was more intense and nervous. Some chewed tobacco, while others smoked and cheered for their man.

Finally, 8:00 p.m. rolled around, and the announcer said, "Let's rowwwwwdy down." The crowd started chanting "Rowdy down, rowdy down, rowdy down." Theme music from *Rocky* played; and when the fighters would just about stop fighting, he would say, "Let's git, git, git, git, git on with it." After someone won, he asked the audience, "Is he macho enough?"

Aeamon Lee's first opponent weighed 230 pounds and appeared out of shape. His fighting name was The Mauler. He was only six feet tall and had a bushy beard. The approach this guy took was the most common approach of most of the fighters. That was to come out flailing away, one swing after another, in an attempt to subdue the opponent. This caught Aeamon Lee by surprise, and he held up his gloves to protect himself and started backing up. The Mauler just kept coming and would not let up. He wasn't hurting Aeamon Lee, just frustrating him. The audience started a chant, "Hit him, hit him, hit him." Aeamon Lee heard

Jo-Nathan above the crowd saying the same thing. While in the middle of the ring, he anchored his back foot and came with a straight cross to the man's face. His corner man heard him say, *"Cogito ergo boom"*[18] just before landing his punch. The blow decked the fellow. In fact, he hit the canvas so hard, the splat was heard throughout the arena. The crowd roared with approval. The Mauler had to have help getting up and getting out of the ring. Instantly, Aeamon Lee became a crowd favorite. He played to the crowd, which was what the promoters wanted him to do. Actually, they wanted a big crowd the next night.

Aeamon Lee's next opponent was a cautious guy, well-built, but not as tall, and nicknamed The Hitman. He counterpunched mostly. By the third round, Aeamon Lee was told he would have to be more aggressive and take the fight to this guy to ensure a win. The opponent was a pretty hard puncher but had not really hurt Aeamon Lee. In that final round, the opponent evidently had been told the same thing, and when he started swinging away, Aeamon Lee was able to get in some hard punches that obviously hurt the guy. The opponent started backing away, and Aeamon Lee followed him and was definitely the aggressor when the fight was over. The decision went to Aeamon Lee based on his aggressive performance in the third round.

On Saturday night, the finals were held before an even bigger audience. The competition was much tougher now, and it would take a stronger effort. Aeamon Lee rested up most of the day and was careful what he ate. Finally, time rolled around, and the handlers encouraged the fighters to tout their toughness in the ring and help build up excitement from the audience.

The number of fighters in the heavyweight division was less than in the lighter weight division, and by Saturday night, there were only four left. Aeamon Lee was now only two fights away from winning the contest and the money.

His first opponent, One Punch, appeared experienced and was bouncing around in the ring, beating the air like he was a professional. Aeamon Lee had heard that sometimes professionals were able to get into the contest. He wondered if this boxer was one of those, but there was no time to dwell on this possibility. He had to be ready for One Punch no matter what.

The fighter was well cut, with bulging muscles, and handled himself like a professional. He jabbed a lot and was obviously trying to set up Aeamon Lee for a strong right. There were several fierce exchanges in the first round, and Aeamon Lee knew he was facing another huge challenge. He decided to make the opponent fight his fight the last two rounds. Aeamon Lee moved into him, brawling and throwing solid punches when the opponent had no defense and when he least expected a punch. One Punch was caught off guard and was hit several times with body punches, which began to wear him down. Aeamon Lee was leaning on him and moving all the time, faking punches and then landing. He felt he had won the second round. In the third round, he continued with his type of fighting, and clearly One Punch was wearing down. When there was an opening, Aeamon Lee landed a one-two combination that decked him for the count.

One Punch's crowd of supporters was pretty disappointed, and many of them came up to the ring and had to be restrained by the guards. The larger crowd, however, was cheering for the Blues Man, but Aeamon Lee didn't react to provoke the supporters of his opponent. He rested as much as he could because the championship bout was coming up shortly. Those sixteen-ounce gloves took a toll on the arms. He told Jo-Nathan, "I can win if I can keep the attitude potes, agendum, couitere?"[19]

By this time, Jo-Nathan just agreed with him rather than keep asking him what he meant. "Whatever you say. I just want you to remember that you can do it, if you want it bad enough," Jo-Nathan said to a smiling Aeamon Lee.

Finally, the time arrived for the championship match. Someone said that the opponent for this final fight was the man who won the contest last year. His ring name was Stump, and it was appropriate because he was built like a stump. He was short, huge around the middle, and had no neck. It was like his head was just set on his shoulders. He was older than most of the other fighters and had a lot of backers in the audience.

In the first round, Aeamon Lee didn't know what to expect, except he thought maybe Stump would just keep coming at him and flailing away. Stump came after him all right, but he was not flailing so as to wear himself out. He moved closer and gauged his punches, which was a smart tactic. Aeamon Lee spent most of the first round trying to figure out how to fight him. Stump was hard to hit, and finally, Aeamon Lee decided that he would mix counterpunching and attempt to land some headshots. This turned out to be a successful tactic. Luckily, Aeamon Lee had not been cut and only had some red spots on his face and body, which would later turn into bruises.

Between the second and third rounds, his handler told him he would have to hit him cleanly and avoid being hit by Stump. In the third and final round, Aeamon Lee began to bury his glove in the man's stomach. This approach wore Stump down some and allowed Aeamon Lee to get some hard punches to the head. Stump opened up a small gash under Aeamon Lee's right eye, but it didn't bleed very much. Aeamon Lee kept going for the head since Stump couldn't get his hands up in time to block the punches. Stump's face was bloodied. When the bell sounded, he was barely standing, and Aeamon Lee was still throwing one punch after another to his head. But he never knocked Stump down.

At the end of the fight, the announcer asked the audience, "Are they macho enough?" The crowd was obviously pleased and responded that both of them were "macho enough."

The patrons cheered throughout the fight and were on their feet by the fight's end. This crowd noise had helped Aeamon Lee not notice how heavy those gloves were. He thought he had won but wasn't sure. It was a split decision, with Aeamon Lee winning the fight and the regional contest. There was, of course, much jubilation. Jo-Nathan jumped up and down, saying, "I knew you could! I knew you could. Now let's get the money and get out of here." Stump took losing fairly well and congratulated Aeamon Lee. There was a lot of fanfare with the announcement of the winner and the playing of their theme song. People wanted autographs and pictures.

The promoters wanted to talk with Aeamon Lee about the next round of bouts and eventually a national championship later in the year. They wanted Aeamon Lee to come to Dallas, Texas, in a few weeks. All Aeamon Lee and Jo-Nathan wanted was to get the $1,000 and leave. He was paid in cash after giving the officials all the information they requested.

As Aeamon Lee and Jo-Nathan were leaving the Coliseum, they noticed a woman right outside the door with three small children. She was in tears and was being comforted by an older woman. Most of the crowd had left, and there were not many people around. Aeamon Lee stopped and just looked at the woman, having compassion on her. Soon Stump came out with $250 he got for second place and hugged the woman. It was obvious that this was Stump's wife and children. Jo-Nathan was trying to get Aeamon Lee to move on, but he went over to the couple and asked, "What's wrong? Are you okay?"

Stump didn't say anything, but the older woman said they were behind on their rent because Stump had been laid off from his job. They thought he would win enough to pay the rent by competing again this year in the contest.

"How much is needed?" Aeamon Lee asked.

"I think they need now around a hundred dollars," the woman said.

Jo-Nathan got in Aeamon Lee's face and said, "Come on and let's go! You don't know if any of this is true, and besides, you are not responsible."

Aeamon Lee said, "It is true, and I'm going to give them a hundred dollars."

"Why, just tell me why, when we've got to get back home ourselves?" Jo-Nathan asked.

"Because it is our raison d'être."[20] He handed them the money over their objections.

Jo-Nathan just shook his head.

The two caught a ride back downtown. Aeamon Lee and Jo-Nathan took turns counting the money. They had about $900 in cash. After a nice well-deserved meal and paying for someone to drive them back downtown, they still had around $870. They also felt they had earned the right to sleep in better quarters, so they stayed in a cheap motel room for the night.

*   *   *

The next day, they walked down to the riverfront after crossing over Riverside Drive. There were several small cruise boats docked, but there was one that was amazingly huge. As they drew closer, they discovered that it was the *Mississippi Queen*, which was regarded as the most magnificent paddle wheeler on the river. Launched for America's Bicentennial in 1976, it was the grandest, largest paddle wheeler the river had ever seen. It had seven decks and, at full capacity, held 450 passengers with overnight accommodations in splendidly furnished staterooms. Each stateroom was named for a river town, state, Civil War battle, or other historic places or personage. The outside staterooms offered private verandas, genuine antique furnishings, and period paintings pertaining to the stateroom's name.

The two of them stood there looking at this elegant boat from top to bottom and from front to back. Easily, the *Mississippi Queen* could have been the dreamboat of Mark Twain.

At the dock, Aeamon Lee started asking questions. It seemed that groups could rent the boat for a cruise down the Mississippi River. This particular cruise began in Cincinnati, with planned dockings along the way to New Orleans. The group that booked this trip was a group of professors, historians, authors, and others interested in Southern culture. On their trip down the river, they heard speeches on various related topics.

When Aeamon Lee asked how long they would be docked there, he was told that the group had planned a dinner in one of the ballrooms at the Peabody Hotel. After dinner, they would return to continue their trip down the river to New Orleans. The passengers would be getting off soon to see downtown Memphis, ride in the horse-drawn carriages, and view the Peabody.

They would witness the famous Peabody Ducks at 5:00 p.m. in the hotel lobby. Just before 10:00 a.m. each morning, a fifty-foot red carpet was laid out, stretching from the hotel elevators to the marble fountain in the lobby. The Peabody Duckmaster escorted the ducks from the Royal Duck Palace on the hotel's roof to an elevator especially reserved for them. With all the pomp and circumstance of a royal event, the five mallards—one drake and four hens—with their red-and-gold jacketed Duckmaster, emerged from their elevator to the music of John Philip Sousa's "King Cotton March."

They marched on the red carpet and then mounted three steps into the fountain, where they splashed and preened for the day. At 5:00

p.m., the procedure reversed, and the ducks ceremoniously returned to their penthouse palace. The riverboat group would witness the 5:00 p.m. ceremony before their dinner. The crewmember that was casually telling Aeamon Lee all about the cruise and the itinerary of the regal passengers then revealed something interesting to him. He told Aeamon Lee that the passengers attending these events at the Peabody were dressed in the costumes of notable Southern figures of both pop culture and traditional culture. He said there would be some dressed up as Elvis, William Faulkner, country music singers, NASCAR drivers, Bear Bryant, Rhett Butler, Scarlett O'Hara, and Miss Americas, to name a few.

Aeamon Lee pulled Jo-Nathan aside and said, "I have an idea, which has taken my imagination by storm."[21]

"What do you mean?" Jo-Nathan asked.

"I mean, I've wondered what it would be like to ride down the Mississippi on a riverboat ever since I read Mark Twain. Listen, Jo-Nathan, we could get on this boat, ride down the Mississippi River, and enjoy the high living of all these passengers. And no telling what else we could find."

"Now you know we can't do that. We'd get into big-time trouble. Remember, I said that I needed to be back home by the end of this week. And we need all that money to get back home on. How do you figure we could possibly get a ride on this fine boat?"

"You heard him say there were close to three hundred passengers, and around two hundred fifty of them are going to be in costume going up to the Peabody Hotel. So all we have to do is find some costumes and blend in with the crowd."

"How do you figure we are going to be able to do all that?"

"I saw a store over there close to Beale that said 'Mr. Abraham's,' which advertised costumes and party supplies. Maybe we could find something over there."

"You are serious, aren't you?"

"I think we can do it."

"Lord, have mercy on us. If my mama knew what all I've already done on this trip, which was your idea, no telling what she'd do to both of us."

"Now, you'll have to admit we've been lucky, had a lot of fun and plenty of excitement, right?" Aeamon Lee asked.

"Well, I'm with you, and you've always taken care of me. Just get me home safe is all I ask."

They took off back downtown until they got to Mr. Abraham's. Several costumes were on display, but one had to ask about other specific costumes. Aeamon Lee had been thinking what he would like to do to make their appearance more authentic-looking. He remembered Big Daddy in *The Long, Hot Summer* and how he looked with that white suit and white hat. Many plantation owners and politicians dressed this way in the Old South. Jo-Nathan thought he could dress up as a house servant, something like a valet. But could they find these outfits? By getting some of the items there and some other places in town to which they were referred, they ended up being dressed up enough to pass as a plantation owner, replete with a cane and his personal servant. They immediately struck out for the Peabody Hotel.

*   *   *

The riverboat tour group was in evidence everywhere they looked. Aeamon Lee instructed Jo-Nathan on how they would present themselves. Since they were so young, they would be students from Samford University in Alabama and just hope that they would not meet anyone else from this school. Their story would be that a Samford professor sponsored them for this trip because they had a special interest in the culture of the South. Jo-Nathan would let Aeamon Lee do most of the talking and try to act out his role as valet.

They strolled around the loading dock, speaking and wanting to be seen by enough people that there would be no confusion when they attempted to board the riverboat later on that evening. Boarding, they made their way to the banquet in the Peabody ballroom. Aeamon Lee struck up a conversation with a tour member from the University of the South at Sewanee, Tennessee. The history professor spent a lot of time boasting how exclusive the school was and its history of attracting some of the best prepared students for college in the South. He dominated the conservation, which meant that Aeamon Lee didn't have to say much, just agree and nod a lot. He invited them to come see their beautiful campus, which was perched atop the Cumberland Gap at Monteagle, Tennessee.

During and after the dinner, Aeamon Lee really got into the swing of things by introducing himself and Jo-Nathan to many guests and even spoke with the old dialect of a Southern gentleman. "Howdy, ma'am, you sure are charming on this lovely evening. Now, who did you say your daddy was? I thought I may have known him or met him on some of my travels throughout the South." He even got a little bolder with this question: "Now, I hope you won't consider this too personal, but are you all regarded as new money or old money?" This evoked a good laugh from those about him.

There was an after-dinner speech by the same history professor they had met earlier. Aeamon Lee couldn't help but think that he was talking about his family. The professor talked about unique traits of the South, such as the art of quilting, growing fresh vegetables, hog killings, music, pastime games, ideas about people from up North, the relationships between Black English and the King's English, and why and how power had been concentrated in the hands of the planter class. Aeamon Lee decided right then that he wanted someday to visit the Center for the Study of Southern Culture located on the campus of Ole Miss.

When the speech and meal were over, Aeamon Lee and Jo-Nathan heard the calliope playing. This was the signal that the riverboat was leaving the dock. This would be the personal maiden voyage of these two itinerate, river-faring strangers because of their brashness and daring sense of discovery.

Those about them were leaving the banquet to return to the cabin deck to change into more comfortable clothes. The two wondered what their next step would be. They knew there were accommodations for over 450, and there were only around 300 guests. So Aeamon Lee figured there had to be some vacant rooms. They attempted to open some doors in hopes they could find a vacant room, but no luck. They asked one of the deckhands about a key to their room, which they identified, but he simply instructed them to go to the main information desk. They would have to identify themselves, their names would be checked, and they would certainly be discovered. They decided they would simply have to figure out a way later on how to get into a room. In the meantime, they found a public restroom to hide in.

They noticed that people were now congregating on the deck, drinking at the bar, smoking cigars, and socializing in small groups. Aeamon Lee figured there had to be a poker game someplace, and now that he had some cash to play with, he asked around to find where the game was. In his jovial way, and still in character, he inquired until he was told that there were several games going on in very discreet places. Finally, he was told where to go to ask.

It was on the observation deck in a room off the Grand Saloon. Since Aeamon Lee was still in costume, he was taken more seriously and eventually was led into a smoke-filled back room where there were some passengers not associated with the group of professors. One player seemed a little suspicious of Jo-Nathan, and he said, "Who is he? You two work together or something?"

Aeamon Lee said, "There's no need to worry about my friend. Right, Jo-Nathan?"

"Right," Jo-Nathan said. He turned and took a seat away from the table against the wall where several other nontalkative men sat. He could see these were men who took their poker quite seriously. They had on their intimidating poker faces to prove it.

Aeamon Lee was informed that they needed to see that he had cash money in his pockets with which to play. He also had to agree to play straight poker (five-card draw). Aeamon Lee was elated about the choice of games because he always thought there was too much left to chance in Texas Hold'em. Anyway, Uncle Jerome had taught him all the tricks to playing five-card draw.

He showed them his cash, and they all laughed and said he could play but that he probably wouldn't be around long. This signaled to Aeamon Lee that the stakes could get high later on, but to start off, the minimum was ten dollars. This meant that he had to win early in order to accumulate more cash to stay around. He asked a few dumb questions to make it appear he was not all that familiar with the game. "Now, let's see, does four of a kind beat a full house?"

About this time, Jo-Nathan got up and asked Aeamon Lee if he could speak to him. They went outside the door quickly, and Jo-Nathan told Aeamon Lee that they needed to make sure they kept enough to get home on.

"Now don't you go and lose all our money. We got to save some. We're a long way from home, and we might need it," Jo-Nathan reminded.

Every time Jo-Nathan thought about all that they had already been involved in on this trip, it made him sick to his stomach. It was too new and too much fun and new experience for a kid from Goshen Wells who had not been to all these fancy places and events. And now they were where they didn't have a legal right to be. Being in such a precarious situation made Jo-Nathan uneasy.

Aeamon Lee reassured him, "You know how I play poker. Don't worry about a thing,"

As Aeamon Lee started the game, the others thought of him as an easy mark whose money they would win right away. He knew what they were thinking and played right along, asking some questions about the procedures. Remember, his greatest asset in all competitive situations was his profound sense of intuition, not just his ability to card count or read other players along with a few other tricks of the trade. The pile got all the way up to $400 on the first hand with three players still betting when there was a call. Aeamon Lee had four jacks to win the pot. The other players, after a few moments of astonishment, then began an uneasy laugh. One could tell they were thinking beginner's luck, and Aeamon Lee played along.

He had a little more money now to play with, but he knew he couldn't win every hand. He would have to win several small pots in order to win really big later on. The show continued with Aeamon Lee acting as though he had good hands and then losing small pots.

Finally, Aeamon Lee decided he had better win what he wanted and get out of this game. He could tell these were men intent on winning. Not only that, these players did not appear to be associated with the Southern culture group. They never cracked a smile, and they played their game very well. So Aeamon Lee started winning while the other players grew impatient and restless with him. They stared at him, obviously attempting to figure him out. Finally, one of them asked him his name again and where he was from.

He then said, "You know, I don't remember you two when we all boarded."

Aeamon Lee kept his composure and said, "We didn't get out of our cabin much. Remember, we're students, and we had to complete a writing project."

One of the men wrote down their two names, making it obvious that they were going to be checked. Aeamon Lee had to do some swift talking.

"Listen, I'll just play one more round with y'all. I know some of you want to win back some of your money. Jo-Nathan and me, we got to go anyway."

This reply seemed to satisfy most of them even though there was a sense of urgency in the atmosphere and a whole lot more tension. Aeamon Lee could not resist the temptation to win this last round. So he acted out like he had once before when he lost. The betting was fierce, and the pot grew to nearly $2,000 when the call was made. Aeamon Lee had a full house, which beat one of the player's three of a kind. He immediately started talking about how they were late being someplace else, all the while raking the money into his pockets as quickly as possible. One man was steaming mad and started making charges against him. The man accused "that n—— over there" of somehow helping Aeamon Lee win his hand. Several others in the room agreed even though Jo-Nathan had sat quietly and remained calm.

They rose and grabbed Jo-Nathan, cussed him, and led him from the back room out onto the deck. Jo-Nathan was trying to convince them he had nothing to do with anything that went on in that room. But it seemed the men only got angrier. They accused him of not being on the boat legally, and two of the guys took over. About the time Aeamon Lee got out onto the deck where they were, they had wrestled Jo-Nathan to the deck rail in an attempt to scare him, but they pushed too hard. Jo-Nathan fell overboard, into the swirling waters of the Mississippi River. He yelled as he fell into the waters.

Aeamon Lee's heart sank. He immediately shed his coat and shoes and jumped into the dark river to save Jo-Nathan. He didn't give it a second thought because he had promised Mama Kate that he would take care of Jo-Nathan on this trip and return him home safely. His best friend was possibly drowning in the river. He had to find him and get him safely to the bank.

The first thing Aeamon Lee did was to be aware of the paddle wheels coming toward him. He made a strong effort to move himself away from the boat as much as possible, though it felt like the water was pulling him closer to the boat. The boat was moving so fast that he got only a few feet away from the boat, fighting as hard as he could to move away. He missed the paddle wheel by inches, and the water swept him back up the river some. He went under the water several times. Using what he had learned from swimming in creeks and watershed lakes with Jo-Nathan back in Goshen Wells, he was able to come back to the top.

He looked around to try to find Jo-Nathan but couldn't see him anyplace. The boat was proceeding down the river with only a little moonlight and some other lights in the distance. He began to holler for Jo-Nathan in a desperate attempt to find him. He started swimming back toward where he thought the boat was when they went overboard. He was becoming frantic in his hollering and swimming, trying to find his lifelong friend and brother.

Jo-Nathan suddenly surfaced about fifteen yards away. Aeamon Lee yelled to get his attention as they swam toward each other. He told Jo-Nathan to stay calm and stay afloat, and they'd get to the bank. They had become disoriented as they attempted to identify where the nearest bank was. Aeamon Lee decided on the western bank but didn't know at the time whether it was east or west or even what state it was. He told Jo-Nathan that they would be smart and swim like they knew how to swim to get to the bank.

As they started, the swirling waters became eddies that almost took them under several times. Each time, they escaped from the pull to continue their swim toward the bank. Jo-Nathan yelled that his clothes were getting heavy. Aeamon Lee encouraged him to keep swimming hard because they were almost to the bank. Both were hoping there would be some snag heaps they could rest on, but none appeared on their voyage to the bank.

The two young river rats were exhausted when they reached a small sandy beach area with a high bank at the back. They dug their hands into the sand while finally realizing that they were going to make it. There was not much light to help them ascertain exactly what was around them. They knew they had to climb that bank somehow. The two sojourners in a strange land started their way up the bank, grabbing and holding onto limbs and grass, each helping the other until they finally reached the top.

"I'll bet there are snakes around here bigger than we are," Jo-Nathan shouted.

"I wouldn't worry about snakes. We've made so much racket, those snakes have gotten out of our way," Aeamon Lee reassured his friend but wondered how many snakes they had actually walked and swam over.

"What happened to you when you fell over the boat?" Aeamon Lee asked.

"It's a thousand wonders I didn't get killed," Jo-Nathan said, trying to get his breath. "I went under the water, and it was dark, and I heard this loud racket, and I just went down deeper and deeper into the water. I was afraid that boat was going to run over me. And suddenly, the water just carried me in one direction. I don't know which direction that was, and when I came to the top I had to swim away from that current. And I think those paddle wheels went right over me. But you'd be proud of one thing. When I was falling into the water, I remembered what you said one time about always getting your shoes off, and that was the first thing I did while I was going under."

Jo-Nathan yelled out, "Thank you, Jesus! How did we survive *that*?"

Aeamon Lee said, "I thought we would make it because I haven't found my mission yet. But that was a close call, my friend. I couldn't let anything happen to you—I promised Mama Kate."

"Well, I know one thing. I ain't never going to even be around close when you play poker again. No more, ever, period. Did you hear that?"

"I know what you mean. There were some tense moments playing with those poker men."

About that time, Aeamon Lee ran his hands into his pockets to see if all that money he had crammed into his pockets was there. It was! Soaking wet, but there.

"It's all here, I think."

"Good, I just hope we've got enough to get back home on," Jo-Nathan said wishfully. This was about the fourth time Jo-Nathan had mentioned going back home since the two young wanderers had left on the bus for Memphis.

"Where in the heck are we, anyway?"

The two young survivors, who had just had a brush with death, with a daring feat of skill in the Mississippi River at night, stood there safely on the bank. They didn't say anything while each one attempted to find a light and decide where they were.

Finally, Aeamon Lee said, "I think we are at the edge of a field, and the rows end right about here." Jo-Nathan kept looking down around his feet and making sure there was no snake where he was standing.

"I tell you, I'm not for going very far barefooted at night knowing what I might step on," Jo-Nathan said.

Aeamon Lee spotted what appeared to be cotton wagons not far from where they were. They had been parked there for the season, and given the circumstances, he decided they had just better stay there for the rest of the night rather than try to find a road. It was way after midnight, and it would be morning soon. They were beginning to feel the chill one finds on a night in May.

They crawled up into the wagon, took off each item of clothing, and attempted to ring it dry. They put the still wet clothing back on as they attempted to find a warm spot. In the darkness and cold of the night, they got a little warmer by lying back-to-back on the floor of the cotton wagon. Neither said anything to the other about it, and the warmth of their bodies was the best they could share. Aeamon Lee did say, "Did you know there is a Bible verse about this?"

"What do you mean?"

"'If two lie down together, they keep warm, but how can one be warm alone?'"[22]

Jo-Nathan said, "I don't care if it's in the Bible or not. I don't want anything ever said about this, do you understand?"

*   *   *

It was the middle of the morning when they woke up, and the sun was shining bright. Aeamon Lee took the cash money and laid it out bill by bill in hopes that it too would dry off. They looked around and saw that they were on the edge of a large field. No houses were in sight, but in the distance, there was what appeared to be a place of business of some type. Seeing no cars or a road, they stayed in the wagon and slept a while longer.

When they woke, they knew they would have to look for some food and a way back home. So they left their overnight lodging in a cotton wagon and began to walk toward the place of business. By this time, some trucks and cars had arrived at the business. Reaching the store, they discovered that it was a beer joint that opened around 11:00 a.m. It had a sign on the front that said Frog's. They figured there were some food in there also, so Aeamon Lee said, "Okay, we're going to go in and see if they'll get us something to eat."

"Why don't you go in and get something for both of us, and I'll wait out here," Jo-Nathan said as he surveyed the place cautiously. Jo-Nathan continued, "We don't know where we are, and most of the time, these joints don't like to see black people coming around."

"Now don't you go talking like that again. You know how I feel about that. They can't legally stop anybody from coming into a public establishment," Aeamon Lee said.

"They don't care what the law is. They just come by your house later and shoot it up."

"We're a long way from home. How are they going to know where to go?"

"You don't even know where we are."

Aeamon Lee looked around and said, "We are either in Arkansas or Louisiana. I think we are on the western side of the Mississippi River. Now they don't know us. Besides, we won't be there long."

He almost had to pull Jo-Nathan along. So the two bedraggled kids with no shoes on and with wrinkled costume clothes went inside Frog's for something to eat. They went to the bar stools and observed four men sitting at tables. The owner was behind the bar with his arms folded. There was no talk among the men, but their eyes were focused on the two young strangers.

The tall man behind the bar said, "We can't serve you anything to drink here." He said this in hopes the two would just leave.

"We're not here for beer. We just want to get something to eat. Can you make a sandwich?"

Jo-Nathan kept looking around the place while observing the four men and began to feel uneasy. The four men still didn't say anything even though they were watching every move and listening to every word.

"Maybe I can make you two ham sandwiches, and y'all can be on your way."

"Make us two ham sandwiches," Aeamon Lee instructed as he started toward the drink machines to get some drinks and chips.

Finally, one of the men at a table yelled out, "You're not going to serve a n—— in this place and allow him to stay in here to eat with the rest of us, are you, Wayne?"

"Yeah, we don't cotton to drinking our beer with a n—— and a n—— lover," another one of the men bellowed out.

When Aeamon Lee returned with the drinks to the barstools, Jo-Nathan told him under his breath, "I told you I don't need to be here. Let's pay for this and get out of here. I know what I'm talking about!"

Aeamon Lee looked at him and said, "No!" And where everyone could hear him, he said, "We're staying right here and eat our food and leave in peace, you hear."

"Aeamon Lee Mistral, I'm begging you to let this go and let's be on our way."

"Look, 'we boil at different degrees.'²³ I'm tired. I'm hungry, and when I'm hungry, I get cranky. Besides, I've had to fight four of the toughest men in the South. I've had to jump into the Mississippi River to save a friend of mine. I've had to swim that river and spend the night in a cotton wagon. And I am going to eat something, and I'll be danged if these characters from—is this Arkansas or Louisiana?"

"Louisiana."

"As I was saying, nobody from Louisiana is going to keep me from eating my meal."

One of the men said, "So you know where you are now? I can tell you're not from these parts. And you and your n—— friend here have come into this respected place of business and insulted all these fine upstanding citizens. You'd be stupid if you think we are going to sit here and let you talk this way to us. You hear that?"

Another said, "I think they've escaped from someplace. You sure you're not from that Parchman prison. Look at them! No shoes on, and look at their clothes, and did you say you swam that river? Call the sheriff, Wayne, and let the sheriff decide who they are and maybe show them some Louisiana hospitality."

"Maybe we'll just do that anyway before he gets here."

Aeamon Lee told Jo-Nathan to go and sit in a chair next to the wall and stay there. He added, "We'd better decide now if we are going to be fearless men or scared boys."[24]

He then walked toward the front door as the men really opened up with a barrage of taunts and insults and moved toward him. They all thought he was leaving. But Aeamon Lee picked up a huge two-by-eight board and placed it across the front of the door and into two hooks on either side of the door. This was how the owner secured the front door when he closed. Now, no one else could enter, and he turned around. The men were startled for a second but continued their taunts again. They moved toward him with bottles and chairs in their hands.

Aeamon Lee realized a while ago that he would have to fight these guys. He sure wasn't going to leave on his own. He had never walked away from what he saw as injustice or unfairness, and he wasn't going to start now. He was now ready to fight all of them.

He hit the one out front with a right cross that sent him back into the arms of his comrades. They started coming at Aeamon Lee with weapons in hand, and the brawl was on. Chairs, broken bottles, parts of chairs, anything they could get their hands on were flying around. Tables were broken, and windows were shattered. It was an old-fashioned barroom brawl one would see in a Wild West movie.

Wayne, the owner, was shouting for them to take the fight outside, but no one listened.

Some four-by-fours around in the room held up the joint's ceiling. One by one, these braces started to shake loose or fall completely down. Jo-Nathan saw one of the men coming up behind Aeamon Lee, so he ran up to him and hit him over the head with a chair leg. Finally, when another four-by-four went down, the ceiling started to fall. With that, the flat roof fell because it relied on those braces.

The fighting slowed down some as the men in arms attempted to keep the ceiling and roof off them. Actually, there was only one man left fighting, and Aeamon Lee finally knocked him down to stay. He and Jo-Nathan tried to crawl toward the door but couldn't get out that way, so they headed toward a broken window and crawled outside.

Evidently, the owner had called the sheriff when the fighting started. They could hear the sirens in the distance. They took off down a cotton row back toward the river. They could hear the sheriff's car and the sound of dogs. The sheriff's car stopped at Frog's, and the sheriff surveyed the damage before they saw the running boys headed toward the river. The sheriff assumed that the boys had robbed the place. The sheriff thought, too, that they might be escaped prisoners from Parchman. They immediately set the dogs loose, and the dogs started running after the boys who had now reached the banks of the river.

Aeamon Lee and Jo-Nathan sure didn't want to be caught by a Louisiana parish sheriff. They started running alongside the river until they arrived at a place where the bank was not so high and they could get closer to the river itself.

"What are we doing?" Jo-Nathan asked.

"We're going to have to swim the river again." Aeamon Lee saw that those dogs were loose and that they could inflict some real hurt on them before the deputies arrived.

"No, we're not. I'm already out of breath."

"It'll be easier this time because we'll be swimming down the river, and the water will carry us, and we'll gradually swim across to the other side. It's going to be that way. Now come on, and let's go for it."

Jo-Nathan continued his complaining all the while Aeamon Lee led him toward the water's edge. Then the two runners began their second swim in less than twelve hours across Old Man.

The waters were swift, and it was true that the currents easily carried them down the river while they swam through rough and muddy waters. They missed an eddy or two and dodged debris floating down the river. They could hear the dogs on the bank and men talking, but they were far enough down the river that they couldn't come after them. Slowly the two swimmers made cuts across for fifteen yards and then let the current carry them until they had crossed the mighty river.

They got to a beach area and came ashore. It appeared that they were almost a mile down the river from where they entered. They quickly got up the bank and into some tall undergrowth so they could not be seen. They had a feeling that the Mississippi sheriff in whatever county they were in would be notified by the Louisiana sheriff. Staying away from roads, they finally found a fairly secluded spot and then rested from the ordeals of their escape.

Aeamon Lee again repeated the ritual of taking the rolled-up bills he had in his pocket and trying to dry off the money the second time in one day. "After a while, that money ain't going to be no good if we keep getting it wet," Jo-Nathan observed. When they had rested awhile, Jo-Nathan told Aeamon Lee he had something to say and that he really meant it.

"You know, Aeamon Lee, I was afraid when we left on this little trip of yours. I never have been to many places in my life, and new people and new towns get to me. I've been afraid every day we've been gone from home, and I was afraid playing poker on the street, in that fighting contest, on that blamed boat, in that beer joint, swimming this river—*twice* in one day—and I've heard that you are not supposed to be swimming no river this wide."

Aeamon Lee started to say something, but Jo-Nathan interrupted, "No, wait a minute till I finish. I've slept on the street and in a cotton wagon. I've done things I promised my mama I would never do. Now I've had enough of this trip, and I'm ready to start going home. I don't even know that we can make it home. We're probably wanted men right now. They're going to be looking for us. I just know it. Listen, I think it's time to go home. Agree?"

"Agree. We'll start making our way back toward Jackson and then home. I think we're somewhere around Natchez." This seemed to satisfy Jo-Nathan.

But Jo-Nathan wasn't finished. He asked Aeamon Lee what he was supposed to say if anyone ever found out about all his poker playing and how he was present. "You know some people think it's wrong to gamble for money."

Aeamon Lee responded, "Not if you gamble your money on Wall Street. Have you noticed how rich people make up this elaborate rationale that allows them to gamble with their money on Wall Street? Sometimes they win, and sometimes they lose. But they will turn right around and condemn us for a little poker game. A person should use sound judgment and common sense, but I resent the hypocrisy."

*　　*　　*

They started walking until they came to the edge of a town and noticed a dollar store. Even though they've gone barefooted most of their lives, they were ready for some shoes and also some different clothes. Only remnants of their costumes were left for clothing. They went into the dollar store even though they looked a mess and found some shoes that fit, a shirt and pair of pants for Jo-Nathan, and a shirt for Aeamon Lee. He couldn't find any pants that would fit, so he just continued to wear the white dress pants of an old plantation owner.

They saw a long grain truck parked with a load of grain on it, commonly seen in the Mississippi Delta. This gave Aeamon Lee an idea. He told Jo-Nathan that they could get in the back of that truck and cover themselves with grain and maybe get back to Jackson. He had noticed that the truck had a Hinds County tag on it, probably headed back home.

"Here we go again," Jo-Nathan said, but he went along with the plans of his friend. They climbed aboard and dug into the grain with no one watching. They finally sank down enough that no one noticed them. And as luck would have it, the truck headed northeast toward Jackson. The truck stopped at Raymond. The two decided that they had better get off there; and by hitchhiking, asking for rides, paying for rides, and walking, they finally arrived in Jackson.

Aeamon Lee had heard of Roscoe's, a sporting goods store in Jackson that had a good stock of sports equipment. Most of the coaches in the area used the store for their athletic purchases. He explained to Jo-Nathan that he had a plan, and it would require him to stop at this store. There was still around $2,000 of the gambling and boxing money in his pocket. Upon arriving at the store, he explained to a clerk that he wanted an aluminum baseball bat, a glove, some baseballs, and a college regulation football. He also got a pair of football shoes and a pair of baseball shoes. He wasn't used to wearing these type of shoes since he didn't participate in the sport during high school.

Jo-Nathan was curious about Aeamon Lee's plan and wanted to know more.

"I'll tell you more when we get home. I've been doing a lot of thinking about our future. This is an important time for us. We've got some big decisions to make. We're young, healthy, and strong, and the future belongs to us."

So the two fellow travelers made their way, again by using various means, back home. They were weary and happy to be home where they were welcomed, with much relief on the part of both sets of parents. The parents wanted to know all about their trip to Memphis—what they saw, did, who they stayed with, and what lessons they had learned.

"Did you go to the zoo in Memphis? I've heard that it really is nice." Martha asked.

Jo-Nathan said, "Well, you know, Aeamon Lee, that was one place we should have gone. I didn't think about that."

"No, I didn't either."

"Where did y'all sleep?" Martha continued with her questions.

"Well, since we didn't have much money, we stayed at various places. It was all right except the night we had to sleep in the same bed." Jo-Nathan looked at Aeamon Lee, and both of them shook their heads, thinking about the night in the cotton wagon.

"We met some people who helped us out and took us around Memphis."

Jo-Nathan added, "And we got to go down to Beale Street."

"Now, boys, I don't know about that being a good place for you to be. Why, all kinds of things go on down there on Beale Street, I've heard," said Mama Kate.

"That was the worst place we went, Mama. And we didn't go back." Jo-Nathan wanted to switch the subject before this went on any longer.

The boys asked, "Tell us about what all went on here while we were gone."

"Nothing much, just the same ole thing. We were worrying about our two boys," Mama Kate said.

"Well, there was nothing to be worried about. We saw Memphis, and we saw the Mississippi River up close, real close." Again, the boys looked at each other and smiled.

"We've had our senior trip, had some fun, and now we're ready to go to work." They never told their parents the full story of their adventures and how close they came to meeting their fate.

*   *   *

After they got their resting up done, Jo-Nathan came up to Aeamon Lee and said, "I want to know about this plan you talked about."

"While we are getting caught up with some crop work, I want us to start working out and get in good shape, both of us, because we've got to be in good shape if we do what I think we can. That means we start running several miles early every morning. June is coming up, and the weather later on in the day is going to be hot, so we need to do it early in the morning and late in the evening."

"Why do we have to be in such good shape? We proved on our little trip that we can swim, run, and fight." Jo-Nathan laughed.

"We're going to have to do even better than that, much better. All right, I'll tell you clearly what I have in mind. Now listen! And don't laugh! I believe we can get in really good shape, practice our running and lifting skills, and be able to go to the University of Mississippi, walk on this summer, and make the football team. Maybe even win football scholarships and play football at Ole Miss. You and me."

"That's what you've been thinking about all this time? That's why you bought that football in Jackson?" Jo-Nathan asked.

"Now, I know you probably think this is an impossible dream, but I think we can pull it off. We just have to be prepared and ready and good. They'll let you walk on, and you get at least a chance to be looked at. I know that it seldom works out, but sometimes it does. I can put myself in that ethereal state of mind, and I believe I can bring you along, and we can make it. I've always heard it said that if we always do what we always did, we'd always get what we always got. We've lived on this hill nearly all our lives. We've faced resentment. We've felt it. But we have something in our character that cries out for something better. It's like the caged bird singing.[25] In the meantime, we've got a lot of hard work to do because, once we are there, we've got to do something really dramatic to convince them that we can play."

"Listen, Aeamon Lee. I wouldn't put a damper on your dreams, but that sounds like an awfully tall order. We didn't even play in high school. You remember what they did to you when you tried to play. We have no experience, no record."

"Jo-Nathan, that's what the aristocrats want us to believe. They own the land, all the business, the flow of money, and the opportunity. No telling how many times they tried to get Daddy's land right here. When he got hurt, the bank wanted to buy the place. I believe that if he had missed a payment for one day, the bank would have taken it. We did without basic necessities, so we'd have enough money to make the next payment.

"They pretty much determine who gets a chance to improve their life. They want people like us to stay in our place. Plantation owners used to compliment slaves for being tractable. That means they were easily controlled, because I looked that word up. We're supposed to be quiet, accept our place, and not complain about it. When I questioned Hollis Clanton for knocking my crippled daddy down, he called me an 'uppity piece of white trash.' That's how the people that have feel about us. But I admit, it is hard to break the cycle. But it can be done, and we'll find a way.

"I read something about the caste system they have in India. There, you are born in one of five castes, and it doesn't make any difference how well you do—you stay in that same caste for the rest of your life. It seems to me that our class system is similar to that. It's unlikely that rich people will lose their wealth. They know where all the safe investments are. They hire accountants to keep up with that sort of thing. And it's also unlikely that the poor and working people will ever move out of their class. Though it is theoretically possible."

"I know all that," Jo-Nathan said, "but what are the ways out of that cycle?"

"I've been doing some thinking about that. In fact, I've made a list. I'll go over them. First, we could inherit a fortune from a rich aunt."

Jo-Nathan said, "I don't have no rich aunt. Do you have a rich aunt?"

"No, so let's go on down the list. Except, you know that's how most rich people got their money—they inherited it from someone else as an accident of birth. That inherited wealth, even though they didn't have to work hard at something and be successful, has given them the status of high living. They're living off someone else's good fortune. When you inherit a lot of wealth, you inherit a lot of other advantages as well. And what I've observed is that it doesn't make any difference how the money was made. Everybody wants these folks to walk through their door. It's like they are better than other folks."

"What's next on the list?" Jo-Nathan asked.

"You can have a rare skill for which there is a great demand by the public, like singing, acting, or being good in sports. That's how Elvis made it."

Jo-Nathan perked up and said, "Hey, maybe you can become a famous singer. You sing and play with the Willie Rivers Band at Sorghum Hill."

"That's a good suggestion, but, Jo-Nathan, that's really a long shot. It usually takes a long time for someone to be discovered. Outside of this little area, no one has even heard of Willie Rivers or Sorghum Hill. There are hundreds of small bands and singers that meet on Saturday night to make music all over the country."

"What else you got on your list?"

"You could get elected to public office and be successful in political campaigns and move on up to higher office. But, of course, you have to have the financial backing of the big political fat cats, which, in turn, means that you are obligated to their interests. You would be bought, owned, or rented by the people with the big money. Once you went against them, you would be destroyed. We could never do anything like that, could we? Because we have principles."

"Next," Jo-Nathan said.

"I've always heard it said that you could marry more money in five minutes than you could make in a lifetime," Aeamon Lee said while going on down his list. "But the problem with this one is that the parents of the rich girls make sure they are placed in social settings, like colleges and social groups, where they are most likely to meet and marry someone within their own class. Sometimes, it is a scandal in their family when they don't."

"I think that one is pretty much out of the question too. What else you got?"

"The most common way to move up the social ladder and have more access to health care, jobs, and opportunity is to get a lot of education. Once you've gotten that diploma, they can't take it away from you. But again, it seems to me that forces are at work to make higher education the privilege only of the upper classes. They want to carry us back to the 1920s. A lot of colleges want to be havens of upper-middle-class students by raising so-called standards and raising the costs. Oh, they'll have their minimum of minority students to get by accrediting agencies and government requirements."

Aeamon Lee continued, "This makes me so blamed mad that I'll fight these forces of elitism and exclusion in ways they've never seen before. I swear by all that is right and good, they'll never kill my spirit.

They don't control my mind. Working people still have a few freedoms. You know, Jo-Nathan, we're better than they are anyway."

"How do you figure that?"

"We may not have their social standing, but we have something that they don't."

"And what is that?" Jo-Nathan asked.

"We know what injustice is. You and I know that that is one thing God has always rejected."

"Does this mean you're going to go the route of making the football team and getting a scholarship? What are some other ways?" Jo-Nathan asked.

"Of course, a person can join the military and learn some employable skills. When they get out, they can usually get some more education," Aeamon Lee said.

Jo-Nathan said, "I'm glad you said that."

"What do you mean?"

"Oh, I'll get around to explaining that. So tell me, what do we do?"

Aeamon Lee responded, "I believe that 'life is not a matter of holding good cards but of playing a poor hand well.'[26] But we need to go ahead and list every negative thing we can think of. We need to give all the reasons we can't do it. We'll make a long list. Let's get it all out of our system, because once we start, we're not looking back. We've got to get our sights firmly set inside of us because 'all serious daring starts from within.'[27] The first thing we've got to do is to get into shape physically. That's where all the running comes in. Then we've got to get our timing down in the forty-yard dash. We've got to run it in four point five seconds or less."

* * *

Jo-Nathan said, "Remember, I kept telling you how I had to get back home by the end of the week? Well, there is something that I haven't told you. Several weeks before we left on our little adventure, I signed up for the marines, and I leave in twelve days. I need to spend some time with Mama and Daddy. I also need to do a lot of what you're talking about, getting into good physical shape, because it's going to be tough."

The news stunned Aeamon Lee. "Dang, I was thinking so much about myself that I didn't stop to remember that you have to be the master of your own fate, the captain of your own ship.[28] You have to make your own decisions about what's best for you. It sounds like I can't talk you out of it because you've already signed up. I hear that you need to start in great physical shape. Maybe we can do that part together. What we're both aiming for requires that we be in tip-top shape. It'll take a while for this to sink in, Jo-Nathan. I guess you know what you are doing. Man, I was going to make a wide receiver out of you, and we would go to Ole Miss together. Now, who is going to help me pick the blackberries in July?"

Jo-Nathan tried to make his decision more acceptable to Aeamon Lee. "I've thought it through, and that recruiter was really helpful and told me all about the careers I could get into when I get out. He explained all the assistance I could get to go to college and a lot of other things."

Aeamon Lee tried not to make him feel badly about his decision. It was too late anyway. Instead, he attempted to get adjusted to the idea and to help his friend get ready as much as possible in a short period of time.

They rose early every morning and ran. It was hard at first; but the more they ran, the more they discovered that no matter how tired they were at night, they woke up the next morning feeling like a million dollars.

Just before sundown, they ran again, up and down the country roads that ran by their houses. They developed a trail through the woods, and eventually, they were able to run farther and farther. They did as many different calisthenics as they could. They had a chinning bar in the barn, and they did push-ups till they dropped.

Jo-Nathan finally suggested that he could help Aeamon Lee develop some more specific skills that he would need if he succeeded in his quest. "Maybe we can come up with some skills that no one has used. You've not only got to be fast, you've got to be quick and illusive so they can't catch you. What is around here that is hard to catch? Look at the animals, they know when to fight and when to flee and just do it instinctively. Maybe, if you can learn how to imitate that, it will be something different."

Jo-Nathan listed several animals that were hard to catch, and Aeamon Lee said, "That's right, and we're going to learn to make the same type moves they make—the deer, horse, chicken, snake, fox, dog, squirrel, caterpillar, goat, and others. You're right, every one of them has its own way of escaping and avoiding capture. We can learn a lot of practical things from nature right here on this farm. We should be able to do this better than anyone else. Even the Bible says, 'Ask now the animals and let them teach you.'"[29]

During the day, between crop chores, they worked on perfecting other skills. There was a lot of extra chicken wire in the barn. They took the wire down to a hollow below the house and stretched that chicken wire from tree to tree until they had closed off a section of that hollow. They made it about ten feet high, placed some salt inside the wired-off territory, and waited for a deer to enter. Finally, early one morning after they had finished running, they noticed a deer inside the fence. They sneaked up close, ran toward the opening, and closed it off with the deer inside. The deer, however, kept running and jumping on the fence until it found a small opening and ran right through it to freedom. They realized then that they would have to patch all possible openings to keep the deer inside.

A short time later, they trapped another deer inside, a doe. This time, the deer didn't escape. But they didn't know how long it would stay in the pen. Aeamon Lee tried to catch the deer. Each time he leaped toward the deer, he fell to the ground. With greater determination than before, he got up and tried again. Even with the same effort, he landed on the ground with the deer out of his grasp. He was skinning himself really bad, but he kept going after the deer.

Finally, Jo-Nathan went up to Aeamon Lee and shouted, "You don't have to catch the deer. All you have to do is learn how to run like the deer."

That piece of advice made so much sense. Aeamon Lee just got off the ground and started a new approach. He noticed how the deer could jump from one place to another place, zigzagging, and no one knew which direction the deer would jump. The deer ran straight for a while and then would do the jumping routine and change directions. Aeamon Lee practiced these moves until he ran remarkably like the deer.

They noticed the moves of the other animals and observed how they could get away from intruders with various techniques. The fox could stop on a dime and change directions completely. The cat could come to a screeching halt and reverse its direction, quick as lighting. The horse could sway its body and lope around and away from someone trying to catch it. The snake, when cornered, could assume a defensive position and strike back. It could weave in and out of tight situations. The goat could take on an adversary head-on with fierce aggression. The dog could sometimes leap for an object from all angles, but it also had the ability to catch the object when it was low. The caterpillar used its whole body to plow ahead. Aeamon Lee practiced these moves until they were perfected. At every chance during the day, Aeamon Lee would suddenly make one of these animal moves toward Jo-Nathan as they joked around with each other. When Jo-Nathan swung at Aeamon Lee, he would jerk his head around and say, "Now that was a cow!" Aeamon Lee learned so much from the animals because he seemed to have a special rapport with them.

Aeamon Lee told Jo-Nathan, "Now we're going to practice passing the football, and I want you to catch anything thrown in your direction. I'm going to be the quarterback, and you're going to be a wide receiver."

"You know, I heard that whoever plays quarterback at Ole Miss is more popular in the state than the governor," Jo-Nathan said.

"I don't care who is more popular. I'm not going to worry about anything else. I have to trust myself because 'self-trust is the first secret of success.'"[30]

Jo-Nathan knew that Aeamon Lee's plans were more unrealistic than his. He didn't completely share the enthusiasm that Aeamon Lee had, but he went along and didn't try to discourage. He knew that Aeamon Lee was serious; he didn't want to pour water on his plans. He had seen him do some really remarkable things, and maybe he could achieve his goal. Anyway, he helped him prepare the best he could.

They set up old tires hanging by ropes; some were high, and some were low. Aeamon Lee passed the ball through the tires at various distances. He learned how to do it with zip, with quickness, and with tight spirals. He threw to Jo-Nathan, who was instructed to run various routes and who learned how to make moves that would separate him from the defenders. They changed the speed of the ball and type of passes thrown. He perfected the fade pass, the fly, the post, the slant patterns, and how to lead the receiver. Occasionally, Aeamon Lee would pull the ball down and start to run. Visualizing the defenders, he adjusted by using the various moves of the animals. Jo-Nathan said, "Just remember, now when the breaks are going against you, run like the animals."

They continued to do chin-ups and push-ups. Aeamon Lee found some barbells and a bench at a yard sale. He bought them with some of the remaining gambling money. Together, they lifted weights every day and were eating carefully. Initially, Aeamon Lee lost a few pounds, but then he began to maintain his body weight. He was still six feet and four inches tall and weighed around 210 pounds.

They were approaching the time for Jo-Nathan to leave. Aeamon Lee didn't take up too much of his friend's time because he knew Jo-Nathan wanted to be with Amos and Mama Kate during the short time he had remaining.

*   *   *

Aeamon Lee and Jo-Nathan visited Sorghum Hill one last time before leaving home. Willie Rivers and the Willie Rivers Band was playing, and Aeamon Lee sang a few songs as he usually did. After his last song, he addressed the crowd.

"For as long as I can remember, I've been coming to Sorghum Hill on Saturday nights. I want to thank all of you for making me feel welcomed. We've had some great times here. I'll never forget the night we sent Castor Nuckolls and his friends on their way. I am saying all this to say that shortly, as some of you know, Jo-Nathan Markum will be leaving us to join the Marine Corps. And I will be leaving home to go to Oxford, Mississippi. I plan to walk on with the football team at Ole Miss and try to make the team, and if I do, I'll be enrolling as a student. This is something that both of us have to do. The sad truth is, 'most of us will go to our graves with our music still inside us.'[31] We can't let that happen. Think of us and pray for us as we go chasing after our dreams. We'll be back every chance we have."

Most everybody there came around to wish the two of them good luck. Several of the older boys talked about how they wished they had done something like that, that they felt they could have amounted to something. Maleah Marcelles, who had helped them with Caster Nuckolls, followed Aeamon Lee when he started to leave. She had always had an eye on Aeamon Lee but never expressed any feelings for him. She thought that this could very well be the beginning of the end. Times would never be the same after this night. Aeamon Lee would leave and find his fortune and life someplace else. But she knew if she did not say something, she would regret it the rest of her life.

She followed him outside, and at first, Aeamon Lee didn't know she was behind him. Suddenly, he turned around, and there she was. She stopped, looking deeply into his eyes. Aeamon Lee didn't say anything.

Finally, she said, "I can't let this moment pass without being honest with you. And I know I would regret it if I didn't tell you tonight how much I care for you. You have respected us and treated all of us right. You helped us out when you could have gotten yourself killed. I never told you this, but you were the one who made a difference in my life. I was able to get rid of all those demons that seemed to be around all the time. Many others like me were giving in to all the dirt that was there, but it never bothered you to stay away from all the bad. Because of that, I can be proud and thankful for living the life I have now. We were both brought up in hard times, but you never gave in to the things that could have gotten you down. That really helped me to make better decisions. I have always felt that you would never notice me, so I never said anything about how I felt toward you. But I just can't stand here and let you leave, knowing I may never see you again. I know, too, that you have big plans for the future. And I wouldn't want you to give up on those plans. You'll do good. I know you will. I just want you to know that wherever you go, there is someone right here on Sorghum Hill who will always stand by you."

Aeamon Lee waited a moment before saying anything. Then he said, "I've always tried to treat you as if you were what you ought to be, and this has helped you become what you are capable of becoming.[32] I'll keep what you've said deep in my heart."

There was silence for a while as the two of them just looked at each other. A breeze was blowing against the silence, and in the moonlight, an awkwardness kept them at a distance. But the sincerity of her heart was something Aeamon Lee couldn't ignore. He smiled, took her hand, embraced her, and slowly began to draw away. He then turned around and walked away.

*　　*　　*

On Sunday night, while Martha, Plea, and Aeamon Lee, along with Jo-Nathan, were sitting on the front porch, they began to talk about their decisions. It was decided that Aeamon Lee would leave after he had laid by the crops in late July. Jo-Nathan would leave on the bus for South Carolina the next morning.

Aeamon Lee walked with Jo-Nathan back to his house. Jo-Nathan told him, "I know you wanted me to go with you and try to play football, but I'd only be in your way. I'm not that good. I don't have the skills you have. We must not allow any negative thinking to get in the way of our plans. One thing for sure, there is nothing here in Goshen Wells that we can build a future on. I have to have a dream to follow, and I can't put it off."

Aeamon Lee said, "And you must not put it off. 'What happens to a dream deferred? Does it dry up like a raisin in the sun? Or fester like a sore—and then run? Does it stink like rotten meat? Or crust and sugar over—like a syrupy sweet? Maybe it just sags like a heavy load. Or does it explode?'"[33]

"I'm doing what several in my family have done, those that have done well, and as you said, I'm not going to defer it. When I get out of the marines, I'll be able to choose from several different options."

"Listen, Jo-Nathan, I'm with you, my friend, but I need to tell you something that recruiter didn't tell you. I've got to remind you of this, or I'll be sorry. You are going to be in the armed forces, the military. You'll be trained to fight in wars, to hate and to kill without feeling. When women and children are killed, they'll just call it collateral damage. They can send you to anyplace in the world to fight, sometimes for their egos. And you could get killed fighting their wars. Are you ready to do that? Because you'd better be." He paused for a moment and then said, "But you have to make your choices in life, and once you've made a choice, you have to pursue it with everything you've got and leave the consequences to God."[34]

"I know about the dangers, but I'll just take my chances. They need volunteers. Besides, for some of us, this is the only chance we have of getting ahead. I'll just have to take my chances. I've talked with Mama and Daddy, and it's all right with them. They're proud that I have enough ambition to want to do something like that."

Aeamon Lee just looked at him and then turned around and hung his head. Jo-Nathan said, "You have the courage and guts to make this football plan work for you. I don't want to get in the way. And I'll be proud of you, and I'll keep up with what happens. I've never told you this, but I am amazed at what all you can do, what you've already done in your life. You don't let nobody tell you that you can't do something. You just go out and do it. I've learned from that, and I'm going to apply it myself."

"It won't be the same without you," Aeamon Lee admitted. "You've been a friend who sticks closer than a brother.[35]

Remember that no one can make you feel inferior without your consent.[36] And never, ever give up."[37]

For the last evening, both families sat on the front porch and talked. Instead of talking about the marines, they talked about light things. Several of Jo-Nathan's family stopped by, and the subject came up about favorite movie quotes. It was not that they had seen many movies, but over time, they had seen some of the old movies on television. Occasionally, they got to go see movies at a drive-in or a walk-in movie house. Several mentioned lines like "Wherever there is a fight so hungry people can eat, I'll be there."[38] One was "You're going to need a bigger boat."[39] Someone mentioned the line "What we have here is a failure to communicate."[40] They asked Aeamon Lee for his, and of course, his line was a little long and on his pet topic: justice.

"I saw this movie called *Billy Jack*, and it's one of my favorites. In the ice cream parlor, these town jerks had poured some flour over the heads of a little Indian girl and another girl. Billy Jack walks in and says, 'Bernard, I want you to know that I try . . . When Jean and the kids at the school tell me I should control my violent temper and be passive like they are, I try, I really try. But when I see this girl of such a beautiful spirit so degraded and when I see this boy so flogged out by this big ape here, and this little girl that is so special to us that we call her "God's little gift to sunshine," and I think of the number of years she is going to have to carry in her memory the savagery of this idiotic moment of yours, I go *berserk*.'[41] And we know what happened then."

Jo-Nathan said, "I don't think you would last one week in the marines." These moments of simple conversation on that front porch would long be cherished in their memories of their home and family.

The farewell at the bus station was filled with optimism for Jo-Nathan's sake, but deep inside, there was great sadness. Aeamon Lee went with the Markums and had little to say. Jo-Nathan said, "I can't be calling except in emergencies, but I can write letters."

Everybody promised to write. The two hugged, and Aeamon Lee had to walk away from the scene so that Amos and Mama Kate could say their goodbyes.

*   *   *

Later that summer, Aeamon Lee spent time bush-hogging around the crops. Plea always kept the fields clean around the edges after laying by. By that time, the grass and brush had grown around the ditch banks and at the edges of the field. Aeamon Lee always tried to do these things the same way his father had done them. Besides, it made the fields look cleaner and nicer. People made observations about whether a place had been allowed to run down or if it had been improved. They could surely say that Aeamon Lee and Martha had improved their place.

In the time left, Aeamon Lee completed several work projects around the homeplace because he knew it would be a while before he returned home. He still had money left over from his trip to buy some clothes. Martha had sewed some new shirts for him that he liked, with the three-quarter-length sleeves. It was a time when students were fashion-conscious, but these trends never affected him the way it did most kids. Someone had written *The Preppy Handbook* several years before, and many students used this book as a guide for how to dress.[42] These were not the primary matters on Aeamon Lee's mind as he prepared for the unknown. He knew everything would depend on his making the team. He also knew this was a long shot.

In the evenings, Aeamon Lee spent a lot of time just talking with the family about the past and the future. They sat on the porch a lot and reminisced over the many and varied experiences they had together. Underneath the exterior was a little anxiety about what lay before him.

It would be an uncertain time, but he would be certain and maintain his air of invincibility and confidence. He wanted above all to know that Martha and Plea were okay with his effort, and he looked for every hint of encouragement from them to pursue his goal.

Those evenings on the front porch lived in his memory. After a hard day's work, everyone was hungry, and Martha warmed up the big dinner, which had been left on the table. A large tablecloth was spread over the table to keep the flies off. At night, the dishes were washed, and everyone had a clean plate and tableware.

After supper, the family retired to the front porch. The windows of the house were opened in order for the house to cool down after a sunny, hot day. In the meantime, the family shared the day's activities and their feelings about each other. A lot of philosophy about life, living, and its meaning were learned in those evening hours on the front porch. Aeamon Lee thought of it as their continuing to discover *summum bonum*.[43] At various times, their neighbor Maleah came by on these evenings to hear Aeamon Lee's bits of wisdom and to offer some of her own.

Often, Aeamon Lee picked and sang a few songs—some he had written, and some he had heard. The evening was not complete without singing a gospel song, and often Martha would join in. They recalled how Jo-Nathan made his way to their front porch and joined in as one of the family.

* * *

Late one afternoon, Aeamon Lee had been out practicing, running, and passing the football. While walking along, he stepped beside a piece of iron that sprang up and scratched his ankle. Getting to the porch was as far as he could go. He stretched out on the porch and even ate his supper out there. Afterward, there were several of the Markums there with the Mistrals, talking and laughing with Aeamon Lee while he rested his ankle.

After a while, one of the Markum girls and Maleah Marcelles, who had stopped by to visit, came over; and Maleah had a pan in her hand. She drew some water for the pan and came up to Aeamon Lee. She took a rag and started wiping off his feet and leg without saying a word. Her long hair fell down on his leg as she washed it clean of all the dust, dirt, and blood from the wound. She then took a tube of what she called special ointment and put some on his wound and told him it would make the wound heal faster so he would be ready for his big day. There was silence among all those present as she did this considerate deed. It was like a mysterious act that no one could quite understand.

Before Maleah left, she gave Aeamon Lee an envelope and asked him not to open it until he was on the bus. She added, "There is something else in the envelope. It's a list of some wise sayings I found that you might find useful. They're not as fancy as some of those you have on those cards you've memorized, but I think you will find them handy at just the right time."

CHAPTER 3

The Quest Begins
AUGUST 1983

Aeamon Lee received verbal agreement from Assistant Coach Arrington at Ole Miss that he could report to campus on August 8, 1983. He was given instructions on where to report as a walk-on and what to bring. Coach Arrington didn't mention where he would live during this time, and Aeamon Lee didn't want to bring it up. He would have to make some arrangements for lodging for an undetermined amount of time. Anyway, he wanted to arrive a few days early so he could get acclimated to things in Oxford and on campus and maybe have a chance to meet some of the players and coaches.

Finally, the day came for him to leave Goshen Wells, his beloved family, and the nearby families of his youth. He knew someone who would take him to Jackson, where he would board a Trailways bus bound for Oxford.

His ride was to pick him up at his house around 10:00 a.m. Throughout that morning, several of his friends and neighbors dropped by the house to wish him well. He packed only one fairly large suitcase. He knew his chances were slim in winning a football scholarship, which would allow him to enroll for classes. He packed carefully the newly washed, clothesline dried, starched, and ironed shirts Martha had sown for him. Martha and Plea were doing all that they could to make this a happy time, but underneath those feelings were fears of uncertainty.

His parents realized that their son was leaving and things would probably never be the same. There was still the uncertainty of their being able to continue the crops and work Aeamon Lee had done for the past five years. Aeamon Lee was still bothered by the fact that he had been unable to motivate his father to do something constructive with the capabilities he still had. He was still hoping that the custom-made carving set would occupy his time. He knew that if his father would just start a challenging task, he would find some satisfaction. But he decided not to bring the matter up anymore, certainly not on this day. In the past, it had only brought disappointment and hurt feelings.

Martha handed him a cardboard box tied with string. She said, "Aeamon Lee, I want you to give these sweet potatoes to Alice Ruth in appreciation for putting you up there at their place for a while." Alice Ruth was the wife of Frank Lorance and a sister of Martha's who lived a few miles outside of Oxford. Mr. Lorance had been a successful cattleman for a number of years, and they had built a fine house and a modern barn. Alice Ruth told Martha that she supposed they would allow Aeamon Lee to stay a while with them. He could pay for his upkeep by helping Mr. Lorance with the cattle and horses.

Over the years, there had not been much contact between Martha's family and the Lorances. Alice Ruth and Frank never attended the family reunions and had felt so proud of their financial success that they felt out of place with the rest of the family that had not done as well. Martha never spoke disparagingly about them and just assumed that they would still befriend a family member in need of lodging for a short period of time.

When Aeamon Lee saw that cardboard box full of sweet potatoes, he really didn't want to carry it to Oxford on the bus. He didn't want to admit that he would be a little self-conscious about it, but he didn't want to offend his mother either. He said, "Mom, are you sure Aunt Alice would want or need these sweet potatoes? I imagine they have sweet potatoes in Oxford, don't you think?" He could tell that Martha really wanted him to take the sweet potatoes, so he didn't mention it anymore. He took his suitcase, the box of sweet potatoes, some money he had left from the poker game, and made his way to an unknown future.

It was almost time for the ride to come by, and they moved out toward the road to be ready. This was where they would say their goodbyes.

Martha said, "Aeamon Lee, I just want you to know—and I don't think I've ever really said this to you though it's been in my heart ever since you came—you were a special gift, and we had waited a long time, as equal partners, for you to come. We kept feeling that someday you would come. We had almost given up hope. We've always known, as I explained, that you would have a special mission in your life, and I know that someday you will find it. We don't know what it is exactly, but we've got to let you start out on your journey. You've been a good son to us, and what you've done for us could not be matched by any son. We'll think about you every day, and we'll pray for you every night. I'm going to ask the church this Sunday to have a special prayer for you. Now don't you worry about us. You know we'll make it all right."

Aeamon Lee hugged his mother and when he finished, Plea knew it was his time to speak, and he knew he wasn't good at this sort of thing. Plea put his hand on his son's arm and said, "Son, I've always regretted what happened to me because it put so much weight on your shoulders long before a child should have to feel this much responsibility. You've done well for us. I only wish I could have been of more help." After all these years, he still felt guilty and responsible for his disability.

"Daddy, you don't have to say these things, you know that. I just did what I could. I learned a lot about getting an old tractor cranked and a lot of about driving nails."

"Well, if things don't work out, you know you can come back home."

To that, Aeamon Lee said with determination, "'A great flame follows a little spark.'"[44] In his mind, there was no room for retreat, for failure. Oh, he would come back home, he hoped, but as a warrior who had been in many battles, all won.

"Dad, you know every time we meet after a long time or when I'm leaving, we sort of shake hands? Well, Daddy, that's foolish for a father and son to just do that. We're flesh and blood, and you're my daddy. I love you, and I'm going to give you a hug, and I'm not going to be embarrassed."

With that said, Aeamon Lee leaned forward and gave his father a big hug. There was emotion building up in Plea, and he sort of hid the tear in his eye. But down deep in his soul, Plea was glad that this barrier between a father and a son had been broken. From that time on, they would always hug each other when they met. Each one was glad and felt better for it.

While he was hugging his father, Aeamon Lee looked upon a distant hill and saw someone he knew. It was Maleah Marcelles just standing there, and she gave him a small wave of the hand. Aeamon Lee couldn't see them, but there were tears in her eyes.

He again looked at Martha and said, quoting the words from a CCR song,

Put a candle in the window,
I'll be coming home soon.[45]

*   *   *

Finally, the ride came for Aeamon Lee to take him to Jackson to catch the bus to Oxford. He loaded up his one large suitcase, the cardboard box of sweet potatoes, and left for Jackson. Martha and Plea stood there silently until the car was completely out of sight.

Everything went smoothly in Jackson, and he got on the right bus to Oxford. The trip up I-55 gave him some time to think about this new adventure as he attempted to anticipate what he might encounter and how he would handle it. He kept reminding himself that he could do it, had every right to try it, even though there was a part of him that wondered about an uncertain future. He kept thinking about living his life on the ethereal plane. So the brash young adventurer would go toward the direction of his dreams with confidence. He would live the life he had imagined.[46]

He remembered the envelope that Maleah Marcelles had given him. He got it out and opened it up. There was $31.68 in it with a note that read, "I know that you will need this. I know you're just like all the rest of us in not having a lot of money. But we admire what you are doing, so some of my friends and I put a little money together to help you out. The others were Georgene Johnson, Pastelle Pulliam, and Omirah Miley." It was signed "Maleah." His heart was moved over such thoughtfulness and generosity.

Then he brought out Maleah's list of wise sayings. There were eight of them, rather short and to the point, so Aeamon Lee memorized them as well, not knowing what a difference they would make as he embarked on his unlikely venture.

As was so often the case with families with this socioeconomic background, each tried to help the other with a little spare money when it was needed. It might be given to help someone get buried, to a family member that was sick, to buy some clothes for a special occasion, or to help someone in their efforts to get someplace in life.

There had always been times in his life when that old negative self-talk popped up in his mind. He fought against the thought that he was only here to survive, to be laughed at, and to be scorned. He could hear the devil side of his nature sometimes tell him, "You're nobody. Don't care. You're not among the privileged. You will never make a difference. You will always work for the man. Nobody cares. You will never be any better. Why try to stay out of trouble? Hit back. Dig a deep hole for yourself." Most of the time, the devil lost this argument. All the dark forces of hell would not prevent him from reaching with unrelenting pursuit.

Aeamon Lee had stuck some of the three-by-five cards in his pocket to read, some with longer quotations because he had memorized nearly all the shorter quotes he had collected over the past several years. He found one card that had a special meaning to him:

> It is not the critic who counts: not the man who points out how the strong man stumbles or where the doer of deeds could have done better. The credit belongs to the man who is actually in the arena, whose face is marred by dust and sweat and blood, who strives valiantly, who errs and comes up short again and again, because there is no effort without error or shortcoming, but who knows the great enthusiasms, the great devotions, who spends himself for a worthy cause; who, at the best, knows, in the end, the triumph of high achievement,

and who, at the worst, if he fails, at least he fails while daring greatly, so that his place shall never be with those cold and timid souls who knew neither victory nor defeat.[47]

He would soon know, in a few short weeks, whether it would be victory or defeat. And he gained satisfaction in knowing that, in either case, he would not be among those timid souls who knew neither victory nor defeat. And it would not be the critic who counted. Oh, there had been many who thought his plans were foolish, only the foolish unrealistic fantasies of a poor country dreamer.

His anxiety and energy level rose with each mile that passed. But he would not live too far ahead. He had always heard about people who lived too many years ahead and failed to take care of the business of today.

*　　*　　*

Aunt Alice Ruth Lorance was a sister to Martha, but since they had done so well financially and had shined in Oxford society, she didn't have much to do with Martha and the rest of her family. Over the years since they had prospered, there had been very little contact. Martha wrote her an occasional letter to let her know about the family and to express family courtesies to her.

Coach Arrington had written a letter to Aeamon Lee explaining the procedure for walk-ons. He mentioned that the players lived in the athletic dorm during the weeks before classes started. But Aeamon Lee did not understand that this was all free and that he got free room and board during this time. This was why he had sought out arrangements to live with the Lorances for a period of time. Since he couldn't afford the extra expenses, he thought he had to provide other arrangements. So he would practice with the team but get his sleep and food elsewhere.

He got his large suitcase and box of sweet potatoes off the bus and found directions to Highway 6 that lead to Pontotoc. The Lorances only lived a few miles from Oxford on their large cattle and horse farm.

There was a Quick Stop at the edge of town on that highway, and he walked to it to see if there might be a ride out to their place. He simply asked people who had stopped for gas if they were going out that highway and, if so, if he could catch a ride for two miles. Several refused, but finally an old gentleman asked him what was in the box. "Well, sir, they are sweet potatoes my mother sent for my aunt and uncle." The man must have thought that was the truth, because you just don't run into a seventeen-year-old every day carrying a box of sweet potatoes to somebody's house.

The Lorances had remodeled an old home to make it appear quite Old South, with large columns out front, painted white with green shutters, and a lot of porch furniture. The yard looked like it had been manicured, with shrubs, flowerbeds, and shade trees all around. The farm had expensive-looking fencing around the house for the horses. The cattle were kept away from the house, but the fine horses were there close enough for all the visitors to see.

When Aeamon Lee walked up the driveway to the house, there were several Lincoln town cars in the driveway. When Alice Ruth came to the door, she said, "Oh, it's you already. I thought you would get here later. We are just finishing up our little bridge party with some of my friends."

As part of Oxford society, Alice Ruth had made it a point to join several of the more prestigious society groups of ladies in town. One of these was a bridge club in which a small number of ladies would take turns meeting at one another's homes in the afternoons to play bridge and gossip. Each one would try to outdo the other in providing some special Southern dessert recipe they had found in *Southern Living* magazine, but they would never admit that that was where they got it.

It was an obviously awkward moment for Alice Ruth because she couldn't send him off someplace with Frank. Frank was not home yet, and the ladies appeared anxious to meet her gentleman guest. So Alice Ruth took Aeamon Lee into the recreation room where the ladies were. She instructed Aeamon Lee that he could leave his large suitcase and "that box" in the foyer while they went in to meet the ladies. Alice Ruth began to apologetically explain that she had a sister who lived in the middle part of the state, in a place called Goshen Wells. This was her son, who had come to visit with them only a few days until he could find a job and then go to Ole Miss. In the meantime, he was going to be helping Frank on the farm to earn his keep, and that he had gotten there earlier than she thought.

One of the bridge partners, Clara Diane Channing, said, "Why, Alice Ruth, you've never mentioned that you had a sister down there in Goshen Wells." She pronounced *Goshen Wells* a little louder than the other words, as if this would further embarrass Alice Ruth. "I must say he's a fine-looking young man, and he appears to have nice manners."

Alice Ruth then introduced each one of the ladies to Aeamon Lee. There was Annie Lee Shanks, Clara Diane Channing, and Margaret Nell Branding. Ms. Channing said, "And your name is Aeamon Lee, and your last name is?"

"Mistral, ma'am."

"What an amusing name! That sounds French, is that right?"

"Yes, that is correct. Aeamon is Scots-Irish, Mistral is French, and Lee is Southern." At this reference to a Southern name, all the ladies had a short and lovely laugh.

Ms. Channing continued, "Well, it's always nice to have a gentleman that knows something historical about his name and is not ashamed of being from the South." These three guests of Alice Ruth were from old money families, and Alice Ruth was obviously new money. Old money families know that it is not proper etiquette to flaunt one's wealth, especially in the presence of serfs. But Alice Ruth had a different approach. Her kicks in life came from performing a well-orchestrated party in which she could impress guests of her high culture and the lifestyle her newfound money could afford.

"Ladies, I apologize if I interrupted your bridge party. You know bridge requires a lot of skill and attention, so you really have to stay focused or you will lose. I'm just curious. Which one of you fine ladies won today?"

Ms. Shanks spoke up shyly and said, "Well, I was the lucky one today, but you didn't interrupt, Aeamon Lee. We all had finished the last hand, and we were ready to leave."

"Ms. Shanks, I would love to have the pleasure of someday playing a game of such skill with you and these other ladies." She blushed, and by this time, Alice Ruth could see that she had lost control of the conversation and that this noncredentialed relative was performing better than she was.

"Oh, Alice Ruth, have you told your nephew about the special evening you and Frank are having with your guests and the fine dinner you've planned? *Fine* is just not the word for it. Maybe *exotic* would be more descriptive."

"No, I haven't told Aeamon Lee because, frankly, I thought he was arriving at a later time on a later bus, but with Rosa Sue's help, I think we can still have everything we've planned."

Aeamon Lee apologized. "I didn't realize that I would be interrupting something special for you, Aunt Alice. I can go somewhere else and come back."

"No, it will be fine. You'll have plenty of time to freshen up, and you did pack some nicer clothes, I hope?"

"I imagine I can find something you would consider nicer, or I don't even have to attend whatever you've planned."

Ms. Shanks spoke up, "Tell him, Alice Ruth, what Frank is doing tonight. I think this is so considerate for a husband to do for his wife."

Alice Ruth just lit up with that request. "Well, Frank has been wanting to do something special for me and started thinking that it would be nice to have Jessie and Molly Worthington, whom you all know, over for dinner. Then one thing led to another, and I thought how nice it would be to have something rare and exotic to serve. Of course, Frank didn't know anything about that, so I helped him out a little and came up with this meal, most of which is being flown into Memphis all the way from Alaska. It is called Copper River salmon, and it is really a big deal in the Northwest when it arrives from the Copper River in Alaska. Why, it's the very best in the world!"

Alice Ruth didn't tell the whole story, but it is true that this salmon comes from a river that is almost three hundred miles in length. It is a wild rushing river that empties into Prince William Sound at the town of Cordova. These salmon grow in the strong, chilly rapids and develop to be strong, robust creatures that have a healthy store of natural oils and body fat—simply loaded with flavor. All these qualities make the salmon among the richest, tastiest fish in the world.

Alice Ruth also didn't say anything about the real motive behind this special dinner. She had learned about how to have this salmon shipped to you by reading *Southern Living* magazine, but she didn't tell anyone. The Worthington's were an old money family in Oxford with whom Alice Ruth wanted to cultivate a relationship as well as impress with her own ostentatious flair. Of course, the other bridge partners knew this was her motive, but they would not dare say anything except pay compliments. It's part of the social games upper-class Southerners learn early in life, and it becomes a part of their socialization into the lifestyles of the rich and wealthy.

To reinforce Alice Ruth's sense of self-importance, Aeamon Lee expressed more interest in the meal, which gave her an opportunity to brag some more.

"Well, for the appetizer, we're having crab spring rolls with pink grapefruit, field greens with glazed walnuts and feta with a raspberry vinaigrette dressing, then the main course. We're going to bake the salmon, of course. For dessert, Rosa Sue has made Key lime pie with berry coulis. It's a good thing Rosa Sue started on this meal yesterday, but you won't be in the way, Aeamon Lee, even though you've arrived much earlier than I was expecting. I just don't know what I would do without Rosa Sue."

"Alice, the rest of us are a little envious. Maybe someday you'll want to impress us with such a meal." Ms. Summers's indirect observation flew right over Alice's head.

"And perhaps soon, Diane."

Then Alice Ruth turned to Aeamon Lee and said, "Of course you can join us for dinner. I'm sure the Worthingtons wouldn't mind. And I know it will be a unique experience for you since I'm sure Martha never gets to prepare meals like this one."

This put-down of Aeamon Lee's mother by Alice Ruth touched a nerve. He hadn't planned on saying anything that would reflect negatively on her since she and Frank were putting him up for a few days. Aeamon Lee always had this problem with his perception of calloused insensitivity and how to respond to it. There was one injustice Aeamon Lee would not bear, and that was when his mother or daddy were belittled.

"Aunt Alice, the meal sounds great, but I'm a little curious. The Copper River salmon season is from mid-May to mid-June, and it's a little late in the season to be serving it now. Also, since it is late in the season for the type limes you're using for the dessert, I'd be afraid they're not going to be tart enough. If I had been deciding about the dessert, I would have gone with the chocolate Grand Marnier soufflé. It's pretty heavy but quite a delicacy.

"And I guess you haven't heard about the superiority of the Yukon River salmon, the gold standard of Alaskan kings. It's usually shipped out to other countries from Alaska, but if one tries hard enough, they can get some shipped to this part of the country. But I'm sure your meal will be fine, so don't worry about it."

A certain consternation came over Alice Ruth's face, and she was at a loss for words.

To break the silence, Ms. Summers said, "Well, I certainly am amazed at the language skills, knowledge, and refinement of one who is only eighteen years of age."

"Actually, seventeen, but I'll soon be eighteen."

"Well, you can come over to my house anytime to help me plan some meals, young man. You must have traveled a lot already. And I would love to talk with you about your travels."

"Actually, ma'am, earlier this year, a friend of mine and I were in Louisiana, but we didn't get to stay long."

"Oh, heaven's sake, I was so glad when I cross that river coming back to Mississippi," Ms. Summers said.

Aeamon Lee said, "You know, ma'am, I felt the same way after I got back across that river."

"Well, I tell you what. You just come by sometime, and we'll have some tea in the afternoon, but not today because by the time I get home, I'll be absolutely famished."

"Well, thank you for your invitation and hospitality. 'There are few hours in life more agreeable than the hours dedicated to the ceremony known as afternoon tea.'"[48]

The ladies stood in amazement at Aeamon Lee without making a comment about his timely quotation.

Margaret Nell Branding had been silent through most of the discussion, but it was obvious that she was not as sensitive to feelings with basic respect like the others. "I hear you're entering Ole Miss. You think you're ready? You know to really be somebody on campus, you have to conform to the fashion code. You think you're ready for that? Surely, you brought more than what is in that old suitcase. Anyway, I'm so pleased that Ole Miss has returned to the style and grace it had when I was there. I remember a time when one always had to consider whether or not they could dress appropriately before coming to Ole Miss. You know in the 1960s and '70s it seemed that most of the students just didn't seem to care what they wore. But it was that way all over the country, pretty much, I was told. Said they were trying to identify with the underclass. Why, they were an embarrassment. Thank goodness we're out of that era and designer clothing has returned, along with more manners and refinement."

With a forced smile, Aeamon Lee said, "Ms. Branding, I certainly wouldn't want to embarrass anyone. I'll try my best not to do that, ma'am."

Margaret Nell looked at Alice Ruth and said, "Alice, why don't you do your nephew a favor and take him down to the square and get him fitted out with several IZOD outfits. That would be a nice gesture for you to do for a family member, and he wouldn't have to worry about his clothes. Now you can do that Alice, I know you can. You know what I heard? There are some students who will buy IZOD socks and cut off the little alligator and sew it onto their shirts to make it look like they are in fashion."

Aeamon Lee said, "I have my own conviction about that. You see, I make my clothes. My clothes don't make me." It took the ladies a while for that meaning to soak in.

Before she could say anymore, Frank drove up from his trip to Memphis. Alice Ruth asked Aeamon Lee if he would help Frank unload his valuable cargo, which would be served for the evening dinner with their prized guests. As the ladies got to the front door, Margaret Nell Branding said, "You know, I know I'm not supposed to be nosy, but I just can't stand this any longer. Aeamon Lee, what on earth do you have in that box?"

"Why, those are some of the finest sweet potatoes you could ever find. I brought them special for Aunt Alice, just as a small token of my appreciation for allowing me to stay a few days." Aeamon Lee decided to take the blame for this himself rather than say that his mother was the one who wanted to send her snobbish sister something to indicate their supposed closeness and appreciation as family.

Ms. Summers was amused and said, "Why, Alice Ruth, if your dessert doesn't turn out, you can serve sweet potato pie, right, Aeamon Lee?"

"Yes, that's right, and you know that sweet potatoes are a superfood." This observation didn't seem to impress the ladies.

Aunt Alice didn't respond one way or the other but rather showed the ladies to the door while they talked about their next bridge party. The ladies all wished her well in her anticipated dinner for the evening. They entered their town cars and left.

*   *   *

Aeamon Lee and Frank greeted each other, and then Alice Ruth and Frank had a sort of private conversation. Aeamon Lee could tell that

Uncle Frank wasn't too pleased, but he came back and asked Aeamon Lee to come on outside. He would explain the work he expected and some other matters.

Aeamon Lee fetched his suitcase, wondering what Aunt Alice would do with the sweet potatoes, and left to go with Uncle Frank. As they walked away from the house, Uncle Frank said he would have to hurry because they had these guests coming tonight, and they still had some things to do to get the dinner ready.

As they walked, Uncle Frank began to tell Aeamon Lee about their newfound recreation in which they had gotten involved quite heavily. It seemed that Racking Horse shows had become quite in vogue in Alabama, Mississippi, and Tennessee. A friend of his living in Germantown, Tennessee, had a large Racking Horse farm that he had visited and had come away really impressed. When they attended a show in Germantown last year, Alice Ruth was thrilled over the social trappings of the event. There was old money and new money on display, and she had always heard that having an interest in horses was the sport of kings. She got to thinking that since they had a large enough place to have one, maybe they could come up with something that would become the envy of Oxford. She was not aware of anyone else around there that was very involved with Racking Horses.

The Lorances discovered that the Racking Horse was legendary for its beauty, stamina, and calm disposition in equine history. Their interest increased when they heard of the horse's noble popularity in the Southern plantations before the Civil War. Frank explained that the *rack* of the Racking Horse was a bilateral four-beat gait, which was neither a pace nor a trot. The attractive and graceful Racking Horse's gait was called single-foot because only one foot strikes the ground at a time. Frank added that such things as boots, chains, and all other action devices are not allowed, nor are four-reined bridles or set tails.

Any use of artificial training aids, forcing stimuli, drugs, or any painful substance was strictly forbidden.

So the Lorances made the decision to go all out. Some new fences were built, and a small track was built for training. Next, they constructed a new barn. Frank had seen his friend's barn in Germantown, and it was something he had never before witnessed. In addition to the finest stalls and haylofts, Frank added many conveniences into the construction. There was a place to park a truck, loading ramps, and even living quarters equipped with a bathroom, kitchen, and anything anyone would need to live there close to the horses. It had ten stalls, a fourteen-foot-wide hall, a washing stall with hot and cold water, a feed-and-tack room, an automatic fly sprayer, and a seventy-five-foot round pen with dressage footing. The living quarters were attached to the back at one end.

*   *   *

Frank had a cattle farmhand named Toe Foot who had worked for him for a long time. He had been trained how to care for the Racking Horses. He was an older African American man who had no wife, and his family were all settled elsewhere. When the barn was completed, they moved Toe Foot into one of the two living quarters. They thought he would appreciate living there with the horses better than the little house he had lived in on the place. Alice Ruth had Rosa Sue fix him a plate of food from the leftovers each evening after supper. Toe Foot would take it back to his room at the barn where he could fix his own tea to drink by using the appliances in the barn.

Toe Foot would get to go to the shows and stay with the horse at the trailer and was there to help with whatever needed to be done. The Lorances bought him an appropriate outfit to wear, and Toe Foot felt like he was a vital part of the job that had to be done. While it was different than anything he had known before, he had grown to enjoy the attention he received. It made him feel needed and that he played an important role in the entire performance.

Frank had bought some horses at an auction in Germantown. But to really compete well in the Racking Horse shows, one had to have an impressive rider who would dress up as an English country gentleman, where the sport had originated. The rider was expected to possess a certain graceful style, and the horse needed to prance smoothly so that the rider hardly moved in the saddle.

Frank found a young lady from Germantown with long, flowing yellow hair who was a good rider. She was hired to be their rider even though she didn't often get down to practice at the track. In more recent years, the involvement of young women had become a little more prevalent and acceptable in the shows.

What Frank didn't mention to Aeamon Lee on the way to the barn was that his job was to help out Toe Foot, mostly early in the mornings and the evenings. And after showing him the new barn, for which he was so proud, he told him that he would be staying in the other room in the living quarters—Toe Foot in one room, and Aeamon Lee in the other. They would share the same bathroom. He kept trying to emphasize how convenient this arrangement would be since they would be working together. But Aeamon Lee knew that he was staying in the barn because of Alice Ruth. She had felt embarrassed in the presence of her socialite friends when Aeamon Lee offered a better menu for her to serve to her valued guests for the evening dinner. He had done this only after she had belittled his mother's cooking. It probably wasn't Uncle Frank's idea, but Alice Ruth had a lot of control over him. He was more passive, trying to get along with everybody, and seldom stood up to his wife.

Aeamon Lee met Toe Foot, and they immediately hit it off because of Aeamon Lee's background with African Americans. They divided the work in such a way that allowed Aeamon Lee to run some early in the morning after he got all the horses fed and watered. During the day, as it was understood by the Lorances, he would go into town to get acquainted with the townspeople, the university, and hopefully, some of the coaches and players. Then late in the afternoon, he would make his way back to the Lorances for his evening work with Toe Foot.

"How did you get the nickname Toe Foot?" Aeamon Lee asked him.

"Well, it seems that when I was born, I had this large big toe, and as I began to grow, that toe got bigger and bigger. When I started having to wear shoes, they would have to cut out a place on the shoe where the big toe was so I could wear them. The doctor told them I would be called Toe Foot because of that, and sure enough, he was right. And I've been Toe Foot ever since."

After supper, they swapped stories and listened to some radio music. Aeamon Lee shared his plans and reminded Toe Foot that he didn't think he would be there very long. He thought he would have to live on campus at some point after his successful quest to win a football scholarship.

"Well, I sure hope you do, son, hope you do. I don't know a lot about those things, but I would imagine it's going to be hard, real hard." He looked up, smiling, and said, "But you can try. A fellow has to keep trying, and one day, you never know what door is going to open for you. I grew up around Pinsonville, and there were no jobs for black men, not many for white men either. I didn't know what I could do. I'd been around horses and cows all my life. A white fellow saw me one day and told me about this white man in Lafayette County who was looking for a man to help him on his cattle and horse farm, but he didn't want a family. He just wanted one man. And he asked me if I might be interested. Course, I didn't know what to expect, so one day, he drove me up here, and Mr. Frank had a small vacant house I lived in for a while until he built this fancy barn, and I moved into it. Oh, I gets back to Pinsonville now and then, but overall, it's worked out real good. Sometimes you just have to take a chance at life, and that's what you're doing. You'll always regret it if you don't at least try it. That's what I did, and now I'm glad that I did."

Aeamon Lee said, "That story reminds me of something I read: 'do not go where the path may lead, go instead where there is no path and leave a trail.'[49] That is what you have done with your life, and what I want to do with my life."

Toe Foot's story was what Aeamon Lee needed to hear. Wonderment and fear had been his most prevalent emotions since leaving home. The totally new experience around new people in a new environment caused him to wonder how he would cope. He was not physically afraid, but he wondered if because of his inexperience, something might come up that he should already know. When he seemed to be at his lowest, such as that afternoon listening to his conceited aunt brag around those socialite women, he kept being beckoned by the confidence and challenge of the ethereal plane.

One night, while they were listening to the radio, the conversation focused on music and what each one liked. Aeamon Lee told Toe Foot that he played the guitar some and sang. Toe Foot said that he knew a fellow down the road who had a guitar. "I'll borrow it for a few days so you can play it."

The guitar was in pretty good shape, and Aeamon Lee got it tuned. Together they played and sang some old songs they both knew. Aeamon Lee said, "We need to write a song about you." He tried out several little tunes and finally came up with this:

I've got a gal in Pinsonville.
She won't go out with me,
But her sister will.
It's the Toe Foot boogie.
It's the Toe Foot boogie
Played by Toe Foot Lewis.

They were playing, laughing, and singing so much that night it seemed Aunt Alice Ruth got annoyed and decided all that noise would scare the animals. She sent Frank out there to see what they were doing and to ask them to quiet down a little.

At suppertime, the Lorances invited Aeamon Lee to come inside and eat with them, but he declined, stating that he was too dirty to come inside and that he would just eat with Toe Foot. So both of them would go to the back door, and Rosa Sue would hand each one a plate of food. Toe Foot, it seemed, liked sweet tea and made his own in the barn since there was a refrigerator and other kitchen appliances.

Toe Foot picked up on the ambitions of Aeamon Lee, and every chance he got, he would say something philosophical to encourage him in his efforts. "What I've noticed is that you've got to have strength, toughness, quickness, deception, and a little fight in you, and when things are not going your way, you have to find a way to win. You know there are a lot of ways to win a ball game."

Later, Toe Foot said, "It seems to me that winning at football is a lot like winning a Racking Horse show. First, no matter what it takes, you've got to have a stable of good horses. Then, you've got to have a rider, like a quarterback or a coach, who can get the most out of the horses. Finally, you've got to have an edge of some kind. Now, Mr. Lorance thinks his edge is having that young female rider with that long yellow hair blowing in the wind. And, you know, sometimes it works. That edge in football could be having a player that's just better than everybody else or the ability to deceive the offense and defense or many other things. But, you know, you can still have all that and still lose because of that great equalizer—the shape of that blamed ball. You never know which way it's going to bounce. Sometimes it bounces your way, and sometimes it doesn't. You just never know."

"That's right, Toefoot, you have to risk it anyway." At that point, Aeamon Lee remembered one of Maleah's wise sayings. "A good friend of mine gave me this, and it fits perfectly with what we're talking about: 'When you dig a well, you may fall in. When you demolish an old wall, you could be bitten by a snake. When you work in a quarry, stones might fall and crush you! When you chop wood, there is danger with each stroke of your ax! Such are the risks of life.'[50]

"Toefoot, I'm going to do what you did. I have to take the risk and see what happens."

*   *   *

Aeamon Lee rose early to do his running. Then he would do his work before going into town. He walked virtually all over the town, including down the streets where mostly African Americans lived. He met a lot of people by just going up to them and asking friendly questions. One thing that amused him the most was the Oxford town square, where he found several bookstores. They even allowed him to sit down and read some of the books for sale. He apologized for not having enough money to buy any of the books and expressed his hope that they didn't mind him spending so much time in their store.

One of the patrons of the bookstore offered to take him to Rowan Oak, the home of William Faulkner. Aeamon Lee was captivated by all the stories he heard about this legendary writer. He noticed the quotation in the Ole Miss library taken from Faulkner's Nobel Prize acceptance speech in Stockholm, Sweden, in 1950. In fact, while at Rowan Oak, he read this speech several times. He was inspired by this great writer and thought of the line "Lives of great men remind us we can make our lives sublime and, departing, leave behind us footprints on the sands of time."[51]

He also got to see the Center for the Study of Southern Culture, located in the Ole Miss campus. This was a fulfillment of a goal he had ever since he heard the lecture on Southern culture at the Peabody Hotel during the past summer of adventure and peril. He would go by every chance he got to read and look around. He always had an interest in understanding how one incorporated the values and norms of his own culture and subculture. He felt that the automatic acceptance, without questioning of whatever those values were, could be detrimental both to society and to one's own growth. On the other hand, he felt it was useful to both understand and appreciate the unique cultural traits to which one was exposed while growing up in a particular subcultural region. Only then could one objectively determine and evaluate his identity.

He was concerned about the ethnocentric feelings he often found in some Southern churches. He looked for insight into this regrettable perspective. It bothered him that the cultural perspective seemed narrow when the biblical perspective was unto all the world.[52]

He was convinced that the church would be the last social institution in the South to overcome racial intolerance.[53]

* * *

At the Ole Miss campus, Aeamon Lee learned his way around the buildings and especially the sports facilities. He did ask for Coach Arrington, who had sent him the letter about walk-ons. He finally got to meet the coach even though he was busy getting ready for the start of fall practice and the two-a-days. There were some other walk-ons he met who were trying to get into good physical shape. Many of them had been in summer school.

Most all college football programs allow for walk-ons to try out for the team. Usually, they are comprised of young men who have always wanted to play football but weren't quite good enough to be offered a scholarship. They think, *Well, maybe* I am *good enough, and I'll just show them that they made a mistake.* Others came from schools where they didn't make it but heard that maybe they could make it here because the team had a weakness at a certain position. And then there were those like Aeamon Lee Mistral, who saw it as a way of increasing their life chances. Finding his mission in life by this means seemed like a far-away and impossible dream. Most would only scoff at an ambition like this. They certainly didn't see him accomplishing his mission playing football at Ole Miss.

Coaches are glad to have a fair number of walk-ons to practice against the scholarship players. The truth is that seldom does a walk-on make it to the roster, let alone be offered a scholarship if any are left over to give. Occasionally, however, the coaches find a gem.

Most of the players thought that surely Aeamon Lee would be trying out the tight end due to his height and weight. They didn't think a player his size could be mobile enough to be a quarterback.

He didn't ask any questions about the living accommodations and still assumed he would have to find his own place to stay until the regular semester started with registration and classes.

Several of these potential walk-ons and some scholarship players invited him to work out with them in the weight room. They also did some running but were limited by rules as to the extent they would get to practice on their own. The coaches didn't want scholarship players in any pickup games at this point, for fear that they might get injured. The potential walk-ons could do what they wanted with the approval of facilities personnel. Aeamon Lee got in on one seven-on-seven game of touch and got to run and throw a few passes. He didn't have the practice gear the others had and just took his shoes off and played barefoot. He received no compliments from the other players because each one was so self-absorbed, it was hard for them to notice the potential or greatness of another player.

He was listening to hear positive things about the prospects of a walk-on, but none of these players were optimistic. He was told that even if he were good enough to be noticed by the coaches, it would be the following year before he could get a scholarship. In the meantime, he would have to spend a year in college classes and go through spring practice.

Aeamon Lee searched for some evidence that it was possible for a walk-on to make it that year. He asked if they had ever heard of any walk-on making it and playing the first year. None knew of any during the short time they had been on campus. Some of the other walk-ons told a few horror stories of how it was for walk-ons in some other schools. They didn't know what to expect from Ole Miss, and the scholarship players wouldn't say much except that "you will be given a fair chance to prove yourself." There was talk of the team just wanting some warm bodies out there to knock around in practice to get ready for the season.

The head coach was a grizzled aging man by the name of Marvin Wortham, who was seen as coming close to the end of his tenure. Rumblings had already been heard from the alumni. Coach Wortham was under some amount of pressure to produce a winning season and to go to a bowl game. Deep down, he knew that this could be his last season. All he could hope for was that some player or players would surprise and raise the level of their performance.

Before two-a-day practices started, the Ole Miss coaching staff held a meeting to discuss the prospects for the upcoming season and to plan the conduct of the practices. The staff members present were encouraged to express ideas. They kept coming back to talk about the consequences of two years of poor recruiting. Consequently, they appointed another coach to be in charge of this most important part of a successful program. But the lingering effects were going to show during that season.

The assistant head coach said, "Well, I've looked at the schedule, and I only see three games that we should win fairly easy. Then, there are three in which we could be competitive. But there are five where we will, right now, be the underdog. It is possible, but not probable that we can improve on last year's 4–7 record. There is always the chance that some of our new players could surprise and even excel."

Coach Wortham had the final word. He said, "I want all of you to know that I don't believe we can weather another mediocre season, for whatever that is worth." Not much was said as they left the meeting. Each assistant coach knew what was meant; they needed to be considering the possibility of finding another job at another school at the end of the season.

*   *   *

The time came for all the walk-ons to report, and Aeamon Lee made sure he was there early at the designated place. Mostly, they heard a lot about school policies, the expectations of the coaches, and rules of behavior. Then came the physical exams, and most of the first few hours were routine. They kept being reassured that they were welcomed and that they would play a vital role in the success of the team that year. The coaching staff appeared to be under tremendous pressure to do well this season because the team couldn't seem to get beyond four to six wins a season.

There was an interesting mix of walk-on players between linemen and skill players. Some of these twenty or so players had been specifically encouraged by the coaching staff to walk on. These were players who were not quite good enough in the coach's estimation to deserve a scholarship offer earlier, but they still wanted to play for Ole Miss. There was still a chance of making the team. Their actual performance against the regular team was unpredictable. There were stories told about how well some walk-ons had done. Some had become first team starters and were even drafted by the pros, by their report. There were some who did not have skills to play Division I football but had always dreamed of playing football at Ole Miss.

For this season, the coaches had decided that they would begin the practice with a three-mile run. Categories of players had to run it within a certain time frame. This served several purposes. First, it would tell the coaches who was in good physical shape and who needed some more conditioning. Second, it would cause some would-be prospects to decide right then that the practice was too demanding. This would weed out several players each year.

This was one of the activities that Aeamon Lee knew about and had prepared for with his running with Jo-Nathan back at home and at Aunt Alice's. He felt that coming in first in this race would get the attention of the coaches right away. He felt good after getting the athletic equipment he needed for practice from the equipment manager and was eager to get it going. He had already run three miles several times in his own practice and knew how to pace himself. The assistants had mapped out the route for them to follow.

Aeamon Lee would run with the wide receivers, running backs, defensive backs, and other quarterbacks. The other quarterbacks didn't seem to take the run too seriously, and Aeamon Lee didn't know why. They just wanted to barely come in under the time limit. He paced himself just as he intended and put on a burst of speed toward the end, and he easily came in first place. He thought that the coaches would make some positive comment about it, but rather, they seemed to be primarily concerned about the position players other than the quarterbacks. These other players on scholarship appeared to just want to get it over with and come in under the time limit. They knew they had secured their position. But Aeamon Lee's expectations from the coaches were not met. It was almost as if they had not noticed.

One of the other players came up to him and said, "I know you are wondering why your winning with the best time was no big deal. You see, almost every year, some eager walk-on plans on winning this thing to show the scholarship players up. Everybody knows what is going on, so it is more or less expected."

Aeamon Lee was pretty well deflated by this even though he had won the race by fifty yards. Again, he would keep on with the self-talk. "Don't get down. Don't let anything discourage you. Act like a winner. Never lose the energy and determination."

He remembered, "it is not good enough that we do our best; sometimes we must do what is required."[54]

* * *

The next day would be the start of two-a-day practices. Aeamon Lee had received information about the meals that were provided and access to the assigned equipment. But somehow, he had not gotten the word on where the players stayed at night. He didn't want to ask, and it appeared that after the first day of practice and meeting the players, they went in a lot of different directions. So he made his way each day to the convenience store on the edge of town until he could catch a ride out to the Lorances.

Toe Foot wanted to find out how things went that day, and Aeamon Lee would tell him. "Toe Foot, I found out today that players get two tickets to home games, and I can give them away. So I want you to come if I get to dress out for a game."

"Ah, I don't know about doing that now, Aeamon Lee. I'm not sure how comfortable I'd be actually being there, sitting with all those dressed-up folks." It was clear that Toe Foot was not sure if he would be welcomed to actually attend a game.

"I remember, as a kid, on Saturday mornings, I would go down to Highway 7 that runs through Pinsonville and watch all those Cadillacs, Oldsmobiles, and Buicks drive through town going to Oxford for a big game. All the men had on suits, all dressed up. I never thought then that I would ever see black players playing at Ole Miss or black people attending the games." His head was down as he spoke, recalling a different day and an era of racism and discrimination.

"Oh, it's not that way now. I'll bet more than half the team is black now, and the coaches and everybody I've seen treat players equally. And you can come to a game. That would be something you could talk about for a long time."

"Well, I'll see. You just make sure right now that you make the team."

Aeamon Lee was told he would not have to have any money during the three-week practice and that all the expenses were paid for until classes began. Even though he had some of the gambling money in his pocket, he always got by without having to spend much of his own money.

At practice the next day, the coaches were upset over some of the times they got from the players in that three-mile run, so they had certain players having to get a certain time in the forty-yard-dash. They ran it until they fell below a time set by the coaches. This included the skilled players and the linemen. It was pretty hard on the linemen who were not in shape. At this time, offensive linemen in the Southeastern Conference were weighing an average of around 275 pounds. Ole Miss had some guys who would normally weigh around 250 but put on enough weight so they could play on the line. With their big stomach's hanging over their belts, it was tough on them to reach their time.

During these first few days of practice, there was a lot of kidding by the scholarship players directed toward the walk-ons. Some of the walk-ons had been there for two or more years, and things would be said that reminded them of the time they had spent on the practice field. Most everything said was good-natured kidding about their continued efforts to make the team. Occasionally, the walk-on would act mad and try to fight, but the fight would be broken up quickly.

There were two senior quarterbacks on the team that were listed as starters. Ole Miss was attempting to run a two-quarterback system. One of the quarterbacks was better at passing, and the other one better at running. This approach had advantages and disadvantages, but it became obvious that Coach Wortham had made up his mind to stay with the two-quarterback system. Aeamon Lee wondered how good his chances were with two established quarterbacks on the team. But he knew it would be unlikely he would get to play that year anyway with both of the quarterbacks being seniors; maybe he could be the one next year, if he could make the impression good enough this year resulting in a scholarship. Otherwise, he would have to go back home.

They practiced on two grass fields, one for the offense and one for the defense. When Aeamon Lee made it known that his position was quarterback, he received a lot of kidding.

"Hey, man, you need to go over to the Tad Pad," players would say. The Tad Pad was the basketball arena.

Then, quarterbacks were often not all that tall, maybe six feet or six feet one inch. And Aeamon Lee was now six feet four inches tall, and it was assumed that a quarterback this tall was not mobile enough to play the position. At one point, Aeamon Lee misspoke trying to defend his height and his mobility. There were both players and coaches who heard him. He said, "I know I'm taller than the other guys, but that can be good on pass plays, and if the quarterback can run too, that just makes him a double threat. Besides, Archie Manning was six feet three inches tall, and he could run."

After this reference to an Ole Miss legend, everybody looked up and was silent. Head Coach Wortham was the one who spoke. He said, "Son, you evidently don't know what you have just done. You have compared yourself to Archie Manning, the greatest quarterback and player that ever played at Ole Miss. Nobody, I repeat, nobody around here compares himself to Archie Manning. You got that?" The point was well-taken by Aeamon Lee, and he never again referred to the famous quarterback in that context.

*   *   *

At this time, all the football players stayed in the athletic dorm with the assistant coaches and their wives who were assigned to a floor. They made sure the 12:00 a.m. (in your room) curfew was met. Most of the players' activities, like watching films, strength training, learning plays, and their general influence on the team, were monitored by the coaches.

Aeamon Lee and the other walk-ons, along with some of the third- and fourth-string players, were put through a few short drills. They were given diagrams of plays to practice. The coaches were trying to figure out what they could do well and in what area they needed to improve. Aeamon Lee stayed concentrated, watched the better players' techniques, and showed himself to be a promising prospect. Coach Underwood taught him the finer points of playing the quarterback position.

After two or three days of practice, Aeamon Lee was still going to the Lorances to do his work there. He spent the night in their spacious barn. Back on campus, something came up one night in the athletic dorm as to where Aeamon Lee Mistral was. The coaches had assumed he was there, but he wasn't. They started asking around, and another walk-on finally revealed where he thought Aeamon Lee was. "I told him we could stay in the dorm, but he didn't believe it, I guess, because at night, he goes out in the country and stays with his uncle and aunt. He sleeps—get this, y'all—in a Racking Horse barn."

"He is out in the country sleeping in a barn, did you say?" the coach asked.

The quarterback coach, Coach Underwood, was summoned and told the story and where Aeamon Lee was. He was dispatched to go and find Aeamon Lee and bring him to the athletic dorm. He found the Lorances and the barn. When he got to the barn, Aeamon Lee was getting all the horses fed.

"Coach, what are you doing out here?" Aeamon Lee asked.

"I just want to know one thing: have you been sleeping in this barn?"

"Yes, but you see this is no ordinary barn. This is one of those new extravagant barns that have a lot of the conveniences of a house. The floor is concrete, and me and Toe Foot here have kitchen appliances, beds, closet, and even a bathroom."

The coach didn't respond to Aeamon Lee's explanation. He just said, "Pack up your things and come with me to the athletic dorm, where you'll stay at least until classes start."

Aeamon Lee decided he would not speak with the Lorances and said to Toe Foot, "Tell the Lorances that I am now living on the Ole Miss campus by special invitation and that I appreciated the opportunity to feed their fine horses. And, Toe Foot, I'll be back to see how you're doing and to give you a ticket to a game."

Toe Foot thanked him and wished him well. "See there, I told you that you were on your way."

Coach Underwood explained how they had assumed he was staying in the dorm. "But anyway, there is nothing we can do about that now. You've just got to look forward and do as well as you can in each practice, pay attention, and develop your skills." He wouldn't commit anything else about how he actually felt about Aeamon Lee's prospects.

*   *   *

The two-a-day practices began taking a toll on some of the players, with the hot dog days of the August sun bearing down. It was hard keeping the energy level high. Things began to get a lot more serious with each practice. The walk-ons were called scabs to cause them to remember who and what they were in comparison to scholarship players. There were drills designed to discover where a player had the best skills. A lot of players were being moved around to other positions, from offense to defense and vice versa.

Aeamon Lee was afraid they would want him to play another position since he was so tall. He really made special attempts to show that he could be quick and could run as well. Occasionally, they would bring a player from among the scabs and third and fourth string to challenge for playing time with the first and second teams.

Finally, one day the coaches started looking at the backup quarterbacks. They brought Aeamon Lee in along with two other quarterbacks to run some basic plays with the first team. It was fairly well assumed that the two senior quarterbacks had the position nailed down. But the coaches repeatedly emphasized that they could never assume anything. There could be a time when they had to use a backup.

The coaches mentioned all kinds of things that could happen that might require a backup to enter the game at a moment's notice. The coaches reminded, "You have to be alert at all times to what is going on in the game and be ready if you're needed."

Aeamon Lee was satisfied with the way he performed. He had made sure he had the plays and formations memorized and down pat. The coaches were focusing primarily on the other players, it seemed, and yelling things to them. He wondered if they were even noticing any of his plays and moves.

The other two quarterbacks were trying hard to impress, but Aeamon Lee's speed and quick learning put him a step ahead for that third position on the depth chart. At least that's what Aeamon Lee felt in his own mind. The coaches were noncommittal. The other two quarterbacks had experience, and there was no way to know what they had been promised by the coaches.

The competition for positions on the depth chart was fierce. Occasionally, a fight would break out, and the players intervened to stop it. Two players kept getting into a fight, and finally, the coaches told them to go to the side of the field and fight it out, that the team was going to keep on practicing. The players were afraid of losing their position, so they decided not to fight anymore.

The intensity level was rising with each practice. Some of the scabs and even some of the roster players were hammered pretty good. Some of them would pretend they were hurt and walk off the field for a while, rather than admitting that the going was just too rough for them.

*   *   *

During the last week and a half, before the first game, the game plan was put in place. A combination of remaining scholarship players and scabs were to run the opposition plays against the first- and second-team defense. This was when it really got tough on the players that were down on the chart. Some scabs, on the other hand, were trying so hard that a first- or second-team player would ask them to let up a little. These were guys who already had their position solidified and didn't want to get hurt before the season. Overall, the first team really laid it on the scabs and would say things like, "Welcome to the Southeastern Conference."

By Aeamon Lee's own evaluation, there were two other scabs that appeared to be making an impression, an offensive lineman and a wide receiver. And he thought he was doing well. One of the scabs who had walked on before told Aeamon Lee that if the coaches felt you could contribute, and if they really wanted you on the team, they would usually encourage you to stay in school a year. You could keep on practicing with the team, and maybe there might be a scholarship the following year. There was some recollection, however, of a player getting a scholarship that first year, but this was really rare. He said that if the coaches liked you, they would call you in privately and talk with you.

Nevertheless, Aeamon Lee felt he needed to do something on the field to be among the two or three they would notice and want to keep. So near the end of the second practice one day, he was playing quarterback for the scabs against the first-team defense. The offensive coordinator was calling the plays they were running. The defense could recognize the plays, and the ball carrier would get crushed on nearly every play at the line of scrimmage. The defense was enjoying the domination and supposedly building up their self-confidence in preparation for the season opener.

Aeamon Lee came up with an idea. The coaches had threatened certain players with making them run the bleachers if they didn't correct their mistakes. Everybody knew this was the hardest exercise anybody could do. There was a lot of jawing back and forth. So Aeamon Lee made his move. He stepped out of the huddle and challenged the first-team defense.

This indomitable outsider looked at the defense and boldly said, "You think you're hot stuff against the scabs. But I can pick some players left over, and we can put the ball on the twenty-yard line, someone will call the game, and we will go the distance and score. If we don't score by game rules, then we get to run the bleachers. But if we score, then you have to run the bleachers. And besides that, I want to do something." He took off the yellow net jersey all quarterbacks wore—meaning, no one could tackle them—and threw it to the sideline. He actually thought the coaches would make him put it back on, but to his surprise, they didn't. The coaches were talking among themselves. It was toward the end of the day, and they obviously felt that this little experiment would not take long. They figured it would be over within four plays, so they decided to let them do it. The defense was laughing and eager to get it on.

Aeamon Lee said, "I want to pick the players." The coaches agreed, and Aeamon Lee picked the best of the lot. There was a wide receiver he had seen that he liked because he appeared to be a really good possession receiver and could catch the passes anywhere around him, including off the grass. They ran several practice plays using different receivers sent in, and none of them worked well. Finally, Aeamon Lee walked toward the sidelines and yelled, "It was a li'l white boy, dangit." They looked around, and there stood this five foot eight inch, 165 pound white scab with the great hands that Aeamon Lee wanted. He would be known thereafter as Li'l White Boy, though his name was Milo Millon.

He knew that if this would even come close to being successful, they had to deceive the defense some. Aeamon Lee said to him, "Since I dared to make this challenge, I want to make only one request: I get to call the plays in the huddle." The offensive coordinator didn't know at first but finally conceded because, again, they all thought this wouldn't last long.

The defense didn't hear them talking about putting in some wrinkles. So on the first play, they lined up in a formation commonly used when running a delayed handoff to the running back. In the huddle, Aeamon Lee called the play but told the running back that he would fake to him and that he would run off to the left side of the line. He whispered this to him and didn't let the other players know that was what he was planning on doing. The play looked familiar to the defense. The offense acted according to plan, and the running back carried through with the fake. The defense converged on the running back hard while Aeamon Lee hid the ball for a second or two while running to his left and saw an open field. He ran the ball all the way from the 20 to the 45-yard line before they caught up with him.

The defense was upset with all the ribbing they got from the sidelines, and from now on, there wouldn't be any letting up. They would go full speed and kill the quarterback or anybody else who had the ball. On the next two plays, Aeamon Lee set up a formation that appeared to be pass plays but had quick handoffs, which the defense stuffed hard. By this time, his offensive-line boys had been pancaked, knocked out, or creamed so badly that, in the huddle, they were sweating, huffing, and groaning. It was obvious they were already wearing down, both physically and psychologically. They were ready for a time-out, and Aeamon Lee had to get their attention.

It was no ordinary talk. He moved them away from the line of scrimmage where he could talk privately to them after replacing one or two players in the line.

"Listen up and listen well! The way you become a loser is by practicing.[55] Every single one of us has had dreams a long time about this moment. Being on the practice field at Ole Miss and going up against the first team. And we've imagined success. We've thought about that for a long time, and we've run it through our minds more times than we can count. I was given a bit of wisdom from someone that fits all of us right now: 'Dreaming instead of working is foolishness.'[56]

To them, we're scabs, just warm bodies to knock around, no better than tackling dummies. This is our moment of truth. And what is the truth about you, and you, and you, and you? Only you can answer that. But we're having an opportunity that we can tell the rest of our lives to our grandchildren, the day that a bunch of cast-offs stood toe-to-toe with the first-team defense and rammed the ball down their throats. I'll be danged if I'm quitting, and you're not quitting, you hear! 'Purity of heart is to will one thing.'[57] This is the last chance you'll ever have like this on this field. Play smart, tough, and line. Just get in their way for about three seconds, and we'll do the rest. Walk off now if you're not willing to make this a good memory."

Aeamon Lee slowly looked at each one, and their eyes were opened wide, and they were breathing hard and tensing up their bodies. He knew they were ready. "Now let's go get this first down." It was third and ten, and he told Li'l White Boy to go down ten yards and go down low, and he would hit him with a hard bullet pass. He would have to catch it right off the top of the grass. The play worked perfectly. First down!

They had now crossed the 50-yard line. After several more plays, both running and passing, there were more first downs. A penalty against the defense for hitting late helped. The ball was now on the 8-yard line. By this time, the defensive coaches were having a fit, yelling, screaming, cussing, and threatening.

Aeamon Lee called a play where Milo caught a reverse pass, and he plowed to the 2-yard line before being crushed. It was third down on the 2-yard line. Aeamon Lee didn't want to trust the tired running back and wide receivers with the ball at this crucial point. He had a strong intuition that told him what the defense was thinking. They were going to play back, thinking that the brash quarterback would attempt to pass it into the end zone. He set up to make it appear like that was exactly what he intended to do. Then he faked to the back and reversed his field and looked for an opening. He would have to use his brute strength and speed to get the ball in. He cut sharply, and with three defenders riding him, he dragged them across the goal line.

There was a celebration that was indescribable among the scabs. They were making big piles of human flesh, jumping up and down and yelling and taunting. The defense was completely silent. They offered no congratulations to the scabs but just stood there, wondering how this could have happened.

By this time, most of the sidelines were cheering for the daring upstarts. And this bunch of no-name players, sarcastically referred to as scabs, would be able to tell their grandchildren about the day they scored against the first-team defense at Ole Miss. This bunch scored because of Aeamon Lee Mistral, who conducted that march down the field like the captain of a ship, a commander in battle, a fearless leader who got his team to play for about twenty minutes far above their heads.

Several of the players were looking over at the bleachers where several retired coaches were seated. They were enjoying a hearty laugh at the events on the practice field. People said they still cast a long shadow over the entire football program.

Naturally, the thing that occupied Aeamon Lee's mind was whether this bold move got the attention of the coaches. The coaches congratulated the offense in general tones without singling out any particular player, but there was even more enjoyment to see the defensive coaches make these tired defensive players run the bleachers.

By the time they had gotten off the field, showered, and eaten supper, all the players seemed to calm down later in the dorm. There were a few positive comments extended to Aeamon Lee but still no word from the coaches.

*   *   *

It was late at night when the players had gone to bed that Aeamon Lee thought about home, Martha and Plea, and all the good neighbors and friends. Was Plea trying to do more than he should? Had he started using the carving knife set yet? Was he still depressed? And what about the crops?

And he thought about Joe-Nathan, far off in South Carolina, going through marine boot camp. Was he tough enough to withstand the abuse, the belittling, and the attempts to make him into a different kind of person—a fighting and killing person? A soldier who could kill another human being with an adrenaline rush and think nothing of it?

Aeamon Lee asked around among the walk-ons, especially those who had been through it before, when one would know what his status was with the team and the coach's opinion of them. What he learned was that the coaches talked privately with the ones they thought could possibly get a scholarship the following year or those they wanted to be on the team this year. Even though the team had already started preparing for the first game against Memphis State, no one had spoken privately with him to let him know anything about his future. He had even taken snaps with the first-team offense and ran all the plays in the game plan. Still there was nothing, no word or hint, and he sure wasn't going to ask the head coach.

Then he heard the word from one of the walk-ons that the coaches had decided on which ones they liked. He was told they liked a certain wide receiver and an offensive lineman and that they would encourage them to enroll in classes and stay with the team throughout the season. They would help them with Pell Grants and available monies for which they qualified in order to get through the year financially. Actually, one of them could pay his way, and that left only one they would need to help.

Aeamon Lee asked the guy specifically whether there were any others he might have heard about, and he said, "No, I think that was about it. I'm not really sure."

Little did Aeamon Lee know that the coaches planned to speak to him the next morning. The more he thought about it, the more his emotions ran wild. He went over and over in his head the practice sessions and his accomplishments. The only negative he could think of was his ill-advised statement comparing his mobility to that of Archie Manning, but he felt he had done everything he could to get their attention and to prove he could play in the Southeastern Conference. But the feeling that he had not succeeded gave him a light feeling in his stomach. He couldn't eat. His mind was swirling around and around. What should he do?

Aeamon Lee was not prone to irrational actions. He decided he would make his presence known the next morning in the athletic office building, and maybe he would be told something. He was there walking the halls and speaking to the staff as he saw them, and everyone responded in kind. Little did he know that Head Coach Wortham had told the quarterback coach to tell him to meet with them at 11:00 a.m. that day. But Coach Underwood had not been able to find him, and therefore, Aeamon Lee still had not gotten the message.

After hanging around their offices for about thirty minutes, Aeamon Lee finally decided there was nothing else he could do, because he knew that he couldn't enroll with little to no money. Besides, he felt he had proven on the practice field that he deserved a spot on their roster. He knew he was at least the third best quarterback there by granting deference to the two senior quarterbacks.

There was an internal groaning like he had never experienced. He tried to fight it off. He had lived and practiced above the ordinary realm. He knew how to live his life on that ethereal plane. But somehow, it had not worked, he concluded. With weakness all over his body, he walked back to the athletic dorm and packed his clothes in the large suitcase. He headed toward the bus station downtown.

All the way there, he kept having flashbacks of all his successes. He could see himself excelling and competing and winning. His head was spinning in all directions as he grappled with his thoughts and disappointment. Leaving the scene of his greatest endeavor was not easy. Nothing seemed to console him in these moments of despair.

Many questions could not be answered to any satisfaction:

"Where did I fail to impress?"

"Did I break any rules?"

"How will I explain this to Jo-Nathan, Mom, and Dad?"

"All that preparation and practice, was it for nothing?"

Aeamon Lee proceeded on his way, getting the ticket and waiting for the bus to take him home, all the while his mind was swirling with confusion, despair, and doubt.

The twist of fate occurred when Coach Wortham reached the bus station after he heard what Aeamon Lee had done and led him off the bus to his car and headed back to campus.

When they arrived at the athletic office, Coach Wortham, the assistant head coach, and their position coaches met with the three walk-on players. They talked with them about what they wanted from each of them. They would be enrolled in classes. The other two had to live in another dorm, but Aeamon Lee would get to live in the athletic dorm. They expressed confidence in their abilities and attempted to set a fire under them to keep them committed to their goal. The next year of their life was planned out, and the impression was that these coaches and the whole staff would take care of them and their needs.

* * *

Coach Wortham explained that he was putting Aeamon Lee down as the third quarterback on the depth chart. "As you know, we have two experienced quarterbacks, and they are seniors. We're going to play them, and I think you can understand why. But in this game, we never know what might happen, and you might be needed. I don't like to play true freshmen, but you appear to be more mature and stronger than most first-year guys. I guess we didn't let you know enough about how we felt about your skills and potential. You thought we weren't watching at times when we were. We talked a lot among ourselves.

"Now you will live in the athletic dorm. I don't know how long, because the NCAA wants the athletes to live in the general population of students. We don't think that is a good idea. Now, we can have some of the coaches to stay in the dorm, and this has worked fine for us. We get to be close to the players, and to tell the truth, we're better able to keep them out of trouble."

There was new meaning to the one-a-day practices now. Aeamon Lee had received the congratulations from all the players. He began to think differently toward them because his mind-set before had been to think of all of them as his challengers and competitors that he had to subdue. But now he began to think of them as teammates and friends who must now rely on one another. The camaraderie between players was phenomenal, and they hung around together, both black and white.

It was reassuring to Aeamon Lee how well the white players got along with and accepted the black players, who had not been in the conference more than fifteen years. He could not remember a time when there was any racial tension among the players. They stood by each other, and the coaches and the administration treated them equally.

* * *

Each fall, before the first game, the chancellor, athletic director, and some university organization would sponsor an outing for the whole football team. It was usually an outdoor party with a catered meal and a small musical band. This year, it was held at the spacious home of one of the women of the University Association of Women (UAW).

Aeamon Lee had never seen such an ostentatious display of Old South values. He had only read about the Old South in books and was not aware there were still some families holding on to some of these lifestyles. The yard had close to three acres of grass and shade trees. Tents were set up with the food, tables, chairs, and flowers. The University Association of Women owned an antebellum home near the campus, and each morning they met to drink their mint juleps and gossip. Otherwise, these women were quite friendly and gracious in most areas.

Surveying the spacious area, Aeamon Lee couldn't help but think how they had a good garden spot not being used—a good place for a barn, truck patches, and at least two to three more houses.

Some of the older players were used to this event and were comfortable with the scenery and the manners expected of them. They paid many compliments, knowing that it would please these ladies very much. The chancellor and athletic director attempted to mingle and shake hands with all the players and extend a personal welcome to Ole Miss and the team. The occasion gave them an opportunity to get to know the players on a different level than seeing them on the campus.

The newer players were not as comfortable in this setting and didn't know exactly what to do or not to do. The setting, and the behavior of the ladies, made them feel a little uncomfortable; so they attempted to be polite and as inconspicuous as possible. They knew it would be embarrassing if they messed up in some way.

Aeamon Lee found himself again in a social setting requiring him to display knowledge of etiquette and confidence. Beneath the exterior of his daring behavior, he often wondered if he had the qualities expected in this different setting. He soon learned that using a well-chosen and well-timed word from the vocabulary of the well-heeled would dispel doubts about his assumed pedigree among those to whom this mattered.

Several ladies who had asked to be a part of this event approached Aeamon Lee to gush over him. Now these breezy exhibitors of ostentatious flair were a part of that small group who met in the antebellum home to carry out their subcultural rituals.

"You must be that new player I've heard about. Why, I've even heard you might be our quarterback of the future, as they say."

Aeamon Lee said awkwardly, "I don't really know about that."

Soon the party was over, and Aeamon Lee felt like he had conducted himself in an acceptable manner.

Practices became more intense in anticipation of the first game. Aeamon Lee was the third quarterback now on the depth chart and therefore took a lot of snaps in practice. It didn't take him long to absorb the playbook and the game plan. As previously stated, his memory was excellent, and he began to get a feel for the aspects of the game of football that he had missed in high school. Other players began to show more and more confidence in him, and he was now treated as a team member rather than as a scab.

Since the first game was not until September 3, Aeamon Lee had enrolled in classes, purchased his books, and was assigned to another room in the athletic dorm. His roommate was the quarterback rated fourth on the depth chart named Webster Warren. The coaches liked for quarterbacks to room together so they could share information and reminders about their role in the games. He was a friendly guy, active in the Fellowship of Christian Athletes, and had a picture of the US president on his dorm room wall.

When Aeamon Lee walked into the room, they exchanged pleasantries and divided up the room agreeable to both. Webster had a closet full of khaki pants, white shirts, button-downs, and power ties with some shade of red in them. Later in the fall, Aeamon Lee noticed that Webster draped his sweater over his back and crossed the sleeves in front. He read *GQ* magazine, which told readers what current designer clothes were in style. The values reflected by Webster and Aeamon Lee would lead to some frank, but respectful, exchanges of differences in their views of the world.

Even though he had expected to move up on the depth chart this season, Webster appeared to accept Aeamon Lee's position on the team fairly well. The roommate believed God determined these things. If God had wanted him to be ranked third on the depth chart, then God would have made him third. This acceptance by Webster was fine with Aeamon Lee and would mean one less hurdle to get over.

Being in a new environment with so many new experiences, Aeamon Lee had to ask a lot of questions. He was observant in his efforts to discover how to fit in and do things the way that was expected. One area that was definitely different was the way he dressed versus the way other students dressed. But his choices in clothes had never bothered him before, and he would not bother now because he never felt the need to conform to every societal norm.

The early 1980s were a time when the pendulum had swung from a period of social consciousness in the 1960s to the present values associated with materialism. It was the time for preppies (white upper-middle-class college students) to make all the connections (called networking) that would result someday in them becoming yuppies (young urban professionals). College preppies yearned to become a yuppie once they graduated from college. Bringing their rich-is-in-vogue imagery to the 1980s meant the emergence of social Darwinism—the survival of the fittest. These winners became the glorified movers and shakers, who became role models for the new generation. If these were the winners, then that implied that others were losers. This was a label given to those who didn't jump on this new revolution's bandwagon. Aeamon Lee despised this term and would never allow himself to be so described because he didn't join the movement.

*   *   *

The daily routine was now more intense, and Aeamon Lee had to focus on all the requirements of time for a scholarship football player. He basically had two full-time jobs: One consisted of meetings, watching film, strength training, long practices on the field, and learning the playbook, which was like a textbook to be memorized. The other job was carrying a full load of classes and meeting all the academic demands of college life. At times it appeared that each professor thought his or her class was the only one being offered. Then there were one or two professors who appeared to be antisports and used sarcasm to describe football players in their classes. Additionally, there were always campus events, off-campus activities, and parties to attend.

One had to be really disciplined to keep this schedule and maintain stability in his life. Aeamon Lee began to realize that the grand myth among the sports public was that football players only played football. They also had to be concerned about passing all their courses and maintaining academic requirements. But he was determined that somewhere in his weekly routine, he would find the time to engage in some of the same activities he experienced in Goshen Wells.

*   *   *

One thing Aeamon Lee had to arrange was the washing, drying, and ironing of the shirts Martha had made for him. He always liked that clean, fresh smell of washing and drying clothes the way they did back home. So he found some time to go into the African American section of town and began to ask around for women who ironed for the public. It didn't take long at all to find a woman who would. But she was already overloaded with work for some white families and some students. While there, he spotted a black washpot and asked if he could borrow it.

On early Saturday morning, when most in the athletic dorm were sleeping late, Assistant Coach Arrington and his wife were awakened by the smell of something burning. They jumped up to check around and then opened the door to the side of the dorm. Coach said, "What in the devil is this?" What he saw was a clothesline stretched from the corner of the dorm to a small tree, and it had shirts on it to dry. There, with that water-filled washpot and a wood fire burning underneath, was Aeamon Lee stirring the clothes with a long wooden handle.

The coach's first thought was, *What would happen if LSU got a picture of this?*

"Morning, Coach," Aeamon Lee said, as he continued to stir. "I'm trying to get through before people start getting up. I'm just about finished doing my washing for the week. As soon as the shirts dry, I'm going to starch and iron them inside. Now, I'll be through washing right away, but it may take several more hours before they dry good enough that I can iron."

Coach Arrington had already discovered some of Aeamon Lee's idiosyncrasies and knew he was from a different breed of young people. He didn't want to come down on him immediately and was able to control his composure until he decided how to respond.

"Say, you're about finished washing? I think it would be good if we could get that fire out as soon as possible. You know it's going to attract some attention pretty soon."

"Okay, this is my last load, but I need more clothesline. If you help me find some clothesline someplace, I'll finish a lot quicker." Coach Arrington quickly found some line that would do, so he got the shirts on the line to dry. Coach and some campus security personnel helped him get the fire out, but they had to wait a while for the pot to cool. Coach grew impatient and used a water hose to cool it down enough so that they could put it out of sight in the truck of a friend.

He allowed Aeamon Lee to dry his shirts on the clothesline this time but told him that after the shirts were dry, they would need to talk about this. Afterward, Aeamon Lee agreed, not that he fully understood though, that he would make other arrangements to get his shirts washed and dried. He had around twelve of these special shirts his mother had made for him. In the meantime, he made arrangements with Ms. Pearl, the African American lady from whom he had borrowed the washpot. He would bring his clothes over there to her house. There he would wash them himself, and together they would dry, starch, and iron them.

*　　*　　*

One day, Aeamon Lee's roommate made some comment about his "rather strange-looking shirts" and wanted to know where he bought them. "I picked out the material and the designs at a fabric store, and my mother did the rest after I drew a shirt design I liked. There is one design I like, but I haven't found the material yet. It is black and has white dots on it. Mama is still looking for that design. My mother can sew shirts as well as Serafina in *The Rose Tattoo*. Have you seen that movie?" Webster had seen the movie, he thought, but he didn't remember her sewing.

"And it doesn't bother you to wear those shirts even though they are not in style?"

"I'm not style-conscious. You know, I have enough self-confidence that I don't need to feel I must conform to some fashion trend. As I recently explained to some socialite lady in Oxford, I make my clothes. My clothes don't make me." By this time, Aeamon Lee felt a little indignant since this was the second time he had to explain something about his shirts. He did not see clothes fashion as that important. He thought it unfairly took away from emphasis on the personality and character as being more important.

Aeamon Lee and his roommate got along well as long as they were talking football plays and the quarterback play on the team. When they disagreed, their discussions were civil and cordial. They usually disagreed on what the important things of life were, but now their attention must be focused on the beginning of the football season.

*   *   *

There is a new spirit, a new energy, and a new anticipation growing throughout the Southland in late August. Actually, it started with a letdown in January, when the last football season was over. Hunting and fishing only served one's joys temporarily until it was football time in the South. Some husbands get reacquainted with their wives during this down period. Slowly but surely, one's life is gradually revived and grows in intensity with each passing month. There is a daily countdown to the first game.

The time has finally arrived on those calm, cool nights with the smell of freshly mowed grass and cigar smoke. Sweat becomes the sweet smell of perfume. The team's schedule is written on the calendar. Depth charts have been carefully drawn for each position. One searches for every bit of information on who will be backing up the starting left guard. One lives from one Saturday to the next. Young men dream of performing superhuman feats on the gridiron. Old men dream of an earlier time when they performed superhuman feats on the gridiron. Preachers preach on Sunday from texts that reflect the team's score on Saturday, such as Matthew 21:10.

The usual yearly rituals to prepare for game day must be performed. Family members must not interrupt this routine, because one must be concentrating to stay focused on what is coming. All house and yard projects must be completed before the first game if they are done this year. One makes sure that all the paraphernalia with the team's colors are ready and in place. The clarion call is in the sound of the band drummer, who summons the fans quickly to the glory of yet another season. One escapes into a world that takes away all that would beset a man with worries of a different sort. The time has come, and it is great.

Many wartime battles have been won using the football model. There must be a strong air attack. Then effective forces must be ready to carry out their mission on the ground. One must strike when the opposition least expects it. One must not signal one's plans to the enemy. One tries to figure out their strategy so one will be ready to destroy it. Defensive formations are important in order to hold the ground you've already taken. Even the combat military and football uniforms are similar.

During the game, players from both teams block, tackle, blitz, kick, pancake, push, and fight for position. This controlled aggression against one another goes on for two and a half hours. But when the last buzzer has sounded, players from both teams will shake hands, congratulate, and pat the other on their behinds. Then some players from both sides will voluntarily assemble in a circle in the middle of the field to thank God for his blessings. What a game!

CHAPTER 4

The Historic Season
SEPTEMBER 1983

The first game of the season was coming on September 3, against Memphis State, and Ole Miss nearly always had a tough game with them. Memphis State could make their season just by beating Ole Miss. The practices were intense. The senior quarterbacks received nearly all the snaps in practice, but Aeamon Lee did go through most of the game-plan plays with the first team at least once. He paid close attention and got all the plays down in his mind and concentrated on the signals called from the sidelines. He would be ready if and when his time came to direct the team.

The team left on Friday and stayed in the famous Peabody Hotel in downtown Memphis, which was headquarters for the team and the fans. The team was treated in a first-class manner, and Aeamon Lee tried not to be too conspicuous, looking around at everything. Of course, he knew a little something about Memphis and the Peabody Hotel, having spent part of his summer there. But his activities then were a little different from those he was now experiencing. He dared not reveal any of his summer events in Memphis. This time, he would not be looking for street poker games or amateur boxing contests. Since this was the first game of the season, there was much anticipation by the coaches, players, and fans. It was a perfect season at this point. There were pep rallies, parties, and efforts by the coaches to keep all the players in line and focused on the game. It was a night game, and the time finally came. Aeamon Lee found out that he was not the only one with butterflies. He kept telling himself it was not smart to be anxious and that whatever he did would be on a higher plane.

Liberty Bowl Stadium was packed, and it helped that half the crowd appeared to be Ole Miss fans. The team, however, had problems from the very beginning of the game. The coaches tried to alternate quarterbacks to see if they could get something going offensively, and nothing much worked except Ole Miss kicked two field goals.

Then tragedy struck at the end of the first quarter when the senior passing quarterback went down with a high ankle sprain. The other quarterback liked to roll out and either run or dump the ball off short to a receiver. The Memphis State defense adjusted and stopped every drive. At halftime, the coaches were obviously planning on the same quarterback playing the rest of the game. The usual offensive and defensive adjustments were made for the second half.

When the third quarter started, the score was 17–6 in favor of Memphis State. Suddenly, MSU scored on a 40-yard pass play they had not previously run. This made the score 24–6. Then the second tragedy for the team occurred in the middle of the third quarter. The running quarterback tore his anterior cruciate ligament and would be out for the rest of the season. When it happened, Aeamon Lee felt regret for both the seniors, but at the same time, he had this heightened energy, knowing that he might be called upon to go in. Would they let this freshman with no experience go in to direct the team, or would they go with Webster, who did have a little more game experience?

The call came from Coach Wortham for Aeamon Lee to get ready. He only had time to make about two practice pass attempts until Coaches Underwood and Wortham began to tell him what they expected. It appeared to Aeamon Lee that they didn't expect much, nothing anyway that would get them back in the game quickly. He had noticed that every time Ole Miss lined up in one formation, they ran the same play. And this was the play they wanted to start with, but Aeamon Lee had other plans.

After the play and formation were called in the huddle, Aeamon Lee whispered to the running back, who was supposed to get the ball and run off right tackle, that he would fake the ball to him and he would run around the end. This was something he had done before when the scabs challenged the first-team defense in practice. He didn't tell the other players so that in no way would the play be signaled. Memphis State knew the formation and lined up accordingly and converged to the left to take down the running back. When they did, virtually no one was left on the left offensive side, which was where Aeamon Lee was running with the ball. He was a good ten to fifteen yards downfield before Memphis State figured out what was happening. Aeamon Lee ran the ball untouched all the way to the end zone for about sixty-five yards.

When he came off the field, he stayed down at one end of the sidelines to avoid seeing the coaches, because he had not run the play they called. Of course, the coaches got him up there in their presence, and Coach Wortham said calmly, "Be glad you scored on that play." Now, Ole Miss was only down 24–13. This reenergized the team, both offensively and defensively. Memphis State's offense was stopped, and Ole Miss got the ball on their own 35-yard line. Aeamon Lee led the offense down the field to the Memphis State 5-yard line. He had run most of the plays called from the sidelines, but there were times when he felt the offense was too predictable for the defense. He would add some kind of wrinkle, and it seemed to work well.

He determined out on the field that the following week, he would discuss the offensive game plan with the coaches. He wanted them to give him some discretion on plays. He even made some checkoffs at the line of scrimmage, which is unusual for an inexperienced quarterback. As the game wore on, his self-confidence increased. Winning the game was now in sight.

From the 5-yard-line, it was third and goal; and he rolled left, hitting the running back with a pass out in the backfield. He barely got it over the line. Now the score was 24–20. This really whipped up the fans, and the stadium came alive on both sides. The competition was fierce, and there were several personal foul penalties. It was killing Memphis State that they were letting Ole Miss back in the game that they had well in hand. But they had never competed against a quarterback like Aeamon Lee Mistral.

The radio announcers didn't have much information on Aeamon Lee except that he was a freshman, was six feet four inches tall, weighed 210 pounds, and was from Goshen Wells, Mississippi—wherever that was. His consistent and hard-nosed play quickly won over the fans and the players, even though the players knew from practice what he could do. They didn't know if he could do it again in actual games on the field. Often, one does not perform well in the actual game under game conditions controlled by a clock. Aeamon Lee's quick learning, intuition, and determination were now paying off. But they were still behind in the game.

In the fourth quarter, the teams swapped possessions, and then Ole Miss started a drive late. Aeamon Lee was not about to give up the clever play-calling and changes he had been making. He decided he would just take the heat for it the next week. There is an old saying that it is easier to get forgiveness than permission. He didn't think they could be too hard on him, especially if the game was won. He mixed up the plays that included him running and passing. He was even telling receivers and running backs what to do on some plays different from what the play called for. He would put a man in motion when he called it from the line of scrimmage. The defense was fairly confused, and from the fifteen, he went back on a three-second drop-back pass play. Everyone was covered, and he rolled out to find some time, and again everybody was covered. He didn't stop running, and suddenly, he tucked the ball and ran around and through some players to the end zone. This touchdown now put Ole Miss ahead 27–24, and the Ole Miss crowd was letting their identity be known for the Memphis State fans.

The Ole Miss defense held. Now with less than two minutes to go in the game, Ole Miss had the ball, and the coaches wanted Aeamon Lee to run some time. It was third and three, and it appeared that they could not run out the time because Memphis State had only used one time-out. The sideline called for a safe play, but Aeamon Lee spotted a wide-open receiver downfield and couldn't resist hitting him on the run for a final touchdown, which now made the score 34–24. And that was the final score.

The coaches wanted the players to get off the field fairly quickly after the game. Some players from both schools met at the center of the field and had a short prayer. Aeamon Lee did not participate in this ritual much, though he never spoke negatively about the practice. Someone asked him later about his nonparticipation. Aeamon Lee stated, "The Jesus that I try to follow didn't like public prayer very much. He preferred that we pray in our rooms.[58] I have a prayer on my mind often, but it is not something you can see. I'll join the group prayer occasionally."

As he walked off the field that night in Memphis, he heard something that inspired him more than he could imagine. The Ole Miss band was playing "From Dixie with Love," and he noticed that the music mixed "Dixie" and "The Battle Hymn of the Republic." He thought that this was an appropriate symbol of reconciliation and unity to portray to the rest of the nation. It seemed to him to be the perfect melody to play following a game, whether they had won or lost. The sound created chills, and it endeared loyalty and feeling to Ole Miss and pride in being an American.

*   *   *

The coaches congratulated the team but reminded them of their loss of two starting quarterbacks. Coach Wortham pointed out the great amount of work they had to do for the rest of the schedule. He told Aeamon Lee, "I'm glad for the win, and I know you did some spectacular things out there tonight, but tomorrow, we've got to talk." In a quarter and a half, Aeamon Lee had rushed for two touchdowns and passed for two with 225 yards of passing.

Overnight, the buzz throughout the Mid-South was about this freshman quarterback at Ole Miss that led the team from behind to win late in the game. The Memphis *Commercial Appeal* played it up and reported the disappointment of Memphis State for losing the game when they were up by eighteen points. After the game, reporters flocked around Aeamon Lee, but he knew not to say anything more than the usual clichés after a win.

More than anything else, he wanted to talk with his family and Jo-Nathan. He knew he could only talk for a short time. The phone was reinstalled at his house before he left. The phone had been one of the expenses sacrificed when his daddy got hurt and couldn't farm anymore. But he knew he needed to talk with them occasionally. He was pleased to find out that Plea and Martha had listened to the game on the radio. They stated that they really got anxious when they called out his name. As far as they could determine, it sounded like he played well. This was what they stated to Aeamon Lee by way of reassuring him and trying to make him feel good.

He asked about Jo-Nathan, who still had more training to undergo until he would be a United States Marine. Jo-Nathan would later write how hard it was but that he was becoming a man he never thought he could become. In his letters, Aeamon Lee thought he sounded older and more mature, even though it had only been two months since he had last seen him.

*   *   *

At the coach's news conference on campus, many of the questions had to do with Aeamon Lee and whether this unproven freshman would start the next game. The coach was noncommittal and stated that they would see how the practices went for the week before naming a starter for the Tulane game in New Orleans. The coach did say, "Well, I think he proved himself quite well when he was in the ball game, didn't he?"

It appeared that one of the senior quarterbacks was out for the season, and the other one could be out eight weeks or more. It was unusual to lose two starting quarterbacks in one game, and the coach stated that they would put the other quarterbacks through some tough drills to find their best two.

As the week unfolded, Aeamon Lee and the experienced Webster took most of the snaps. Aeamon Lee was able to help Webster with his technique and understanding of the speed and flow of the game. Webster, in turn, helped Aeamon Lee with other matters simply because of his game experience.

The grumbling from the alumni and students was that it would be a long season, especially after losing two senior quarterbacks. And since Ole Miss struggled against Memphis State for most of the game, the expectations were being modified downward. Many thought it would simply be one of those "developing character" seasons. Even though Aeamon Lee's play had been phenomenal, he was still an unknown, and the end of the first game was viewed as one of those proverbial quirks.

The most eventful thing of the week came early when the coaches on the offensive side of the ball met along with the head coach. The offensive coordinator came to Ole Miss from Tennessee and was attempting to make the same assumptions about the talent at Ole Miss that could be made about Tennessee's teams. The Vols had consistently been able to recruit top offensive linemen from around the country, and therefore, they traditionally had a good rushing team, mostly relying on it to get them down the field. It was hard for the coordinator to realize that Ole Miss was not as blessed with this amount of talent and had to be more creative and imaginative in the play calling. Therefore, the offensive scheme was far too predictable, and it simply was not working. But the coordinator was not ready to give up on it.

The coaches argued for forty-five minutes about what changes were needed on the offensive side of the ball. They called Aeamon Lee and Webster into the meeting, and Coach Wortham announced that they could not duplicate what happened in the Memphis game, that they all had to be on the same page.

"I don't mean any disrespect, Coach, but I could not stand to see our running backs getting squashed at the line of scrimmage. It is true that I arbitrarily added some wrinkles to some of the plays. My point is that it worked if you saw the game I saw. It crossed up their defense, and we were able to move the ball because they couldn't figure out which side the ball was going. I am hoping that you will recognize the need for some changes. When you come up with a multiple offense that allows for some on-the-field adjustments, I will run that offense, and we will win with it."

Aeamon Lee's self-confidence was asserting itself, so he continued, "Another thing I feel that I must mention. Before I went into the game, and while I was in the game, I began to get a feel for what was really going on out there. What I mean by that is that I had a keen intuition of what their defense was going to do, and I felt like I knew what play would work best in a given situation. I know that sounds arrogant to you, but I'm just telling you the truth."

At this point, the offensive coordinator said, "Well, I can't believe what I'm hearing. So you want us, the coaching staff, to let you, an inexperienced freshman player, develop the offensive and defensive game plan each week?" Actually, there were some profanity thrown in so that his remarks would get attention and possibly intimidate Aeamon Lee.

"Oh, no, sir, I'm just being honest with you, and I've not made a request like that. I'm just sharing something that could, I believe, help all of us. And, yes, I would like to make some simple suggestions after I've viewed their film."

Aeamon Lee thought that he might have been too brash after only playing a quarter and a half and being a freshman at that, so he quickly stated, "But, sir, I will run the game plan I'm given to the best of my ability."

Coach Wortham spoke up and stated, "Well, we sometimes look at film together, and maybe we can let you sit in and discuss it with us. You can tell us what you think after you have viewed the film if we can't do it together."

"That sounds good to me, and thanks for agreeing to this. We are all on the same team, and we'll win together."

Aeamon Lee and Webster were then allowed to leave the meeting. Webster didn't say anything for a while. Later, he looked at him and said, "I'm amazed at the audacity you showed back there. Players don't tell coaches what to do. I can't believe you changed those plays on the field. I could never have done that. I thought they were going to kick you off the team for insubordination."

Aeamon Lee didn't respond to him but thought to himself, *And this is why you're not starting. You're not wanting to win like I want to win.*

* * *

The week of practice was hard work. It was back to basics as far as the coaches were concerned. Mistakes were pointed out, and they were worked on until the mistake was corrected. Classes were in full swing, and the demands on the time for the athlete were mounting. It was definitely demanding on Aeamon's time. Coach Underwood, the quarterback coach, worked with Aeamon Lee and Webster on their technique and reading defenses. They watched film on the other team together. Aeamon Lee was able to suggest some formations and plays, and he felt good about the game plan. It seemed that the head coach had nudged the offensive coordinator to give a little in his offensive schemes. Given his offensive record the past two years, his job was on the line too.

The discipline an athlete had to have in order to keep up with everything was astounding. Aeamon Lee had to learn so many new aspects of the football program each week, along with all the demands of a regular student in difficult classes. When he heard people make comments about the easy life of an athlete, it made him downright mad. *Such ignorance!* he thought. *You would think the university would do more to remind people of the dual role of an athlete.* The stereotype of the athlete being dumb had been around a long time, but still, people mouthed this sentiment, having no basis in fact to justify it. The truth was that it was much harder being both an athlete and a student than it was being just a regular student.

Aeamon Lee found that the best time for him to focus on his college studies was to go to the library somewhere around 9:00 or 10:00 p.m. and sit at a carrel where he had privacy. He didn't tell his friends where he was at this time. It was getting to the point where students wanted to talk with him about the team, schedule, or his shirts. He just could not accommodate every request. Other students knew not to interrupt one studying in a carrel. The library staff became used to him coming in late most every night, and they helped to protect his privacy.

Aeamon Lee was always discovering things about himself that he never fully realized before. He knew he had caught on to what was expected of him to succeed really early. Once he had a vision of what the right thing was, he could go out and physically replicate it. His intuition kicked in at times and places when it was most needed, providing answers and insight. He never fully grasped what this all meant, but he would continue to go down that road and enjoy the serendipity. He just decided that it was because he was still tense and attempting at every moment in this new environment to live life on the ethereal plane.

*   *   *

The game plan was in place for the Tulane game, and Aeamon Lee would start at quarterback. The trip to New Orleans was an exciting adventure for him because he had not been very far from home before (except to Memphis and down the Mississippi River). He tried to take in as many of the sites as he could, and other players noticed how observant he was. He definitely was not used to the fine accommodations provided to the team in terms of what hotel they stayed in and the meals provided. He had never seen such a site as the Superdome. It was a lot for a freshman from Goshen Wells, Mississippi, to take in.

The game was an offensive shootout. The Tulane team had one of the best offensives in the country with their passing attack. Ole Miss had to match them touchdown for touchdown. Aeamon Lee had a little less pressure on him than the first game when he only had a quarter and a half to produce the win. Now he had the whole game and game plan, and he began to gain even more confidence and control. The players began to respond to him more positively and gained more confidence in him. His passes were on target. The receivers were now more used to his tendencies, and he knew the routes of the receivers better than they did. There were some plays where he added something different either in the huddle or at the line of scrimmage. Occasionally, a lineman had a false start, but he knew it would only take a little more time for all the offensive players to learn his signals and calls.

The game score was close until the fourth quarter, when Aeamon Lee realized he had seen enough of their offense that he began to anticipate where they were going with the ball. But how could he communicate this to the coach calling the defensive signals from the sidelines? So he moved close to him on the sidelines, and at one point, looked the coach in the eye and said, "They're going to throw an out pass in the flat on the right." The coach didn't respond to him because he was getting his calls from the coach's booth upstairs. When the plays went exactly as Aeamon Lee had called several times, the coach called the formation and then shouted to the left-side or right-side players to be ready. This input helped the defense to stop them, and the other team had to punt. The assistance turned out to be the opening Ole Miss needed to get ahead and stay.

Ole Miss won the game after the defense began to stop them, allowing the team to get two touchdowns ahead. The final score was 45–28, with Acamon Lee passing for 344 yards and four touchdowns.

He also rushed the ball for fifty-eight yards and one touchdown. His yardage was more than the highly touted Tulane offense could produce.

After the game, Aeamon Lee walked down to where the Pride of the South band played "From Dixie with Love" and stood respectfully facing the band and the fans. When they got to the part where the band started with the upbeat "Battle Hymn of the Republic," he raised his helmet in the air and started waving it back and forth. The coaches had not noticed that he was down there. Coach Underwood met him while he was running back toward the visitor locker room. The coach said, "I don't know if you can continue to do that. You know what the coach's rule is on getting off the field as quickly as possible."

Coach Wortham had taken notice of him telling the defensive coach where the plays would go. This meant another meeting and more coaches being offended. Coach Wortham interviewed the coach on the sidelines to discover what was going on and the accuracy of Aeamon Lee's calls. The coach admitted that, for the most part, they had been correct. He stated that sometimes Aeamon Lee had failed to get the call made in time for adjustments. This was due to their quarterback not calling a play until he got to the line or switching off right at the last moment. Otherwise, the calls correctly identified which plays were run and which were pass or option. Nevertheless, the defensive coach advised the head coach that he believed the defense could be helped with Aeamon Lee's input on the sidelines. Convincing the defensive coordinator to allow this help might be another story.

The coaches huddled on campus, and Coach Wortham told Aeamon Lee afterward that he could give his opinion to the sidelines coach when he was sure of the other team's play. But he would not be included, for the time being, in the meetings that involved developing the defensive game plan for the next game.

Coach Wortham reminded the team that they had well-earned victories over two unranked opponents. But the schedule would get harder with games inside the Southeastern Conference coming up. The next game, in fact, was against the mighty Crimson Tide of Alabama, who was high in the rankings. And the game was in Tuscaloosa.

* * *

When Aeamon Lee made his brief call home on Sunday, Plea and Martha already knew they were going up against Alabama. He was amused at their growing interest in the game and the schedule. Martha was concerned about her boy's safety. She said, "Aeamon Lee, I've heard that they have some of the best players, and they are big and rough."

"Don't worry, Mama. We know who we are playing and what it'll take for us to stand our ground."

"Well, you be careful, and try not to get hurt."

He knew this was typical mother-son talk, and he reassured her that all would be well.

After talking with his parents, he couldn't help but think of home. By this time, he had started wanting some good home-cooked food like his mother and Mama Kate cooked. He asked Webster if he was hungry for some different food. Webster said he was, though he would often go out and dine in some of the fine restaurants in Oxford.

Aeamon Lee said, "Come with me, and I'll show you how we can get some." They stopped by the library and found that day's Memphis *Commercial Appeal* and looked in the obituary section for Oxford, Mississippi. There were several deaths reported. Aeamon Lee wrote down the funeral homes and the times for visitation.

"Here's one," said Webster.

Aeamon Lee looked and said, "No, that one won't do. They're Lutheran." Webster didn't understand. Finally, Aeamon Lee found one and said, "This is it, Southern Baptist!"

So Webster drove to this funeral home as Aeamon Lee instructed Webster on what to say. They went in and got in the long line to meet the bereaved family and to pay their respects. They explained that they were there to express sympathy and to meet the family of this fine individual. Afterward, they just sort of stood around and greeted people. And then it happened! A lady came up and said, "I know you boys must be hungry. You wouldn't believe the amount of food people have brought. You all just go right into that kitchen and help yourself." Now Webster understood how this thing worked. The boys thoroughly enjoyed an ample amount of the very best of Lafayette County's home cooking.

*   *   *

Jo-Nathan wrote Aeamon Lee, telling him how exciting it was to read about their wins and that he was counting down to the end of boot camp. "The consolation is that I'll know I went through the toughest physical training in the world, but not ever would I want to do it again." He said there would be graduation exercises with a lot of ceremony and hoped that maybe his mother and father would be able to come. He knew, though, that this was improbable. He admitted that he got terribly homesick the first two weeks, but he said they kept him so busy that he didn't have much time to think about home. He said the training started the moment he stepped off the bus. Aeamon Lee could tell that his lifelong friend was becoming a real man now, more independent and able to take care of himself. The recruits could not make phone calls except in cases of emergency, so they exchanged about one letter a week.

With 2–0 Alabama looming, the fans and students were saying, "Now we shall see if we can compete in the Southeastern Conference. This game will tell the tale." These feelings irritated Aeamon Lee all week even though he knew they were partially right. This game would indeed be their moment of truth, so to speak. He expected a hostile environment and breaks would go against them. This was the game when the players, especially the new players, would come of age. After viewing the film, this feeling was reinforced as Alabama had their traditional strong defense but had not shown their capabilities on offense. They had a great running back who was hard to bring down and a return guy who was always dangerous. In short, this game was critical in terms of the team coming to believe that they could compete in the other conference games.

No one had to tell Aeamon Lee what this game meant and what would be expected of him. Instead, he was wondering, not about himself, but about the other players on both sides of the ball. After viewing much film, he knew they had to play with intensity and play smart till the last play. Again, Aeamon Lee got in his suggestions to the offensive and defensive coordinators even though they were still stubbornly cool to him doing this. They only allowed this because Coach Wortham told them it would be all right, and they couldn't argue with success. But this was Alabama, the coaches argued. "Now, let's see how well he can perform under pressure he has never seen before."

For his overriding thought during the week, Aeamon Lee chose "Play smart! It's not smart to be scared. It's not smart to have butterflies. It's not smart to be overanxious. It's not smart to allow the environment to rattle me. It's not smart to get down on the team or myself when the breaks are going against us. It's not smart to be intimidated. It's not smart to be unprepared. It's not smart for someone second and third on the depth chart to not be ready to play the whole game. It is smart to be cool, yet intense and focused. It is smart for eleven guys to carry out their responsibility on every play. It is smart to take advantage of any breaks with deadly determination. It is smart to avoid making stupid mistakes. It is smart to stand toe-to-toe with the opposition. It is smart to play like you are one touchdown behind. It is smart to play hard for four full quarters." He began repeating these reminders in practice and in meetings.

Coach Wortham liked the greater involvement of Aeamon Lee as the leader of the team and encouraged the team to follow. He even adopted that theme for the week, "Play smart."

Over and over, Aeamon Lee reminded himself of the realities of the game: *I don't care how good they are. They can't put more than eleven players on the field at a time. The field is still 120 yards long and 53.3 yards wide. The refs are supposed to enforce the same rules by which we have been playing.*

He knew they would have to rely on deception more than before. Thus, he devised a scheme that was approved whereby on any given play, he could, at the line of scrimmage, call for something that might deceive the defense. The team practiced these possible changes at the line of scrimmage over and over until they understood his signals. Sometimes he might be changing the play, sometimes he could call for some pass route, or it could all be smoke and mirrors. Hopefully, this would allow them to score early and get a lead. They felt down deep that the best way to win was to get the lead and hold it. But Aeamon Lee reminded the team, "If it happens that we are behind three touchdowns going into the fourth quarter, we'll still come back to win. We'll do whatever it takes!"

On the day of the game in Tuscaloosa, Aeamon Lee held his head up walking into the stadium for pregame warm-ups. The hallowed sanctuaries of The Bear were to be seen everywhere. The home crowd was wildly whooping it up, with the Ole Miss faithful and band down in one corner of the stadium. The film of last year's game showed their cheerleaders and band chanting, "Hey, Ole Miss, we just beat the hell out of you." Every time the Alabama crowd roared, Aeamon Lee mentally interpreted this as their jeering Martha and Plea, his mama and papa.

Before the coaches got to the locker room, Aeamon Lee wrote one of Maleah's sayings on the board: "Whatever you do, do it with all your might."[59] When the coaches came in, they took note of the saying and approved by yelling, "Yeah, we'll do it with all our might."

The pregame locker room talk was emotional and filled with old locker-room clichés. Aeamon Lee stood up and said, "We're going out there and have fun playing *smart*, and we'll do it with all our might." Nothing was left unsaid, and they believed that nothing was left that they could have done on the practice field.

Ole Miss won the toss and elected to receive. On the first play from scrimmage, Aeamon Lee saw a weakness in their defensive secondary and called for a crossing pattern for one of the swift receivers. He hit him when he separated, and the receiver went untouched to the end zone. Aeamon Lee could see the Alabama coach cussing out some assistant coaches on the sidelines. After this play, the going would get a lot tougher against their vaunted defense. In the second quarter, their fleet punt-return guy got loose and ran in a punt for a touchdown to tie the score. They would play even till the half.

In the third quarter, the Rebels stopped the Tide on their first possession and got the ball at their own 30-yard line. They began to grind out the yardage on short passes and short yardage rushing. When it was third down, Aeamon Lee would break the pass routes and run the ball himself, picking up two crucial first downs this way. He would sometimes feign going out of bounds, only to cut at the last moment and pick up more yardage down the sideline. Defenses always hate this when a quarterback, of all people, pulls this stunt. Actually, the quarterbacks were inviting some hard sideline hits afterward. From the 25-yard line, Ole Miss ran a fade pattern, and Aeamon Lee connected with his receiver in the back corner of the end zone. The score was now 14–7.

Later in the third quarter, Ole Miss had driven to the 22 and ran the same pattern. The receiver caught the ball just inside the line in the end zone with one foot clearly in bounds. But the referee running down the sideline ruled he didn't have control until he was out-of-bounds. This was a close play, but in the minds of the Ole Miss players, he had control when his foot went down inside the line. There were arguments and booing and delays but to no avail. This call would gnaw at Aeamon Lee for the rest of the game. Perceived injustice created strong feelings of reaction, but on the other hand, he recalled how they had to play smart. Coach Wortham let the refs have a mouthful. The score would have put Ole Miss up two touchdowns, but it was not to be—at least not on that play.

The injustice stirred the competitive juices in Aeamon Lee, and he felt that he could outrun the rush to the sideline on what would appear to be a passing play. It was third down. Aeamon Lee took the ball and sprinted to his right. He outran the defensive ends and linebackers and then cut sharply downfield. His receivers on that side did a great job blocking, and Aeamon Lee did the rest with a hard charge through two tacklers that took him to the end zone. No flags, touchdown! Again, their head coach could be seen in the face of his assistants.

With the score 21–7, Alabama began to claim the fourth quarter, as they usually did, as their own. Their hard-charging running back ran the ball down to the 2-yard line and barreled across the goal line on the next play. They were fighting back furiously and had the momentum. Aeamon Lee knew that Ole Miss was still in the ball game because of the play of the defense, and while no one else wanted to admit it, it was because of Aeamon Lee virtually calling the defensive formations from the sideline. When they broke the huddle, Aeamon Lee picked up a sense of which direction the play was going. He signaled when the play was going to Alabama's left and when the play was going to their right. This assistance helped tremendously to stall their drives.

But the Crimson Tide did get close enough to kick a field goal, which now made the score 21–17. Ole Miss drove down the field with Aeamon Lee's crisp passes and rushing the ball when no one was open. After a missed field goal, Alabama began a drive by pounding the ball up the middle and completing one 35-yard pass play. They scored the go-ahead touchdown with three minutes and thirty-five seconds to play. The score was now 24–21.

The Ole Miss fans and band were really into the game even though they were now behind in the score. The bench and everyone on their sideline believed that they could come back. They had to keep the chains moving to stop the clock. They had to drive from their own 10-yard line. Aeamon Lee kept saying the refrain, "Play smart, but on a higher level of intensity and with all our might." They carefully crafted a drive featuring this young, strong, elusive, and smart kid Alabama had never seen and for whom they were not prepared. They knew he was a freshman and attempted every intimidation act they could. They even incurred a personal penalty for roughing the quarterback.

There was now forty-four seconds to play, with Ole Miss holding the ball at the Alabama 5-yard line. It was third down and goal, but they wanted the win, not a tie. They set up the formation, making it appear like a pass play to the left, but Aeamon Lee faked and ran a cross-buck to the running back that went to the right. The running back was hardly touched until he got into the end zone. The Ole Miss crowd was standing and cheering and gave a thunderous yell, "Are you ready? Hell yes, damn right, Hotty Toddy, gosh almighty, who in the hell are we? Flimflam! Bim, bam! Ole Miss, by damn!" The Alabama crowd had been subdued for a few short seconds with the score now reading

Ole Miss 28 and Alabama 24. Then they revved up the noise for some last-second miracle with their Rammer Jammer chant.

Aeamon Lee quickly got to the defensive signal caller on the sideline and began his intense efforts to use his intuition accurately. After Alabama got the ball to their 45-yard line, Aeamon Lee wanted to go in on defense at free safety. This was the first time he had ever mentioned it, and Coach Wortham had been generous with his requests in the past, but not on this one. Finally, one of their backs that had caught a short pass got tackled before he could get out of bounds, and with no time-outs left, they furiously attempted to get the clock stopped, but time ran out on Alabama.

The team and fans were ecstatic. It was obvious that Coach Wortham considered this game one of his biggest victories. It made the players feel good to see him have such joy inside. Aeamon Lee looked up after they had made a big pile in the middle of the field, and the Alabama head coach was there with his hand stuck out. "Son, that was a heck of a game you played."

Aeamon Lee nodded his head but didn't know quite what to say. He looked him in the eye and simply said, "Thanks, coach."

When Aeamon Lee went down in front of the band, several of the players went with him this time. They were almost overcome with emotion as the band played "From Dixie with Love" right there in Alabama's own backyard. Walking off the field, he couldn't help but think of his family, the dear friends back home, and how far he had come since sleeping in a cotton wagon earlier that summer.

* * *

This game put Aeamon Lee on the football map, so to speak. He was offensive player of the week in the SEC. Articles about him began to appear in the paper. National sports news specifically called his name and gave him credit for leading Ole Miss to an upset win over mighty Alabama. His stats were not quite as good, but impressive enough. He had 305 yards passing and a whopping 89 yards rushing. That's almost 400 yards of offense. The television networks began plans to put Ole Miss in some televised games later in the season. They were 3–0 and ranked twenty-fifth in the nation.

Events were beginning to happen fast and furiously. Martha had told him on the phone that one of his high school teachers, Ms. Babe Markle, the one who had urged him to try to go to college, came to see them. It seemed that Aeamon Lee had confided in her the story of how Plea had been crippled by the falling tree, had been unable to get his disability, and how the family was struggling financially. She wanted to help Plea reapply. She helped to get all his medical records and statements from the doctors, and they sent in the request for reconsideration. She even got her lawyer to help with the process. It would be a while before they knew the decision.

Martha also told him about how the vegetable garden was still producing, how much she had canned and put up for the winter. The corn would soon be ready to be combined. The Markums were getting regular letters from Jo-Nathan. Aeamon Lee reassured her he would be home on their open date, and he would make arrangements for the crop to be gathered.

News reporters and students wanted more of his time, which meant he had more difficulty trying to stay out of the limelight. The fans and students could envision one of those once-in-a-lifetime seasons, and yet they had only played three games. Expectations were running high. The team was playing above its ability, and there were many tough games ahead.

* * *

The next game was supposed to finally be a home game, but instead of playing in Oxford, the game was in Jackson, Mississippi, the state capital. In fact, the coaches complained that there were only three games on campus on the schedule. Two other home games were played in Jackson. They didn't like this and sought to persuade the athletic director to have more games on campus like most other colleges. Playing in Jackson was too much like an away game, having to make the trip and playing on a strange field.

The game was against Arkansas, who was in a rebuilding year in the Southwest Conference. Ole Miss won the game 34–26. Again, the Ole Miss defense was having a hard time stopping the opponents but was able to do just enough to allow the offense to put up more points. The game provided Aeamon Lee with an opportunity to build upon the growing statistics he was accumulating in passing yardage and even in rushing. He was actually second in the conference in total offense. The fans were growing accustomed to his play. The buzz throughout Rebel country was about the unexpected play of this freshman that remained somewhat of a mystery because there were no high school records to which they could point. How long will this last? Could he really be this good, and could he carry the load throughout the season?

* * *

Every week, Aeamon Lee continued to write Jo-Nathan, who had gone through the famed Eagle, Globe, and Anchor ceremony. This signified that he was now a marine, always and forever, one of the few and the proud. On Family Day, the Markums—Mama Kate and Amos—were there, all the way from Goshen Wells, Mississippi, to see the ceremony and the graduation parade. It was an emotional moment they would never forget. They sat proudly and equally with all the other families. Jo-Nathan could hardly speak, knowing that his beloved parents were there to see the pageantry and to celebrate with him a rare accomplishment. They had never been that far away from home. All their family had contributed a little and made up enough money for them to make the bus trip to Parris Island, South Carolina. After the graduation, Jo-Nathan came back home with the family on a ten-day leave before being assigned to the marine combat corps at Camp Lejeune, North Carolina.

Needless to say, Jo-Nathan was indeed proud of his accomplishment, and he should have been. He had undergone the most intense physical and mental training, more so than in any of the other military services. He told Aeamon Lee on the phone that running with him had really helped in his preparation. He told about how he could break a M16A2 rifle down and knew the characteristics of all its parts. He had memorized more codes and rules than he ever thought he could. Aeamon Lee reinforced his good feeling about himself without reflecting the fear he had for his friend.

He was anxious for Jo-Nathan in terms of where he might be sent, especially if he went to a combat zone. He knew that Jo-Nathan had primarily been lured into the marines for the glamour of achieving that status and how this, in turn, would help him with a career. He had heard that there would be less discrimination against him if he were a marine. After combat training, he didn't have any idea where he would be sent. In Aeamon Lee's heart, there were fears, and he had an uneasy feeling for his lifelong friend.

*   *   *

Finally, on October 1, Ole Miss would play the first of only three games in Oxford against Georgia. The atmosphere was totally different than what he had experienced in the previous weeks. They now had a friendly crowd, supportive fans, and no long distance to travel.

The Grove was full of cars, people, tents, food, music, and Southern cordiality. Georgia was always strong and competitive, and it would take another super effort to win this game.

All week, the coaches felt the team needed to be sharper in certain areas. Aeamon Lee put another saying from Maleah on the board before the coaches arrived: "Since a dull ax requires great strength, sharpen the blade."[60] Coach Wortham came in and read the statement and said, "Aeamon Lee, I don't know where you're getting these quotations, but they sure have been on target. I expect everyone to look sharp today in all phases of the game.

Again, Aeamon Lee's combination of running and passing kept Ole Miss in the game, and they only won by three points, 38–35. Even though the score indicated a close game, the biggest gain was in the confidence being generated by players with not as much ability as the opponents.

In the Georgia game, Aeamon Lee again rushed the ball more than a quarterback usually did. Every time he went to one side, there was a cornerback who was prone to taunt the opposing players. No matter if the runner picked up ten yards on him, he would say, "Man, you better not come my way again. Man, you can't endure much more of me."

Finally, Aeamon Lee had enough of this taunting, and when it happened the next time, he got up and grabbed his jersey, pulled him up close, and quoted, "'Man will not merely endure: he will prevail.'"[61] The cornerback walked away, saying, "That man is crazy or something."

The local fans who had not been attending the away games had heard about Aeamon Lee's habit of going down to the front of the band after the game for the playing of "From Dixie with Love." On this day, most of the fans didn't leave immediately. They wanted to see what he did. When he went down to the band and began waving his helmet in the air, the fans really roared. To him, this was the stuff dreams were made of[62] after a great win.

There was another reason for the success: Aeamon Lee's contribution to both the offense and defense in helping the team come up with winning game plans. This was an issue that was kept quiet, and it was occurring only because Coach Wortham insisted that he continue to have input. The coaches would take the credit after the game for their effective game plans. Coach Wortham was always generous with his compliments of Aeamon Lee, however, but didn't want to sound too confident. He would borrow a page from Coach Bear Bryant's playbook and poor mouth about his team's weaknesses and the need to improve greatly if they were going to be competitive.

Aeamon Lee also knew that the mysterious sayings Maleah had provided had amazing effect, and he would continue to use them when he felt they were needed.

* * *

In leaving the field that day, Aeamon Lee couldn't help but notice the numerous Confederate flags waved by many in the crowd. The game was televised regionally, and the cameras paid great attention to the Ole Miss tradition of waving the Confederate flag. This created some amount of cognitive dissonance inside of him. He was playing for a school and fans, trying to win with all his being, and yet he wondered what their agenda was. He would address this matter with his confidant, Coach Wortham, during the week.

After the players changed into their street clothes, they were expected to greet their families and friends outside the dressing room. Even though he didn't have any family there, a crowd of students and fans surrounded him, wanting autographs and trying to gain his friendship. He went through this ritual because he wanted these fans to know how important their role was to the success of the program. He reminded them, "You might not know this, but when we're down there on the field, we notice how much you are with us and giving us encouragement. Keep it up, because it means a lot to us."

There appeared to be an unusually large number of female students who would happen by. There were times when he drove around with them but resisted the urge to ask them out on individual dates. He had mixed feelings about this because he knew they would go out with him; in fact, they would sometimes invite him to go places. The ones that turned him off were the ones who talked like a Valley girl. He knew he didn't have much money to spend on dates, and he didn't think they would understand. There might be a little more money after the crops were gathered, but that would be another month or so. He also knew he had to give priority to what he was doing in classes and on the football field. Many players had let pretty women divert their attention, demanding so much of their time that it showed in other areas of their lives. There was plenty of time for these matters after the season, and he was determined that nothing would interfere with his plans and success. Considering this as simply being smart, he called it deferred gratification.

After the Georgia game, a reporter said, "Well, I know you must be overwhelmed given your success. The team must be asking a lot from you this season, and you must be asking a lot from the team." You know these reporters don't ask outright questions. Instead, they make their own statements and want the athlete to simply respond to their statement.

Aeamon Lee responded, "I don't ask for much. In fact, I only ask for three things: First, that the refs call the game fair on both sides of the ball. Second, that they don't change the rules in the middle of the game. And third, put me in the game so I can compete. That's all I ask, and I'll do the rest."

Well, this response was reported in all the newspapers and sports talk shows. This was quoted over and over again. The coaches usually gave the players some talking points they could use with the media. They also designated the players who were allowed to talk to the reporters. They had not allowed Aeamon Lee to be interviewed, but they decided this one time what he said was okay and that he didn't cross any forbidden line. Although, he did get close with the comment about the refs.

* * *

After this home game against Georgia, Aeamon Lee received invitations to various fraternity parties on campus. It seemed they were competing with each other to see who could get him to their party. But Aeamon Lee missed the time he used to spend on Sorghum Hill, playing and singing with the neighbors and the people with whom he had grown up. He had already asked around about a nightspot with live music on Saturday night. This was what he really wanted to do, but he had a feeling that the students would not understand and would expect him to show up at their parties. He knew he would draw a lot of attention, and the situation would be stiff with him having to watch everything he said. His words quickly spread around campus.

After getting into more casual clothes, he and an African American player, Andre Tinsley, went down to see Ms. Pearl, who washed and ironed his shirts. He asked her again about a place she had mentioned where she thought they made music on Saturday night. Eventually, they found it around 9:00 p.m. It was a small joint called Pappy's Place, which had a small stage band. There were only three men playing, and the place was crowded. Andre and Aeamon Lee went in and immediately felt the soulful spirit that permeated the joint. He had never had any problems with a setting like this. There was something about Aeamon Lee that soon mellowed the crowd at a place where he was the only white person present.

Pretty soon, the word had spread among the patrons who these two guys were. They got some soft drinks and found a place to sit near the stage. He got Andre to tell one of the musicians that he would play with them if they had an extra guitar that was tuned up. A band member asked, "Do you play this kind of R and B music?"

"Sure, I can play most anything. I'd like to play in the background if you don't mind."

"We don't mind trying you out to see if you really can play."

They found another guitar, and Aeamon Lee started playing rhythm in the background.

He played with the band sitting down for about thirty minutes, and then the leader decided he wanted to sing a number. He and Aeamon Lee swapped guitars, and he played the lead guitar for the number. After a while, Aeamon Lee asked them to play "Night Time Is the Right Time." He told them that he could do the vocal on that song, and they agreed to let him try it. He sang the blues song with as much feeling as John Fogarty with Creedence Clearwater Revival. The crowd was feeling the music, and everybody was moving in rhythm with the song. He received applause and continued to play until after midnight. The band invited him back, and that was mainly what he wanted to hear. Andre saw a side of Aeamon Lee he had not seen before. He knew he was eccentric in some ways because he remembered the incident with the washpot and clothesline on campus.

* * *

Aeamon Lee kidded Webster some about his music tapes. At least Webster wasn't into the punk rockers like the Beastie Boys or Bad Brains. It seemed to Aeamon Lee that they had a fatalistic tone to their music while wearing shirts with "I Don't Care" inscribed on them. And

Aeamon Lee wasn't about to give up his idealism and expectation of a better world.

"I get tired of listening to the Bee Gees. Do you have something by Bruce Springsteen or 'Fortunate Son' by CCR?" Then he quoted from the song:

> Some folks inherit star spangled eyes,
> Ooh, they send you down to war.[63]

*   *   *

At the first of the week, he asked to talk with Coach Wortham privately. On Monday around noon, he got his opportunity. He thanked the coach for all that he had done for him and allowed him to do. "There is something I have observed, and before I say anything, I wanted to talk with you." The coach was listening. "It is about the Ole Miss crowd waving those Confederate flags at the games and displaying them all around campus. I've wondered how the black players view this."

"It is interesting you would bring this up," Coach Wortham said. "Confidentially, let me share with you my feeling, which I have expressed to the chancellor and the athletic director. You see, waving that flag has been a tradition for a long time. But that flag has become symbolic of something very negative to our black players and students and many others as well. And it has interfered with my recruiting black players to come to Ole Miss. We don't sign a lot of good players because of that symbol. And this has hurt us in the conference, and I've told the school that they were going to have to do something about that symbol. Consequently, I've gotten a lot of negativity for doing that."

Aeamon Lee said, "I've talked with some of the black players about it, and they said that they just block it out and never talk about it. They are just glad they are getting a chance to showcase their talent with hopes of maybe making it to the NFL someday. And they appreciate the fact that they don't experience any discrimination or prejudice from you, the coaching staff, or the university. They say most of the students are friendly to them, and they haven't experienced any problems of a racial nature to any great significance. I guess that is commendable, but it burns me up to see some fans wave that flag in their face knowing the feeling it generates," Aeamon Lee said.

Coach responded, "Maybe the school will act on this soon. I have spoken publicly about this negative symbol, and I have gone out on a limb on this issue. I know that if I could have recruited certain black players, we might have had a better record. And that is not taking anything away from our black players. I care about every one of them, and the ones we have recruited are great individuals. They are busting their guts out for this program. By the way, you might not know this, but I know full well why we are winning this year."

Aeamon Lee did too, but he didn't ask the coach to explain. "You may not know this, Coach, but there is going to be a meeting of all concerned about the flag issue on campus this week. I'm thinking about going, and if given an opportunity, I might speak up."

Coach Wortham paused as if he were thinking about whether this would be wise or not. "I've had a lot of confidence in you on the field. You know you could pay for doing this because there are many supporters who consider that flag sacred. In fact, you will pay a cost if you speak. Do you understand that?"

"If you can take it, Coach, then I can too. I promise I'll be careful and use some tact."

"All right, I'll trust you again to do the right thing."

Aeamon Lee mentioned to Webster that he was going to this meeting to discuss the flag issue. Webster told him he didn't think he should go.

"Here's why I am going." Quoting from his three-by-five cards, Aeamon Lee said, "'To sin by silence when they should protest makes cowards of men.'[64] I will not be silent nor a coward."

"Isn't your religious group going to present a resolution that describes the Christian ramifications of waving this racist symbol of hate on this academic campus?" Aeamon Lee asked. "They are involved aren't they, since this is actually a moral issue with spiritual overtones?"

"Well, no, we haven't discussed it. You know the tribes of Israel in the Old Testament had tribal banners called standards, or what we would call flags. That's all the Confederate flag is—just a banner like those symbolizing a tribe of God's people," Webster countered.

"I've heard that argument and let me ask you a question: Suppose that Baal worshippers stole that flag and used it as their own. The Israelite tribe didn't object or say a word. The Baal group would use it at all their meetings and rituals for many generations. After a while, people began to associate that particular banner with Baal worship. Do you think the Israelite tribe could start using it again and not expect people to associate it with Baal? Anyway, my church won't say anything either."

"Okay, I see your point."

"It is interesting to me," Aeamon Lee said, "how evangelical Christians cherry-pick the moral issues they want to emphasize. They seem to leave alone the sins against humanity."

On Wednesday night, the meeting was held with some faculty and administrators present. The Student Council was in charge and laid down the rules for discussion. Aeamon Lee sat in the back and had decided not to ask any player to come with him. He would stand alone, but first he would listen. Finally, people from the audience would be allowed to speak. It was explained that there had already been some discussion about designing a flag, unique to Ole Miss, which could be used at ball games. On the other hand, it was stated that there were also many who believed that Ole Miss should not abandon tradition for the sake of a minority. "How do you feel?" the audience was asked.

Mainly students went to the microphone to voice a strong opinion in favor of keeping the flag. They argued that it was tradition that counted and that Ole Miss was allowing outsiders to influence its heritage. They made the "it's a cultural thing" argument. And "my great granddaddy fought for this flag."

"It's our constitutional right to wave this flag."

"Why, it's not a racist symbol."

"If people don't like this flag, they can just go elsewhere."

"Once they take away the flag, it won't stop there."

Aeamon Lee observed that those few students who spoke on making a change were timid, nonassertive, and appeared intimidated by being outnumbered. The advocates for the status quo were making their arguments forcefully. They had set up two microphones, one for those who wanted to keep the flag (and there was a long line there of both male and female students), and another microphone for those who wanted a change because of the negative symbolic nature of the Confederate flag. That line was short.

After more than a dozen people had spoken, mostly students, Aeamon Lee walked to the front with all eyes focused on him, forgetting about the person currently speaking. When he went to the microphone for those who were advocating for a change, many in the audience were visibly surprised. It was probably because of his practice of listening with such reverence to "From Dixie with Love" after each game. Evidently, they had deduced prematurely that Aeamon Lee would be a supporter of the flag with them.

Finally, he was recognized to speak. The hall got very quiet. He held his head up and looked out over the crowd. He had no notes and spoke only from the heart. He had decided that simply being assertive in his speech would be the more effective course to take, not too passive or too aggressive.

He started by saying, "In the minds of some folks, it would be better if I had just stayed away from this meeting as just another football player who can't use a complete sentence. Or as one who has nothing of any substance to say since football players are a little dense and slow anyway." This got a few chuckles from the audience and had the effect of lowering the tension somewhat. "But I am here to say a few things from my heart and the hearts of many others whose voices you won't hear tonight.

"I have five things to say: Number one is that I saw a T-shirt someone had on that said this flag issue was a cultural thing. Maybe it is only that to some people. But if you are into promoting a cultural agenda as a part of your regional heritage, then why in heaven's name are you using the Ole Miss's football program as a place to do that? You don't seem to be using any other medium. There can be no argument that the flag issue directly affects our football program. So my suggestion is that this is not the place for you to carry on your cultural agenda. Do it someplace else, and stop hurting this great university by your cultural hobby.

"The second thing is that I heard some of you swear that the flag is not a racist symbol. You think that, I suppose, by talking only with those who agree with you. The indisputable truth is that it is a racist symbol to many people. And that is obvious. I know you often see the racist groups in our society waving this flag at their parades and in front of their homes. There are many hate groups all across the country that use that flag as their symbol of defiance. You can't deny that. What is interesting to me is that when we see these groups using your beloved flag for obvious racist and hate reasons, what do you do? You don't do one blamed thing about it! Where are your speeches, news conferences, letters to the editor, articles, and outrage? I don't hear you say to these hate groups, 'Why, how dare you use my beloved cultural flag in such a racist manner and distort the South's image!' No, I don't see you doing any of that. I see you silent as the tomb!

"And that brings me to the third point. As children of the South, we are all at fault because we didn't speak up and defend this flag as a part of our history, whether it was for an honorable cause or not. For a hundred years, we were silent, and we allowed these hate groups to take it from us and use it in this hostile manner. Therefore, we have forfeited the right to wave it today. When many people see that flag, they associate it with every hate crime committed against an oppressed minority in our sordid past. As a local and noted historian of the Civil War has stated, 'We failed to defend that flag and failed to take it away from these hate groups.'[65] Therefore, I believe we have forfeited the right to it. In other words, we have no one to blame but ourselves. By the way, the next time the Klan comes to town waving that flag, I'd like to see some evidence of your outrage.

"Fourth, why wouldn't you want to wave a flag that is uniquely associated with Ole Miss? Isn't that what we are supposed to be signaling at our football games? Support for the team and Ole Miss? I want to see a flag that no one can mistake and not some symbol that gives off different interpretations, some of which are unflattering to this university. Any real Ole Miss fan would want to do that!

"Fifth, knowing that this flag is offensive to our black students and black athletes, why would you want to deliberately do that? Why would you want to interfere with our need to be successful? I think it is time for many to reevaluate their motives and learn what it means to be sensitive, moral, and just. While we are here tonight, there are minority athletes on this campus who are spilling their blood, sweat, and guts on the practice field and playing field to make us all winners. How could you do this to them?

"Let tonight be the beginning of a new day of tolerance and understanding at this beloved place we affectionately call Ole Miss. You know we may someday graduate from the University of Mississippi, but one never graduates from Ole Miss.[66] There is a sound reason for you, the Council of Students, to initiate a move to create a flag that is uniquely Ole Miss and to discourage the use of the Confederate flag at football games. Thank you."

Aeamon Lee sat down to a hushed audience. Several in the other line sat down instead of speaking. His speech had been dramatic with him giving emphasis at times, using pause and a forceful yet considerate tone. The meeting adjourned shortly thereafter, and he wondered what the reaction would be. Several students thanked him for coming and participating without giving their own views about the issue. The persuasiveness of his arguments probably helped the committee more than anything else in that it affirmed to them that they were more than justified in creating a new Ole Miss flag.[67]

On his way back to the dorm, after a stop off at the library, Aeamon Lee felt morally justified about what he had done. He wondered to himself if he had mellowed or if he was simply learning how to use vocal, logical argument more effectively to combat injustice. He was amused at himself when he thought about a time in his life when he would have just busted heads when people were so blinded by cultural tradition that they couldn't see the obvious injustice.

*   *   *

On October 8, they played Texas Christian University, also at home—the second of the three games in Oxford. Aeamon Lee wondered if there might be any repercussions from his speech on the flag issue. The crowd was still supportive as ever, but most still waved their Confederate flags. TCU was an improving team in the Southwest Conference. They had developed a wide-open offense and had been putting up a lot of points. The quarterback would take the ball usually in the shotgun position, and there were many options available to him. They were good at running this offense, and Ole Miss knew they needed to keep the ball out of their hands. Their game plan was to sustain long drives. They would use the nickel defense a lot to try to stop their passing attack.

Again, Aeamon Lee helped the defensive signal caller to get the team in the most likely formation that would stop their passing attack. The Rebels started clicking early in the game and began to put up some points. He would have his best game, statistic wise. TCU couldn't contain Aeamon Lee's pinpoint passing and play variations. He ended up completing twenty-eight of thirty-three passes for 418 yards with some of them going for long yardage. He rushed the ball also for seventy-four yards, but the coaching staff constantly discouraged him from running the ball, but to no avail. The final score was 45–19.

Aeamon Lee showed up for a few minutes at one of the frat parties, but he soon went over to Pappy's Place, where the patrons now knew him. The fact that he and Andre came back the second time reassured the crowd that he liked it there. This time he arranged a practice time with the band so he could play and sing more tunes with them. On this night, he sang several numbers and played behind the other lead singer for the group. One of the band members paid what Aeamon Lee considered the highest compliment when he said, "You've got more soul than any white person I've ever met." He appreciated that because he understood that the word meant just the opposite of pharisaical stiffness and emphasized an easygoing acceptance of others with tolerance. Word had spread about his whereabouts after home games, and several students also showed up at Pappy's. This number of white people wanting to attend where he was playing with the band increased and included some reporters who were looking to write stories about Aeamon Lee.

*   *   *

The team was now into the middle of October undefeated, and finally, they had an open date. As it is for all teams, this was the time for the injured to recover and to get treatment for their numerous little injuries, like sprained fingers, ankle sprains, scrapes, bruises, hip pointers, and a multitude of other things that could hinder a person's play. Aeamon Lee had been looking ahead to this date, October 15, as a time when he could go home. This had been the longest he had ever been away. Only the required busyness had kept him from really getting homesick. He had often thought about home, Martha and Plea, and the crops. His one phone call per week, and an occasional letter from Martha who would tell him things she didn't want Plea to hear, had been the only contact.

One of the players with transportation offered to drive him by Goshen Wells. They left a day early because there was a long list of things Aeamon Lee felt he needed to do. On the way to the house out from Goshen Wells, his friend was a little surprised to find that Aeamon Lee lived so far off the beaten path.

"What did you do out here growing up?"

"We worked mostly. On Saturdays, we usually went to town, and on Saturday nights, the neighbors gathered for a time of making music at a place called Sorghum Hill, not far from here. On Sunday, we went to church, and during the week, we worked till dark. We then sat on the porch to sing, play games, or talk till bedtime." To the driver, this sounded like a strange lifestyle for that day and age.

Martha and Plea were of course glad to see him, and they both wanted to talk at the same time, trying to tell Aeamon Lee what they had heard about him since he left for Ole Miss. Aeamon Lee just wanted to look around for a while and mentally take note of all the things he needed to do in three days before his ride would come by to get him late Sunday afternoon. He had developed a strong sense of responsibility in the past six years since Plea had become disabled. No one could keep up the place and get the crops in like he could.

That night, he got in the old truck and drove over to the house of the man who had the machinery to combine the beans and gather the corn. They made about the same financial arrangement they had in previous years and set a date for it to be gathered. They would do all of it because it was getting a little late in the season. He now had the experience to know about what he had in the crops and how much they would bring. Although the man had treated him fairly in the past, he wanted the man to know that he knew what was to be expected. He calculated that the profit from the crops would be about the same as it had been. The last payment on the farm had been made several years before, so this meant that they would have a little more expendable income. He carefully explained to Martha and Plea what was going to happen and what money they would end up having for the year.

Aeamon Lee was anxious to improve Plea's mental state. Plea had wrestled with depression since his accident and, in spite of all their efforts, still had not shaken it off completely. That night, they shared the biggest news with Aeamon Lee. Martha said, "You know that teacher of yours in high school, Ms. Babe Markle? Well, you remember how I told you that she came out here and helped us reapply for Social Security disability. She helped us get all the medical information together, which we didn't do the first time. She sure was nice about everything."

Martha, holding a letter, said, "This is the letter that we received this past week," and she handed it to Aeamon Lee to read.

All he saw was "You have been approved." There would be a check also for some back time. He was filled with relief and couldn't speak. In two years, Plea would receive a Medicare card, which would mean he could have the medical treatment that might make it possible for him to walk again. He hugged Martha and Plea, and he went outside alone. He walked in the darkness and stopped by an old familiar tree and looked up into the starlit sky. He thanked God for this milestone, and said, "Maybe, Lord, there are more good people in the world than I thought."

Even though Plea's monthly check would not be a whole lot, nevertheless it would help out tremendously for a family who had only subsisted for six years. He told Martha and Plea, "It would be good for us to remember, we all have drunk from wells we did not dig and have been warmed by fires we did not build.[68] I'll send Ms. Markle a note of thanks."

The next day, Aeamon Lee spent most of his time bush-hogging and cleaning up places by cutting brush and burning it. He got to see the Markums and spent a little time talking with Amos and Mama Kate. Of course, all they could talk about was their trip to see Jo-Nathan graduate from marine boot camp. They described how hard the training had been but that Jo-Nathan had done pretty well. He attributed it to his being raised on a farm, getting up at daybreak, and working till dark. Amos said, "All that swimming I understand y'all did and all that you did to survive on that trip to Memphis helped too." Aeamon Lee didn't say anything about that because he did not know Jo-Nathan had told his folks the details of that trip.

* * *

Aeamon Lee asked his parents about going over to Sorghum Hill on Saturday night because he didn't want them to think he would rather spend his time over there rather than being with them. They said it would be all right to go, and Aeamon Lee said he would only be gone for a short time.

It was like another family reunion that night. Word had spread that Aeamon Lee was going to be there, and there was a large crowd. Willie Rivers and the Willie Rivers Band were playing, and they wanted Aeamon Lee to come up and do several numbers with them. He explained that he only had but two opportunities to play and sing since he left. But he belted out several tunes, and the crowd applauded this friend of theirs who had returned. It was one of those moments you wish you could freeze in time. No great worries, but Aeamon Lee did say to the crowd, "There is one other person that I wish could be here tonight, and if Jo-Nathan Markum could be here, it would be perfect." The crowd clapped in approval. "But he is serving his country and is now a full-fledged United States Marine. I know he was here a few weeks ago, but I missed him. I hope we'll keep him in our prayers."

He also saw Maleah Marcelles, who had found a full-time job and moved to Jackson, but she came home when she heard that Aeamon Lee was going to be there that weekend. They talked and shared things about each other's lives. She said, "I've been reading about you in the paper. You are something like a star now. I wondered if you would ever want to return to Goshen Wells."

"Now you know I could never leave my family and friends here. You all are never far from my thoughts. There are a lot of demands on my time now, but I'll always come back home when I can," he reassured. "But tell me, Maleah, how are you doing? Are you happy?"

She responded, "I'm doing well. I have the best job I ever had, and it has possibilities for promotion. I'm determined, which I got from you. I've made lots of new friends, but there is no Mr. Right in my life now. I know you are busy, but if you ever want to write or need any help, I live at 345 Mariam Street."

"Listen, Maleah, those sayings you gave me—you have no idea how they have helped me and the whole team. They have been magical." She smiled as she walked away.

On Sunday, he went to church with Martha and Plea at Pilgrim's Rest. Plea used a cane sometimes, and sometimes he would use some crutches. He could get around the house by propping himself up on the furniture. The little church thanked the Lord for Aeamon Lee coming home to see his parents and for being at church. He didn't have time to go over to Zion's Grove and see the church members over there at Jo-Nathan's church. He still had work to do before his ride came to drive him back to Oxford. When he returned to campus, there would be an even greater demand on his abilities in the classroom and on the football field.

*   *   *

Upon arriving that Sunday night, someone asked about a newspaper article about him. He explained that he had been working at home and had not seen a newspaper. They handed him a copy of the Memphis *Commercial Appeal*, and on the front page, the headlines read, "Ole Miss QB accused of crime." He quickly read the article right there in his tracks. It seemed that one of the men he had brawled with back down in Louisiana in the summer at the beer joint had died from injuries sustained in this fight. The sheriff of that parish had somehow tracked down the identity of the two boys from Mississippi who were involved. The article didn't mention Jo-Nathan but did mention Aeamon Lee, who wondered how in the world they found him.

The account of what happened in the joint was not even close to the actual events. The sheriff was quoted as saying, "Ain't no Mississippi redneck goin' to come down here in Louisiana and disturb the peace and tranquility of this community. I don't care if he is a well-known football player. He has come down here and caused the death of one of our fine citizens, and we're charging him with second-degree murder. As far as we're concerned, he's nothing more than a common criminal."

When he arrived at his room in the dorm, Webster said, "The coaches have been looking for you all afternoon. They want you to come over to the athletic office as soon as you get in, and they said for you not to talk to anybody. Do you want me to go with you?"

"You can if you like," Aeamon Lee said in a soft and deflated tone. Webster went with him.

When he arrived in Coach Wortham's office, there were several other coaches, including Coach Underwood and Coach Arrington. Even the athletic director was there. When he walked in, they called the chancellor, who got there shortly. They asked him whether he had read the paper, and when Aeamon Lee stated that he had just read it, they asked him to tell them the whole story. They said not to leave anything out because this matter was in the news, reporters were asking questions, and the students and alumni were concerned.

So Aeamon Lee told them of his summer of adventure with Jo-Nathan Markum that took them down the Mississippi River and the events that led to them being in the beer joint. He recalled the sequence of events and exactly what happened. He explained how they escaped by swimming the river.

Their first reaction was that what Aeamon Lee had said was unbelievable. But Coach Wortham said, "Well, this season has been unbelievable, hasn't it? I think we should assume that Aeamon Lee is telling us the truth. I don't know what the law can do. It doesn't sound like Aeamon Lee was doing anything but defending himself. I don't see how he could be charged with a crime even if one of them died, because they were the ones who started it."

Aeamon Lee walked over to the window and looked out. He said, "'He who steals my purse steals trash . . . but he who steals from me my good name robs me of that which not enriches him and makes me poor indeed.'"[69]

The chancellor cautioned everyone to remain quiet about the details other than simply stating that the matter was being investigated. He said, "Even the governor has called me about this matter because the whole state of Louisiana is up in arms over it, and they think they got something that will make us look bad."

The athletic director observed, "Well, whether we like it or not, we do look bad. There are people by the droves calling Aeamon Lee just another thug and will turn against us if we don't do something."

Aeamon Lee responded, "'The opinion of ten thousand men is of no value if none of them know anything about the subject.'"[70]

It was decided that they would announce to the public that Aeamon Lee was suspended from the team until the truth was known. For him, it was the best of times; it was the worst of times.[71] He was living the life he had imagined, but now he had to deal with circumstances that threatened everything he had accomplished.

Webster swore he would not talk to anyone about the events. The other players were either noncommittal or supportive. Some made jokes about killing someone from Louisiana "who probably deserved it." Everybody wanted to know what happened and what Aeamon Lee's side of the story was, but he couldn't speak. This made it hard on him because it appeared that some students had believed every word of the newspaper story and were turning their backs on him. This really bothered Aeamon Lee—that people could turn against him so quickly with very little information. There was something in the papers every day and every night on the sports news about it. It was unclear what

Louisiana authorities were going to do about it. Aeamon Lee had gotten nothing in the mail or in person about the charges.

At his first chance, he called home to discuss the matter with Martha and Plea. It seemed they had only gotten a small bit of information and didn't know the full ramifications of what was going on. Aeamon Lee had not told them a word about their experiences on their summer trip to Memphis and back home. He reassured them that all would turn out okay and all this would soon pass. Martha offered her assistance because she had always protected him and had not allowed anything in the past to interfere with her plans for Aeamon Lee's future. Even though she had often stood in the background, she had never cautioned him about his sense of justice. Her gift to the world would do well, and he would come out of this bit of controversy all right. But back on campus, the tide of public opinion was turning against him. Now all of his oddities were taken out of context, and he was painted as someone not befitting the Ole Miss program. This hurt him deeply, and he felt helpless to do anything about it.

He spent most of his extra time doing strength training. In his classes, he was generally shunned. Occasionally, a student would say something like, "While you were at it, why didn't you do in a few more down there." It was hard for Aeamon Lee to find humor in this, given the uncertainty of his future.

The uncertainty went on for several days, and then there appeared the miracle revelation. It seemed that a marine stationed at Camp Lejeune, North Carolina, had gotten permission from his commanding officer to call the newspaper and television station in Memphis to explain the truth as an eyewitness about what he had been reading in the papers. He was quoted verbatim about the event and how these men had taunted the two of them. He revealed that because he was black, both of them were ordered out of the joint. He explained how the men jumped Aeamon Lee and how Aeamon Lee had put him in a corner, asking him not to interfere. He explained how they brawled long and hard and how the roof had caved in. He told about how they had to crawl on the floor to find a way out and that they ran because they were scared. And he told the paper that he sure didn't see anybody get killed. "Those men, all of them, chose to jump on Aeamon Lee, and the fact is, they tried to kill him." On the television sports show, they gave the sound of Jo-Nathan's phone voice telling the story. "I know what happened because I was there, and those men in Louisiana are telling a lie." His everlasting friend had now corroborated Aeamon Lee's account of what happened on that fateful day.

The next day, there was another article reporting that one of the men in the fight had come forward to say that what Jo-Nathan said was the way it happened. The Mississippi governor, chancellor, athletic director, all the football coaches, and fans were more than relieved, to put it lightly. Aeamon Lee was reinstated on the team as they prepared for Vanderbilt and then LSU the following week in Baton Rouge. Some players, students, and others wrote letters to him to apologize for believing the worst about him.

*   *   *

In the midst of this chaotic week, there was a letter from Jo-Nathan written before his phone call to the papers. He told Aeamon Lee that he had completed the combat training successfully. Marines from Camp Lejeune had been sent to Beirut, Lebanon, back in March, after some terrorists had bombed the American Embassy. He said, "I've been selected as one of several marines needed to replace some of the marines overseas. Some of the marines have been sent back stateside for various reasons. I can't tell you exactly where I am going, but it is someplace in the Middle East. As soon as I get where I am going, I'll write you.

I guess I'll get to be a real Devil Dog now.[72] Just remember that when the breaks are going against you and your back is against the wall, run like the animals. You know what I mean. Ha."

Included in the letter was a sketch Jo-Nathan had made of a football player wearing Aeamon Lee's number 12 jersey. The caption was "Charm in the arm and heat in the feet!" Aeamon Lee grinned and said, "Hea-vy du-ty."

Webster asked, "What is it?"

Aeamon Lee said, "Oh, it's just something personal I got from Jo-Nathan." He put the sketch, along with the letters, together in one place on his desk. He would often take the sketch out and look at it privately.

Aeamon Lee mailed a letter to him right away, hoping Jo-Nathan would get it before he was flown out. He had to tell him what his phone calls to the papers and television stations had meant in his life. He had to express his appreciation to his friend and his prayers for this mission he was on. It was unclear whether Jo-Nathan ever received it before he left.

Aeamon Lee called the Markums, and they had heard about Jo-Nathan's deployment but didn't know any more than what he knew. He felt an overwhelming sense of fear for his friend's life and safety. Mainly, Aeamon Lee had had this feeling for a long time—that the president actually wanted some kind of confrontation so he could show American military strength. Now Jo-Nathan flew to a part of the world where fanatical religious groups had been fighting for hundreds of years. He knew that these Americans going in and occupying their land would be considered enemies, and there had already been hundreds of threats made against this US military presence. *Does this president actually think that our military is going to be able to scare these people into submission and get all these factions to just give up what they were taught to do since birth?* he thought.

* * *

Aeamon Lee did not have nearly the same concentration he had during practice for the next game, which was against Vanderbilt in Nashville. It had indeed been a roller-coaster week for his emotions. It seemed that Vandy always played Ole Miss close. All week, Aeamon Lee tried to get more information about the troops that were in Beirut. On the positive side, this news helped him put away the sad chapter in which his character and worth as an individual had been called into question. He watched the news every night he could. He looked for articles in the newspapers at the library. Aeamon Lee could not shake the feeling that Jo-Nathan was not safe.

His lack of focus could be observed in the Vandy game. His stats were not nearly as good. And so it happened that Vandy kept close, and Ole Miss had to kick a field goal in the last minute to win it. The coaches asked him about the matter after the game. He told them more of the story of who Jo-Nathan was and why he was concerned. They encouraged him to realize that there was nothing he could do at the moment and that he was doing a good thing by keeping in touch with him. But he stayed pretty much to himself on the entire trip. So much was happening so fast, and he thought things were getting out of control. He wanted the world to slow down a bit so he could get a handle on what was happening.

"You're not in control of what all goes on in this old world, Aeamon Lee. You're only responsible for what you can control," Coach Wortham told him.

After church on Sunday in Oxford, on October 23, 1983, he went back to campus and saw some students gathered around a television. He drew near, and there it was: reporters and film about the marine barracks being bombed in Beirut, Lebanon. A terrorist in a truck had barreled in close to the building that actually looked like a high-rise apartment complex. The truck explosion had demolished the building. There were many casualties, it was reported.

Aeamon Lee walked away with this light, sick feeling in his stomach. He looked for reasons to think that Jo-Nathan might not have been in that building they were calling barracks. He wanted to be alone in his thoughts. "What can I do?" He called home. Martha and Plea had gotten the news about the bombing, but the family knew nothing. Martha had gone down to the Markums and was staying there with them until they got word on Jo-Nathan.

"You know they are bound to be agonizing not knowing," Aeamon Lee said.

Webster was consoling and offered to do anything he could. "Is there any place you need to go?"

Aeamon Lee preferred going to his usual carrel in the library, but that didn't seem to help. He had so much energy he couldn't be still.

He started walking across town, almost in a daze, with the premonition that his friend had been killed in the blast. He leaned on a light post, sobbing until he heard an African American church having Sunday-night services across the street. He could hear them singing,

> There is a balm in Gilead
> To make the wounded whole;
> There is a balm in Gilead
> To heal the grieving soul.
> Sometimes I feel discouraged
> And think my works in vain.
> But then the Holy Spirit
> Revives my soul again.[73]

He walked in knowing that there would be an opportunity to make a prayer request. He felt guilty for not being able to control the situation more. He should have prepared himself when Jo-Nathan went into the service, realizing he would not be able to control the events as he had before when he took care of all the people who lived on those hills at Goshen Wells.

The preacher noticed that Aeamon Lee was emotional and was now leaning forward in his seat with his head in his hands. He could feel the hands of sympathizers on his back and shoulders. The preacher asked if there was anyone present with a prayer request. Aeamon Lee stood up and told his story with a trembling voice.

"I hope I'm not interrupting, but my heart is bowed down with a heavy burden. I'm a student, and today, I received word that my best friend in the armed forces may have been killed in Beirut, Lebanon, where a terrorist bombed their barracks. I've just been wandering all afternoon, and I just wandered into your service off the street. I hope you won't mind. I know his parents and what anguish they must be experiencing not knowing about their son. I just want to ask for your prayers. I don't know what else I can do right now."

The people were deeply moved at his testimony as they had also heard the terrible news about the terrorist bombing. The preacher called him to the front of the auditorium and sat him down on the front pew. He put his left hand on his shoulder and raised his right hand in prayer. They didn't just mention Jo-Nathan's name as they were praying. Several different men prayed for Jo-Nathan, for Aeamon Lee, and for all the families wondering about the fate of their loved ones. And they never even knew whether Jo-Nathan was black or white.

When the service was over, Aeamon Lee walked away with the feeling that he had now done everything he could. There was a calm he had not experienced in a long time. It was a feeling that, whatever happened, all would be well. It was a peace that was indeed indescribable. This was in his heart, but down deep, he felt the worst had happened. He would now just have to wait until he heard something.

*   *   *

The team started preparing for LSU on Monday. Aeamon Lee apologized for all the distractions. The players reassured him that it was not his fault, and they would stay focused. Several of the players, however, wanted to know the full story of his summer adventure. It seemed that a newspaper reporter had decided to find out more about Aeamon Lee and titled his article "Just who is this kid playing quarterback at Ole Miss?" And the article began to try to piece together the events of the summer of 1983. The coaches laid down the law that week. "There will be no more discussion of what the papers were saying. We will concentrate on the LSU game, period." And they meant it.

After practice on Monday, Aeamon Lee was summoned again to the coach's office. He didn't like the feeling because of what happened the last time he did this. He walked in, and the coaches were somber. Coach Wortham finally spoke up, "I guess I'll have to be the one to tell you, Aeamon Lee. We have gotten word that Jo-Nathan Markum was among two hundred forty-one military personnel killed in the Beirut bombing. Some two hundred twenty were US Marines. We know that he was your best friend. The only other thing we know is that it will take a week or so before his body will return for burial. We want you to know we are all sorry, and we'll do anything we can to help."

Acamon Lee was visibly shaken because he had held out hope that maybe, just maybe, he was not in the barracks. The coaches offered to stay there with him as long as he needed to deal with this harsh reality. But he was remarkably strong. Ever since the night before in that little church, he had been developing the strength to accept whatever happened. He received the condolences of the coaches who had suggested that since Jo-Nathan's funeral would not be until at least the following week, the best Aeamon Lee could do was to concentrate on the upcoming game. "Take it out on LSU," the coaches said.

Aeamon Lee called the Markums and his parents, and they had received the word earlier in the day. They were the ones who had called the coaching staff and asked them to convey the news to Aeamon Lee. It sounded like the whole community of Goshen Wells was coming together during this time of loss and grief. It is amazing how community and church leaders want to be there to be seen and heard when one of their own has gloriously died in such a "noble" cause. "He is such an example of patriotism, who was willing to pay the ultimate sacrifice for his country," they said. Aeamon Lee had the unspoken thought that this was not the correct way to explain the loss of this fine nineteen-year-old. He couldn't help but think of the lines "They wrote in the old days that it is sweet and fitting to die for one's country. But in modern war, there is nothing sweet nor fitting in your dying. You will die like a dog for no good reason."[74]

*   *   *

During practice, no one mentioned the events of the past two weeks. Afterward, the players told him how sorry they were for the loss of his friend.

The coaches emphasized to the players that they had to focus on the game. LSU was having a great season and was still in the hunt for the conference championship. This game against Ole Miss would be crucial for both teams and a game that had to be won to gain the championship. The consensus among sports reporters in the South was that Ole Miss was having a remarkable season so far that could end just any week. Outside of a few Ole Miss players and coaches, that seemed to be the universal feeling. It could end this week against the always-tough Bayou Bengals. It was always believed that strange and unusual things happened to teams that came to Death Valley on a Saturday night near Halloween.

LSU was well-balanced and had a lot of depth at every position. The film showed that they covered long pass plays really well, and the Ole Miss game plan was to throw underneath the coverage a lot. They needed some sure-handed wide receiver that could take the punishment by running routes over the middle. Suddenly, Coach Wortham and Aeamon Lee had the same thought. The li'l white boy that Aeamon Lee had unwittingly named during preseason practice came to mind. They thought, *Where is he, and why haven't we used him before?* As it turned out, he had remained with the team and was listed way down on the depth chart. They remembered his name: Milo Millon.

The coaches called him out in practice and let him run some curl routes. He was so excited about the possibility of playing in a game, he was nervous at first. Aeamon Lee reminded him that it was not smart to be nervous. Both smiled at each other, and after that, he showed the level of confidence he would have to have in the game. They developed several plays for him, and he would be in the game at other times as a decoy. The coaches decided to let him run the curl routes, which became timing routes as he and Aeamon Lee got on the same page. They decided to let him run some underneath routes, as they called them, when he would literally go down to the ground to catch a hard bullet thrown by Aeamon Lee.

The LSU game plan and winning the game was not the only thing they had to be concerned about. An attorney down state had gotten word to Coach Wortham that even though it was not in the news, there was no sure way of knowing what Louisiana authorities would do to Aeamon Lee when he entered their state. There had been no final word from the sheriff exactly what he would do even though most everyone had assumed the charges had been dropped since a participant had confirmed Jo-Nathan's account. It could turn out that Louisiana authorities might arrest him right there on the field and charge him. However, Aeamon Lee was encouraged by one of Maleah's quotes on wisdom: "If you wait for perfect conditions, you will never get anything done."[75]

When this possibility of an arrest was announced to the team, they were furious. The coach said, "Now I don't like having to do this, but we have to take some precautions." The coaches devised a plan that called for several defensive actions. When the team stepped off the bus, they ran in groups to wherever they were going. Aeamon Lee was disguised. Some extra Mississippi highway patrolmen were assigned to accompany the team everywhere they went. There didn't appear to be anybody around looking to arrest someone, but the team never knew what could happen next.

The plan called for Webster to wear Aeamon Lee's number during warm-ups and for Aeamon Lee to wear Webster's. They would run quickly into the locker room and over anyone who got in their way. When it was time for the kick-off, there would be a huddle on the sidelines allowing Aeamon Lee to change into his own jersey. At halftime, and at the end of the game, they would bunch together and run to the locker room, knocking down anyone obstructing their route.

When Aeamon Lee first walked onto the field at Tiger Stadium, he marveled at its size. There was something eerie about the place. In his mind, he could see the ghost of Billy Cannon running eighty-nine yards to beat undefeated Ole Miss in 1959. He had seen that on film many times. He could hear the roar of the rowdy crowd. But for Aeamon Lee, none of this bothered him or frightened him. Again, he would turn the sounds of the crowd into jeering Jo-Nathan, which would recharge his batteries. He did wonder about the other players and how much they would be intimidated. But he reminded everyone, "It's not smart to be intimidated." And he wondered whether Milo Millon would be able to be cool and catch the passes.

The LSU crowd was boisterous and yelling "Tiger bait!" as Ole Miss passed by. Signs everywhere said, "Geaux Tigers." Aeamon Lee was most amused by a cheer in Cajun, "Hot boudin, cold coush-coush. Come on, Tigers, poosh, poosh, poosh." The fact that Aeamon Lee's last name was French didn't impress these fans.

As the game got underway, everything was working well, but nothing came easy. Midway through the first quarter, Milo was sent in with a play. He had never been seen on film during the season. He ran a perfect hook route, and Aeamon Lee hit him with a straight shot and, while going down, kicked backward for four or five more yards.

A running play with four receivers in the game, and two more pass plays to Milo, had the ball at the 13-yard line. The call from the bench was to run Milo to the goal line where he would catch one of those underneath passes, which worked perfectly. There was no defense for it as Milo used his great hands to catch it off the grass right at the goal line for a touchdown.

As the game wore on, Aeamon Lee sensed that Ole Miss was playing harder in this game than in any previous game. They were playing old-fashioned, hard-nosed football—and with confidence. The Big Ten Conference called it smash-mouth football. It was evident that LSU was on its heels as Ole Miss put up two more scores and led 21–10 at the half.

The second half was more of the same. Aeamon Lee had never seen the running backs run as hard and fast. The defense was playing with a vengeance. Late in the fourth quarter, Ole Miss scored on a long TD run from scrimmage and was now sixteen points ahead, 36–20. Ole Miss was controlling every aspect of the game. Milo caught more underneath passes in the second half and became a threat every time he was in the game. They had discovered another weapon to use for the rest of the season. LSU had upset Florida the week before on this field, and the fans saw nothing but glory the rest of the schedule. And to see Ole Miss take such a commanding lead was more than most of the crowd could stand. By the end of the game, the stadium was virtually vacated by their fans.

No Louisiana law enforcement official showed up, and Ole Miss left town and the state without an incident. They were now 8 and 0 and appearing to be getting stronger. Aeamon Lee played smart, and he also had dedicated the rest of the season in memory of his fallen friend. He didn't announce it; it was one of those things he worked up in his own disciplined mind. Now that this game was over, he could concentrate on paying respects to his friend and the entire Markum family.

*   *   *

Coaches Wortham and Underwood; Aeamon Lee's roommate, Webster Warren; and team member Andre Tinsley were chosen to attend the funeral of Jo-Nathan Markum. They would represent the football team and support Aeamon Lee. He knew that there would be an opportunity for him to speak at the funeral. Also, they wanted to go and make sure that Aeamon Lee didn't get into any more trouble.

At African American funerals, there is a part of the service when friends of the deceased are given an opportunity to speak a few minutes about their feelings and remembrances. He knew it would be expected for him to speak. But he was torn between two speeches he had. One was a speech in which he would say all the appropriate things for the family's sake. Another speech would reflect his true feelings as to why his friend had died. He had gotten word that there would be some uniformed marine officers that would be present and sitting together.

The little church building at Zion's Grove was overflowing with people, black and white. The singing was filled with meaning and spirit and soul.

> There's a man going 'round takin' names;
> There's a man going 'round takin' names;
> He has taken my son's name
> And left my heart in pain.
> There's a man goin 'round takin' names.
>
> Now death is the man takin' names;
> Now death is the man takin' names;
> He has taken my brother's name

And left my heart in pain.
There's a man going 'round takin' names.[76]

    The flag-draped casket was rolled down the aisle. The preacher asked the audience to stand, and he started quoting scripture while walking slowly down the aisle in front of the casket and standing on the pulpit while the family got seated.

Yea, though I walk through the valley of the shadow
of death,
I will fear no evil for thou art with me;
Thy rod and thy staff, they comfort me.[77]

I will lift up mine eyes to the hills;
From whence cometh my help?
My help cometh from the Lord
Who made the heavens and the earth.[78]

In my father's house are many mansions;
If it were not so, I would have told you;
I go to prepare a place for you.
And if I do and prepare a place for you,
I will come again, and receive you unto myself;
That where I am, there you may be also.[79]

Greater love hath no man that this,
That he lay down his life for his friends.[80]

I have fought the good fight,
I have finished the course,
I have kept the faith.[81]

Then it came time for friends to speak briefly about Jo-Nathan. Aeamon Lee spoke third after Maleah Marcelles and one of his schoolteachers. He looked around the crowd of mourners, at the casket of his friend, and swallowed. He would keep his bitterness to himself.

"As you all know, I was Jo-Nathan's *best* friend, and he was my *best* friend. We *grew up* together. The Markums always lived just *a few steps* from our house. And we've been *all over* these hills and hollows together . . . *Everywhere* I look, my *mind* is overwhelmed with memories." Aeamon Lee had learned how to emphasize certain words in the sentence, how to use inflection, to shake his head and allow the audience time to respond. Not many white people knew how to do this. "He was *not* my brother in the flesh, but he *was* my brother." At this point, the audience was responding to his every sentence. "The *Bible* says that God *knows* what we're made of . . .[82] and God knows that this was *a good* man—a man with a *good* heart who *loved* his family. He made them *proud* every day he lived." Aeamon Lee's voice trembled at this point. "He had a lot of years left in him. But don't you know? The good, they die young.[83] 'Old men declare war. But it is the youth that must fight and die.'[84] He will never get to know the joy of having and loving his own family. He'll never be able to show the world what he could *really* do. *That* is why we are sad today. Not because we sorrow for him, but because we, *all* of us, are *poorer* today for having lost him. I tried to talk him out of joining the marines, but this is what *he wanted* to do—for his family, for his country, and for himself. His purposeful life is reflected in the words of a well-known writer: 'Some people see things and say, "Why?" I dream things that never were and say, "Why not."'[85] The reality of his loss is keenly felt, but we who remain must struggle on. 'No man is an island, entire of itself . . . any man's death diminishes me, because I am involved in mankind, and therefore never send to know for whom the bell tolls: it tolls for thee.'[86] So the loss of this connection to our loved one diminishes our own souls. That is why we need each other."

During Aeamon Lee's tribute, Webster and Coach Underwood looked at each other in astonishment over his style of speaking. They both agreed that he could achieve renowned success either as a politician or as an evangelist.

The funeral service lasted one hour and forty-five minutes. Then there was the slow walk to the cemetery that joined the churchyard. The Markums had Aeamon Lee sit with them, and he walked by their side to the gravesite. Over and over in his mind, he kept thinking that this death was not necessary. He was reminded, "In peace, sons bury their fathers; in war, fathers bury their sons."[87] There was the usual impressive pageantry with the twenty-one-gun salute, the folding of the flag that was presented to Mama Kate, and "Taps": Day is done, gone the sun / From the lakes, from the hills, from the sky; / All is well, safely rest, God is nigh.[88]

The coaches, Webster, Andre, and Aeamon Lee made their way out from the crowd toward the car. They passed near the marine officers and a congressman. The congressman looked at Aeamon Lee and said, "You have something against our military?"

He should not have said this. Maybe he thought that Aeamon Lee would just keep on walking. Maybe he thought his position and the uniform of the officers and the associated aura that went with it would intimidate Aeamon Lee from responding.

Instead, Aeamon Lee stopped, looked at the congressman, and strode toward him. He placed his stern face right in the congressman's face and used his six-foot-four-inch frame to look down at him. He said, "You listen well to me since you asked the question. All that these good and decent human beings ask of your commanders and the commander in chief is that you get the military policy right based on good evidence, that the mission be clearly defined with a success strategy, and that they be given adequate protection. You all didn't do any of that! They didn't mind being put in harm's way, but your mission was not clearly defined, your intelligence was not good, and they were put in what looked like a high-rise apartment complex. This made them enemies of these extremist groups, and you let them gather there as sitting ducks for some fanatical terrorist bomber. And you know what you're going to do about it? Not one blamed thing![89] Whether you want to admit it or not, you and the chain of command botched this mission, and 241 good soldiers died. Yeah, I have a complaint, but unfortunately, it is too late for Jo-Nathan Markum. Why in the devil don't you go and tell that to that grieving mother and father over there?" This response was predictable, given his strong sense of justice, and it reflected his common humanity.

He drew closer and closer into the face of the congressman. The other officers came up to the discussion and heard everything that was said. By this time, Coach Wortham had come back, and he took Aeamon Lee by the arm and led him away. That congressman would never forget the words of this angry civilian. He didn't know it, but he should have been glad that there were only words spoken.

*　*　*

The coaches, Webster, and Andre were able to meet Aeamon Lee's parents and even drove by his house. They said all the usual complimentary things. Coach Underwood asked, "Which one of those houses do you live in?"

"The newer one, the one in the middle of the three houses. I still have some work to do on it."

"What do you mean? Who built the house?"

"Oh, Jo-Nathan and I built it back when I was sixteen, but I still need to insulate the floor and get Mama some more kitchen cabinets."

The others in the car just stared at Aeamon Lee, and no one asked any more questions. Coach Wortham did say, "Well, I'm not surprised. You did a good job with that too. And someday, after this season, I want you to tell me the whole story of your summer."

There were some newspaper stories in the Memphis *Commercial Appeal* and the Jackson *Clarion-Ledger* about Aeamon Lee's connection to Jo-Nathan. A heart-warming article appeared in the *Daily Mississippian*, the student newspaper. They also carried an article about some students who were having their moms cut off the cuffs of their shirts and making the length of the sleeve only three-quarters long.

There had actually been some reporters at the funeral, and the articles were quite moving, which endeared him to the fans, as did his play on the field.

*   *   *

Ole Miss was now ranked fifth in the country in most polls, with three games left on the schedule. If they could win these, a New Year's Day game in the Sugar Bowl was assured. Maybe even a national title would be at stake. They would have to wait to find out, but no one dared talk about it at this point. The wrath of Coach Wortham would be brought down on any player looking ahead farther than the next game.

And the next game was on November 5, in Knoxville, against Tennessee, who was also still in contention for the conference title. They had lost only to Florida early in the season and had rolled in every game since. In addition, the Rebels would have to play before the largest crowd of the season, but their exposure to hostile environments was helped by having already played in Tuscaloosa and Death Valley. And to make matters worse, Tennessee made this game their homecoming. Ole Miss would use this as a motivation to spoil their homecoming.

The autumn colors and a cool fall day made it perfect for college football. Tennessee had shown no respect in the press during the week for Aeamon Lee. The players and coaches had been asked all week how they planned to contain him, and they wouldn't commit to anything or even praise his play. It seemed they wanted to get Ole Miss back for the infamous (their word) Archie Who game in 1969. Ole Miss knew Tennessee wanted this game badly since they were undefeated as Tennessee was undefeated in 1969.

Aeamon Lee had never seen such a sea of orange in a classic football setting. They were loud in the crowd on old Rocky Top. The Rebels had prepared all week for a hard-nosed ground game for which Tennessee was famous. The Volunteers recruited top athletes, always had a lot of depth, and their kicking game was the best in the country. Their offensive line was quite strong, and their two wide receivers were so fast they ran track. The saying of Maleah's he used was perfect for this game: "The fastest runner doesn't always win the race, and the strongest warrior doesn't always win the battle."[90]

This saying gave great confidence to the players. The game was televised, which would give Aeamon Lee more national exposure.

In Ole Miss's long winning streak against Tennessee in the 1960's, they had found them to be vulnerable to the run up the middle. So the Rebel game plan was to exploit this possible weakness and use their multiple attack system. To everyone's surprise, the game was low scoring. Each team had problems moving the ball, and each team had only one scoring drive. Field goals would make the difference. With the score tied 10–10, Ole Miss drove the ball deep late in the game when they kicked a field goal. They held on for the 13–10 win, an extremely disappointing loss for Tennessee. This pretty much put the Big Orange out of the conference title chase. It was reported in the papers that a moving van was placed in front of the Tennessee head coach's house the following Monday morning.

*   *   *

The last home game of the season was against Kentucky, in Oxford. Aeamon Lee had not forgotten his promise to Toe Foot about having him come to one of the games. Aeamon Lee was given two tickets for each home game, and he got Webster to drive him out to the modern barn on the Lorance's farm where Toe Foot lived. Aeamon Lee had to tell Webster about his coming to Oxford, how he lived out there for a while, and how he got to know Toe Foot.

"You lived in this barn?" Webster asked.

"Yes, but you'll see it's real nice on the end with the living quarters."

Webster was continually surprised and amazed at discovering things about Aeamon Lee's life. He never quite fathomed why anyone would have to live that way in the first place since he had always known a comfortable living. He assumed others had the same opportunities that he did.

Toe Foot was really glad to see that Aeamon Lee would come back to see him. He told him how he heard about how well the team was doing. Webster was introduced to him and appeared to be in a state of shock as he kept looking around to determine if this was a suitable place for anyone to live. After sharing a little of what had been going on with both of them, Aeamon Lee gave Toe Foot two tickets to the home game on Saturday. He insisted that he be there, and Toe Foot said he would get his grandson to come by and go with him to the game. "By all means, I want you to be there. I'll be looking for you." Aeamon Lee told him that after the game, he wanted Toe Foot to come around to where the crowd would be gathered at the front of the Athletic Training Center.

On the way back to campus, Webster said, "I'm still trying to figure you out. It seems every week I learn something about you I never dreamed any human being would do or could do, like living for a while in a barn."

"But not just any barn," Aeamon Lee said.

"And all that brawling," Webster added.

"But in the name of justice. Remember, 'justice in the life and conduct of the State is possible only as first it resides in the hearts and souls of the citizens.'"[91]

* * *

The Kentucky game on November 12 was the last home game, and there were several things Aeamon Lee had to see for himself instead of just hearing about it from the other players. One thing was to go to the Grove early on game day and witness the famous and elegant tailgating going on there. He got permission from the coaches because their movements on game day were fairly well planned out. He and Andre Tinsley walked over and saw all the vehicles crammed into the Grove, which was located at the center of campus.

They silently walked through the throngs of fans that were enjoying a feast befitting the opulence of the Roman Colosseum. There were long tables with designer tablecloths and a candelabrum on each end. The table's imposing centerpiece had to depict something about Ole Miss. On the tables were some of the most exotic finger food one could imagine. There were smiling, gracious ladies behind the tables, who obviously had taken much pride in the expert way they had presented their food. Andre and Aeamon Lee found out that if you stopped and said something complimentary, you were probably going to be invited to partake of the tasty cuisine. Unfortunately, they couldn't take up the offers given; they had to eat only what was served at the team meal on game day. In the Grove on game day, Southern manners and hospitality were not vague, cultural abstractions but, in the empirical sense, could be seen and heard every way.

Actually, there were different levels of tailgating on campus. In the parking lots and places where the cars had parked off the street on the grass, there was everything from eating out of a cooler to small charcoal grills that had been fired up. Some of the people recognized Andre and Aeamon Lee. They tried to be friendly while still walking because they knew they couldn't stop. The coaches had cautioned them about talking to anybody else on game day.

During pregame warm-ups, Aeamon Lee looked up into Vaught-Hemingway Stadium where his free seats were, and as expected, there was Toe Foot and his grandson not missing a thing on the field. Toe Foot was all dressed up in a suit like he was going to a Sunday revival meeting.

The game turned out to be the best game of all season for Aeamon Lee. Kentucky had a passing quarterback, and they did put up some points, but Ole Miss's passing attack was like a well-oiled machine as Aeamon Lee passed for 416 yards, scored five touchdowns, and ran the ball for fifty-four yards. This would put him first in the conference in total offense. The final score was 48–31. Each team marched up and down the field. His receivers were especially proud of his passing because it made them conference leaders in receptions. The defense was a little down with their performance, but actually, the Kentucky team was averaging about that number of points per game. The game had been hyped as the battle between two great quarterbacks, but when the dust had cleared, there was no question that Aeamon Lee Mistral was something extra special.

Aeamon Lee couldn't wait to get out in front of the Athletic Training Center to see if Toe Foot was there. He was there all right, talking with players and their families. Aeamon Lee never mentioned it, but when he came out after each of the other home games, it seemed that nearly all the players had someone waiting for them, but he didn't, except those nosey reporters. He missed not having some family there. Oh, there were always the ever-present females courting his attention, but there was always something missing. Except today, he had Toe Foot.

He introduced Toe Foot to some of the players and even took him back into the Center to meet some of the coaches.

Coach Wortham said, "Welcome, I understand that this is your first college football game."

"Yes, sir, and I sure did enjoy myself. And my grandson did too."

"Now how are you two connected?" he asked, looking at Aeamon Lee and then back to Toe Foot.

Aeamon Lee said, "We used to be roommates."

Coach Wortham was silent for a moment and looked at Aeamon Lee, who offered no other explanation. The coach didn't want him to think he was prying, so he didn't ask any more questions about that. This was not the first time, and would probably not be the last time, that he was completely taken back by discoveries in the mysterious life of his quarterback.

When they went back outside, Aeamon Lee heard some lady calling his name. He looked around, and lo, there was Frank and Alice Ruth Lorance, who owned the Racking Horse farm where Aeamon Lee had stayed a while when he first came to Oxford—when she was ashamed of him then. Alice Ruth was acting elated to see Aeamon Lee and made out like they were the best of friends. She stated how great it was to see him because she had heard all about his notoriety. "Why, all my friends talk about you, and would you know, they are speechless when I tell them that you are my nephew and how you spent some time in our home. Actually, I am so glad to see you because I have this great idea: I would like for you to come out to our place some Sunday afternoon where I'll have some of my Oxford friends, and I'll have the opportunity to introduce you in person. They would just love to meet you. I think this would be a great idea. What do you think?"

Aeamon Lee, of course, readily understood what this was all about. It was all about Aunt Alice Ruth showing off her now-successful kin to her socialite friends, all of which was designed to add to her social credentials. "Well, that sounds inviting, but the team is obligated on Sunday afternoon, so I won't be able to come." Alice Ruth was deflated and didn't say much more, and she and Frank left.

Then Toe Foot and his grandson went on their way. "Now, Aeamon Lee, you come back to see me from time to time. There is a lot we could talk about."

* * *

That night, he, Andre, and several other players went to Pappy's Place. Two reporters from Memphis asked Aeamon Lee if they could come along also and whether they would be welcome.

"Sure, you can come along, just don't act too white," Aeamon Lee laughingly suggested. They had no idea what that meant, and Aeamon Lee knew they wouldn't understand.

"We'll behave ourselves," they reassured. But what Aeamon Lee meant had nothing to do with staying out of trouble.

The crowds had increased in anticipation that Aeamon Lee would be there, and the crowd of patrons now claimed him as one of their own. The women liked for him to bring along some of his football friends with him. Since they had now practiced together, Aeamon Lee and the band could play several numbers really well. For Aeamon Lee, this was an experience that would allow him to relax and live, at least for a while, in another world without all the pressures and stress as a football player. It was like Sorghum Hill.

Someone said that Pappy's Place in the past had sold beer, but for some reason, it had lost its license. Anyway, the police didn't come around, and evidently, there was some amount of drinking going on outside. Interestingly, when it came time to end the music-making, those in the crowd, especially those who were inebriated, would request a gospel song; and sometimes would sing along. It was always true in the South that those with an overwrought conscience wanted to end with a gospel song or two after their drinking, knowing that redemption was available the next morning. So Aeamon Lee and the band would perform a soulful rendition of "Amazing Grace" or "Take My Hand, Precious Lord."

Getting to perform at Pappy's Place allowed Aeamon Lee to try out some of his own music. He wrote a song about football and got the audience to sing along in the chorus. It was titled "Football in Heaven." It was so popular that it had to be performed every time Aeamon Lee was there.

> Oh, Lord, I hope there's football in heaven
> So I can see the Steelers and the Cowboys play;
> And if there's no football in heaven,
> Then, Lord, just send me on to Green Bay.
>
> I just can't wait till the fall of the year.
> I start with the games on Friday nights;
> I watch them all day on Saturdays,
> And on Sundays till they turn out the lights.

Chorus:

Oh, Lord, I hope there's football in heaven

So I can see the Steelers and the Cowboys play;

And if there's no football in heaven,

Then, Lord, just send me on to Green Bay.

I have a special place on Monday nights,

But my wife wants me to lend a hand;

But the game has already started,

'And, darling, it's the Oilers and the Miami Dolphins!'

Oh, Lord, I hope there's football in heaven

So I can see the Steelers and the Cowboys play;

And if there's no football in heaven,

Then, Lord, just send me on to Green Bay.

Now I'm living here all by myself,

And I think my wife has left me be;

At halftime, she could not be found;

When the season's over, I'll check to see.

Oh, Lord, I hope there's football in heaven

So I can see the Steelers and the Cowboys play;

And if there's no football in heaven,

Then, Lord, just send me on to Green Bay.[92]

*   *   *

On the Sundays that Aeamon Lee was in Oxford, he would get up while some were sleeping in and go to church. Early in the fall, he found out about this little church of his faith located several miles out in the country. One of the members would drive him out to the little country church. The older members didn't show much knowledge of the football team or how well it was doing. Rather, it appeared that they were curious as to why he was there. Sometimes these little churches show suspicion of new people and treat them as outsiders until they've gone there for several years. They don't realize how visitors picked up on this feeling of exclusion. Aeamon Lee was not the type, however, to allow such spiritual pettiness to bother him. He looked for some opportunity to serve.

There were four teenage boys at this church, and he noticed that they sat in the auditorium during Sunday school with the adults. He asked one of the church elders about why they didn't have a class of their own. It was explained that they did have a class until recently, but the teacher and his family had moved away. No one else was yet willing to take them into a class. Even though Aeamon Lee had never actually taught a class before, he felt he was getting to a point of expanding leadership in his life. So he asked if he could take these boys into a class, and he would teach them. The elders thought it would be okay and finally said he could. This was after they had asked him several questions about his previous church affiliation and involvement.

He had already acquainted himself with the boys by talking with them after church and finding out that they kept up with the team. The next Sunday, he took them into a classroom and began to ask them general questions about their faith, which would determine the direction he would take in the class. He shunned having a workbook and decided he would ask them to use their Bibles as they studied stories that related to their needs. He discovered that their concept of Christianity was to just believe all the right things and make sure you went to church on Sunday. Aeamon Lee knew that this kind of faith would leave a huge void in their lives. Most of the dos and don'ts related to personal acts of deviation, and none had to do with the sins against humanity.

So for several Sundays, he discussed with them Jesus's acceptance into his discipleship of the so-called social outcasts who repented and how he sat down at meals with publicans and sinners. He taught them about the importance of Good Samaritan acts instead of passing by on the other side. He explained how the Good Samaritan, the good guy in the parable, even though he was normally despised in Jewish society, helped a man of another religion, another ethnic background, and a person who had been passed over by others. He showed them how the beaten and unconscious man was given medical care, transportation, and housing. He taught these young men that all these issues were also important to address in being a Christian.

The young men loved what they were doing in the class and felt really privileged to have the Ole Miss quarterback as their Sunday schoolteacher. But things began to deteriorate as the fall wore on. Aeamon Lee thought it would be great if they would host a Sunday afternoon youth rally, invite some other young people from some other congregations, and have refreshments; and he would speak to the whole group. The young men were excited about it, so Aeamon Lee asked the elders about it. He asked the ladies to prepare some refreshments and drinks for the occasion. The elders said they would meet and let him know of their decision.

The next Sunday the men called Aeamon Lee in privately and announced to him that they couldn't have the youth rally because they had decided that he was teaching the young men things they didn't believe in.

"And what are the things you don't approve?" Aeamon Lee asked.

"Well, we know you mean well, but we don't believe we should use the church building for meals. We have never had a meal in our church building. The Bible says, 'Have ye not houses to eat and drink in?'[93] And also, we understand you have been teaching the young men the church can do some things that we don't believe are a part of the church's mission. So we think it is best for you to give up the class. Though we want you to still come and help us out."

Aeamon Lee was sorely disappointed in such reasoning. There was no earthly reason why, in 1983, folks believed this way, he thought. He knew he would have to be considerate of their position as church elders, but there was no reason why he could not be assertive.

"I guess you'll be removing that drinking fountain from the back of the building right away," Aeamon Lee asked.

The men turned around and looked at the drinking fountain and asked, "Why is that?"

"The same verse that you quoted that refers to eating also refers to drinking. You haven't noticed that?"

The men didn't say a word, but Aeamon Lee continued, "If you take the verse that literally, then it forbids eating in restaurants and going on picnics, because it specifies houses to eat in. I know some of you eat in restaurants, don't you?"

Again, silence.

"And besides, that verse could not be referring to church buildings, because the first church building as such wasn't built until about three hundred years later. You all should really think about this, because you should realize that it is just as wrong to make up laws for God as it is to break God's law."

One of the men said, "Well, Aeamon Lee, we couldn't change because we've always practiced this, and it would divide the church, and you know, it would cause problems."

"Which is it? Is it something that the Bible teaches, or is it because you're bound by tradition?"

Another brother spoke up and said, "Well, we've made our decision, and I don't see any need for further discussion. But we want you to continue coming, Aeamon Lee, and we'll find someone else to teach these boys."

The young men were waiting with their families outside in their cars. Aeamon Lee went out there and wished each of them well. He encouraged them to remember the lessons they had learned and said that he hoped they would have a good life. And he left never to return to church there.

*   *   *

As the week started before the final game of the season with archrival Mississippi State, there were still distractions. First, he called home and discussed the family financial situation after harvesting all the crops. Plea said, "Aeamon Lee, we've been figuring some ourselves, and since we don't spend nearly as much as we once did, we think there will be enough for you to get a car or truck to use at college. Maybe it wouldn't be a new one, but one that would get you where you needed to go. And of course, to come home with."

Aeamon Lee had not even thought about this possibility. He stated that the fellows on the team gave him rides to most places, and he had faired okay, but having his own truck would help a lot.

"Are you sure, Dad?"

"Yes, I am sure. Don't worry about us. Now that I'm receiving the disability and the place has been paid for, we're getting by all right."

The week was so full of activities that he hardly found time to go looking for a truck. Another player told him about a particular dealer with whom a lot of the players did business. He made some time to go by this dealer, and he found a two-toned, black-and-white 1977 Ford F-100 with a red interior that had low mileage. Aeamon Lee told them he could only pay a total of $2,500 for the truck. The salesman came back after talking with the owner, and they had a deal. Aeamon Lee would dress it up in time by putting some treated boards behind the cab and down each side. He bolted them together on the truck after painting them. Finally, he had transportation and would not have to bum rides off his friends.

Everybody was on edge the week before the game on Saturday, November 19, in Jackson, with the old in-state rival. Ole Miss had moved up in the polls, and everybody, it seemed, had dreams of an undefeated season, the conference championship, and playing for the national championship. It took two days before the coaches were able to get all the team on the same page. They would not talk about a championship of any kind and would focus on winning the next game. Even though it was designated as a home game, State would have about as many fans present as would Ole Miss. The Rebels had to win this game in order to win the conference championship and get a Sugar Bowl berth.

Aeamon Lee had not been around college football long enough to develop grudges and hatred for any team. He had never felt hostile toward State as many at Ole Miss did. He had always wanted them to win when they were not playing Ole Miss. But he learned quickly that you never pulled for State in anything, and when they were beaten by anyone, you cheered. Everybody was focused and intense all week during practice. The team knew that State would like nothing better than knock Ole Miss from the ranks of the undefeated.

Again, with Aeamon Lee's help, the game plan was developed and installed on Tuesday on a full scale. It was a long practice that even included some hitting. Besides losing the two senior quarterbacks in the first game, the team had been lucky in that there had been only a handful of other injuries. In addition to the usual nicks and bruises of others, one offensive lineman and a defensive back had missed several games. It seemed that everyone had developed as a smarter, more physical player during the season. There was no question that they had vastly improved, and most teams underestimated them.

All week, the emphasis had been on playing as a team. That expectation was reinforced by the timing of Maleah's saying: "A person standing alone can be attacked and defeated, but two can stand back-to-back and conquer. Three are even better, for a triple-braided cord is not easily broken."[94]

Two days before the game, a reporter from the Jackson *Clarion-Ledger* ran a feature article about some comments several of the State players had made about Aeamon Lee. They were so derogatory toward him that Coach Wortham thought it was a deliberate attempt to rattle Aeamon Lee. One of the players was quoted as saying that he was green and not yet an experienced player in the conference. And he went further by threatening, "We had better not get him by himself on the field because we could teach him a few things about playing in this conference." The Ole Miss coaches tried to get Aeamon Lee to completely disregard these remarks.

On game day after the warm-ups on the field, the team went back into the dressing room. Aeamon Lee knew State would have to come out onto the field first, so he slipped out of the dressing room without the coaches noticing. He walked toward the end zone and then to the goal posts by himself. By this time, the crowd had seen him, with one side cheering and the other side booing. By the time State came out of their dressing room for the kickoff, Aeamon Lee was almost to the 50-yard line in the middle of the field with his helmet on but unstrapped. The State players started taunting and inching closer and closer to him. He just stood there stoically. By this time, the referees had noticed what was going on and rushed out to get Aeamon Lee off to the sidelines. When the team and coaches got there, the referees explained what he did to Coach Wortham and called a fifteen-yard penalty on Ole Miss to start the game. Luckily, there was no pregame fight this time. Although, Aeamon Lee felt that State had gotten his message.

When Ole Miss took the field, Aeamon Lee yelled, "Caedite eos! Novit enim Dominus qui sunt eius."[95]

One player asked another, "What the devil does that mean?"

"Never mind, just play like the devil."

The game with State would be the usual knock-down, drag-out type of game from start to finish. There were personal fouls called on each team that thwarted drives. The score at the half was 20–17 in Ole Miss's favor. But at halftime, Aeamon Lee returned to their theme for the year and reminded the team that they had not played smart on every play. As the course of the season had worn on, Ole Miss had developed a fairly good running game, as Aeamon Lee would cross up the defense play after play by sometimes audibling to a rushing play. Being able to mix up the plays was helping. In the second half, Ole Miss played with much more consistency, but it appeared that a stable of players were going down to injury. After kicking a field goal to make it 23–17, the score remained the same until late in the fourth quarter when State intercepted a bobbled pass and ran it back for a touchdown. This made the score 24–23, and the Ole Miss faithful began to worry. "Surely we can't lose to State!"

This turn of events had inspired State, and on the ensuing kickoff, they held Ole Miss on its first two plays. Now it was third and eleven on their own 11-yard line. Milo Millon had hurt his hand on an earlier play. This was bad because this would have been the ideal situation to run him underneath, a play that had worked well. With fifty-seven seconds to go in the game, Aeamon Lee called a fake pass play; and he would scramble, find an opening, and pick up the first down himself.

"This is it guys. We've got to make this play work. Keep on blocking legally all the way down the field."

Buford Jackson, the running back, asked, "Can you do it?"

"Si, se puede,"[96] Aeamon Lee answered, and he broke huddle. Players and other friends of Aeamon Lee had learned just to assume that he knew what he was talking about when he used phrases like this.

The sinewy young quarterback darted through holes, and defensive guys were missing him right and left. He swung to his right after picking up about fifteen yards, and when he looked straight ahead, he collided with a safety. Both players went up into the air. Aeamon Lee was addled but clutched the ball. He stretched out his left arm and caught the ground with his hand and feet, but no knee hit the ground. He quickly recovered, swung to his left, and with his speed, broke free around the fifty. After that, it was a foot race to the goal line. He was caught at the 5-yard line, but his momentum carried him straight ahead, and he plowed toward the goal line with all his might. There were thirty-six seconds to go, and the score was now 30–24.

During the extra point try, Aeamon Lee went to Coach Wortham and said, "I know I've asked about this before, but you've got to let me go in on defense at free safety. I know what I'm talking about."

The old coach looked at him but didn't immediately respond. Finally, he said, "Be ready, and I'll let you know." State returned the ball to their own 35-yard line, with Coach Wortham screaming on the sidelines. He was obviously angry at someone for letting them pick up so much yardage. He looked at Aeamon Lee and said, "Okay, go in. I hope you know what you are doing. I don't know what you are doing."

State moved the ball on two quick plays on Ole Miss's right side down to the Ole Miss 45-yard line. Ole Miss was protecting against the long ball, and now State would have to go long. Or so everybody thought. Instead, they connected on a fifteen-yarder with blockers around. Aeamon Lee broke through the blockers and hit the receiver but didn't take him to the ground. Instead, he wrapped him up good while pushing him on down the field. The officials could not blow the whistle with the play moving forward. State players were trying to call time-out. The receiver was trying to lateral the ball off, but Aeamon Lee wouldn't allow him. He knew there were only seconds left, and finally, the buzzer went off. But Aeamon Lee realized the play was not over until the ball carrier was on the ground. He took him down with the guy trying his best to lateral, fumble, or get out of bounds. It was not to be, and the game was over.

The old stadium literally rocked. Coach Wortham had the traditional barrel of water thrown on his head for winning the conference championship. As Aeamon Lee and the team confidently headed toward the end of the field where the band played, the tall, imposing figure covered with the sweat, dirt, and grime of battle gave the mirage-like image of a ghostly warrior marching on glistening, wavy waters of glory. The ethereal plane had beckoned. He had fought a good fight. He had kept the faith.

Two small children who had gotten loose from their parents ran out to see him up close. He picked up the little girl and held her with one arm while holding his helmet with the other. The little boy stood at his feet gazing admiringly up at his hero. A photographer snapped a picture at the moment Aeamon Lee raised his helmet into the air when the band got to the dramatic beginning of "The Battle Hymn of the Republic" in their version of "From Dixie with Love." That picture appeared on the cover of *Sports Illustrated* with the caption, "A New Legend Is Born at Ole Miss."

After this great victory, Aeamon Lee would say to any players he met, "This is our time. Enjoy the moment. It comes maybe once in a lifetime." Then the band struck up "I Saw the Light." Aeamon Lee had taken off his shoulder pads from under his jersey. He saw one of the cheerleaders he knew, Belva Darren, and they did a little dance together on the field to the beat of the old ballad. Aeamon Lee knew that Belva wouldn't have any qualms about doing this. Players are not supposed to engage in such a flaunting display of jubilation after a game, but this time, forgiveness abounded.

After the game, Coach Wortham stated he was relieved that the eventful season was over. He also reprimanded Aeamon Lee quite severely for his actions but said, "I know why you did it. You felt you had to do it, didn't you? It was an automatic response, wasn't it? At least there was no brawling this time. Maybe that's progress."

*   *   *

Players were about finished dressing when someone came in and told Aeamon Lee about a young woman who was waiting to see him outside. He said, "Man, she is about the prettiest woman I've ever seen. She has beautiful long, unbound hair that flows like waves. You'll want to see who that is."

When Aeamon Lee went outside, there stood Maleah Marcelles and her brother, Landon. She was decked out in a dazzling outfit with a gold-colored scarf. After they shared greetings and excitement, Maleah told Aeamon Lee how they had planned all season to see him play in one of the games in Jackson. Laughing, she told him about telling the fans seated next to her how she and Aeamon Lee kept bad people from Goshen Wells when they were growing up together. She said, "They looked at me in amazement. I don't think they believed me."

Maleah shared how she had been promoted at work and was taking night classes. The evidence was clear that Maleah was becoming a professional woman. She said, "I know you don't get down this way often, but even if you just need to talk, here is my phone number to call, 222-153-1746."[97] Aeamon Lee always felt good whenever he got to see any of his old neighbors from Goshen Wells. But this time, he began to admit to himself that meeting Maleah caused him to have a sense of closeness to this remarkable woman that he had not allowed himself to feel before. "By the way, the sayings you gave me were perfect for each occasion. That old wise man sounded as if he knew all about American football."

* * *

The Southeastern Conference championship had been won, the first one in over twenty years. There was an automatic berth to the Sugar Bowl on Monday, January 2, 1984. There was a rumor spread that the Sugar Bowl didn't want Ole Miss because they supposedly didn't travel well. What this meant was, due to its proximity to New Orleans, many fans would only go down on the day of the game and go back home after the game. This way, they wouldn't spend nearly as much money as other teams farther away, whose fans would stay several days and shell out cash in the city. One bowl official complained, "Those Ole Miss people will start frying up all that chicken early that morning and packing all the fixin's and won't spend any money down here."

The question to be decided was whom they would play. The polls came out on Monday, and Ole Miss had moved to number three in the rankings and undefeated at 11 and 0. The Ole Miss faithful complained about not being ranked higher. Notre Dame, ranked number one and undefeated, was issued the invitation. They accepted on the grounds that they only had to win the game to win another national championship, which they figured they could do. And beating an undefeated team should help as well. The Orange Bowl and Rose Bowl each had a team with only one loss. So how it would all play out after the bowl games was anybody's guess. The odds favored Notre Dame, and they accepted the bid.

* * *

In late November, talk about the Heisman Trophy seriously began. Aeamon Lee's name would often come up because of the undefeated season, and he had Heisman-like stats. He had 36 touchdown passes for 3,453 yards and an astounding 527 rushing yards. This led the Southeastern Conference in total offense. He was selected unanimously as the Freshman of the Year in the conference. The sports reporters, however, would always talk about his glowing statistics and achievements on the field only to be followed with, "But as we all know, he is just a freshman." This latter observation automatically dismissed him from serious consideration.

None of this talk bothered Aeamon Lee because he knew this was something over which he had no control. He had learned already in life that tangible rewards on earth are few indeed. His attitude was to perform on the field, and then others could offer whatever judgment on it they wanted. He also knew that politics and regional bias played a role in selecting the most outstanding football player in the country. In some years, career stats were important, but in other years, they looked only at the performance of that one year. He remembered how Archie Manning was overlooked in 1969 for the Heisman Trophy when he was clearly the most outstanding player in college football. This was why he won the Walter Camp Award for the Most Outstanding Back that year, presented by the Washington, DC, Touchdown Club. A running back out of Oklahoma won the Heisman Trophy, because he had over three thousand rushing yards in his career.

In 1982, Herschel Walker of the Georgia Bulldogs won the Heisman, and they surely would not give the Heisman to a Southeastern Conference player two years in a row. This was one of the reasons why Aeamon Lee was dismissed from the running so quickly. So a running back from Nebraska who was expected to go on and have a great NFL career won the trophy. This was of little consequence to Aeamon Lee and the team. They still had plenty of work to do.

* * *

The team was allowed to go home and spend Thanksgiving with their families. This time, Aeamon Lee drove his new used truck home to show the family. He explained all its features, wanting to hear from Plea and Martha that they thought he had done a good job picking one out. But as soon as he drove up the road to the house, there was heaviness in his heart about losing Jo-Nathan. He kept waiting for Jo-Nathan to pop in any minute and welcome him home. Everywhere he looked brought back memories of something they had done together. He went down to the Markums, and he could feel the sadness all around and in everybody's voice. They were still grieving and were now in the stage of real suffering. All the other family and friends had gone home, and Amos and Mama Kate were left to deal with their loss alone.

Before he left their house, Mama Kate showed him a letter she had received from a soldier that had survived the attack in Beirut. He said that he saw Jo-Nathan standing near the entrance of their building. When Jo-Nathan sensed something suspicious about the terrorist truck, he immediately began to push others to the rear of the building. The blast killed Jo-Nathan while he was saving the lives of others. "I'm able to write you this letter because of him," he wrote. Aeamon Lee choked up, and he and Mama Kate hugged each other in tears.

It was not a very pleasant holiday weekend. He went through the motions of trying to make it pleasant, but it never was. Plea would still sit and stare for long periods of time. He said all the necessary things in an effort to make Aeamon Lee feel good. Underneath, however, was the same old depression. Martha explained that the doctor was trying a new medication for Plea called amitriptyline. This was an antidepressant medication that might help lift the depression fog that had overwhelmed Plea for such a long time. It would take a while before they knew whether or not it would be effective.

Aeamon Lee tried to stay busy, taking care of business matters. It seemed the only satisfying thing they could talk about was the great season Ole Miss had and the role played by Aeamon Lee. Martha said that they had even received some letters from people she didn't know, telling them how well he had done and how happy they should be for him.

Aeamon Lee would not go to Sorghum Hill on Saturday night. He stayed home and watched a little television and read some. On Sunday, he would tell Martha and Plea that the next few weeks would be critical for his studies and preparing for the big game in New Orleans on January 2. He said that he might not even get to come home on Christmas.

Before he left home that weekend, Martha said, "Aeamon Lee, you've been gone out into the world for a while now. Have you found your mission yet?" His mother reminded him through the years of that solemn prediction by the midwife when he was born. Each time, she always whispered her words in his ear. Aeamon Lee did the same by speaking quietly into her ear.

"No, Mama, but it's a start. While the world has made progress in some areas, I have discovered that there continues to be a lot of injustice in the world. It needs a wasteland healer. Maybe I'll start an agency called Justice Unlimited and confront these forces in some dramatic way, maybe with a little less brawling. I do know that first I must be the change I want to see in the world.[98] Maybe the journey should simply reflect the good[99] that emphasizes the inner qualities of the spirit. I am developing a vision of a more humane world, though. There are times when I think big, such as finding the formula for world peace and the cure for cancer. But at other times, I wonder if the mission should be to simply find joy in the golden now, learning how to live to the fullest in the moments of each day. Or maybe it's a combination of the two. I believe that someday, it will be clear."

For the first time, he was glad to return to campus, away from all the reminders of his lost friend.

At times, Aeamon Lee could not resist engaging in an exchange of opinion differences with his professors. After one class, a student told him, "By the way, there is a place in town off the square called the Hoka Theater and Moonlight Café where a lot of people just hang out, discussing issues like ones you have in class. You should go there sometime and share your thoughts. Everybody is sociable, and the whole scene is totally nonthreatening." At this point in the semester, Aeamon Lee had too many commitments to go and check out this place. He hoped that someday he could. It sounded like a place that would tolerate and even appreciate his numerous quotations.

In subsequent classes, some professors sometimes said, "Of course, Mistral might have a different take on that." And most of the time, Aeamon Lee would only smile and refuse to be drawn into another discussion.

* * *

The usual emphasis for the team now that the regular season was over was to give attention to one's academics, to make sure the semester ended well. Finally, there was some time to get caught up on all the required classroom activities. Aeamon Lee used his keen insight and intuitive powers well in the classroom. That fall semester, he ended up with four As and one B. The B irritated him because the professor had made some snide remark at the beginning of the semester about football players in his class. He stated that no player could expect any favors from him (as if they did). It didn't matter what Aeamon Lee did on the exams or what contributions he made in class, the professor was never impressed. Another thing that galled him was that he had been warned before classes started about the bias of this professor, but he assumed that he would have to be basically honest and fair with his grading. A 3.8 GPA was not bad, however. And he felt good that one A came from his Survey of Civilization class.

The coaches were concerned about a long layoff before the game in New Orleans. So they kept up the pace of practice with a lot of conditioning exercises and polishing the offense and defense, kicking game, and special teams play. The defensive secondary, consisting of Ray Flowers, Cliff Clowers, Sonny Bowers, Rennie Jowers, and Terrell Blades, got a lot of attention. The coaches felt that this secondary had the potential to be special. The linebackers were key in the defensive scheme because they were the ones expected to take down the ball carriers after being slowed by the defensive front. The linebackers and lineman with the most playing time were Conley Armstrong, Joe Pinner, Theo Thrasher, Bob Cat Tacker, and Sut Hardy. They had accumulated by far the most tackles on the team. The running backs had developed durability and made the most progress of anyone during the season. Now, Buford Jackson and Linnell Washington were hard-nosed, hard-driving running backs.

* * *

These were glorious days for the team. There was finally a time to relax a little and reflect on their accomplishments, even though there was one more huge test. The team had learned a little more about winning and what it took from everyone involved.

Aeamon Lee was more relaxed and got to play and sing at Pappy's Place some. Word had spread about Aeamon Lee's Saturday-night activities. Now there were many more people wanting to come than could be accommodated. The owner decided to give out tickets to the usual patrons, and they had an extra ticket or two to give out to their friends. He gave Aeamon Lee five tickets, and Andre had five. They gave the tickets to other players and students occasionally. Aeamon Lee had developed a friendship with a television sportscaster named Glenn Conner and also a sports columnist, George LaPierce. They had been to Pappy's several times and had been considerate in not exploiting this part of Aeamon Lee's life. So they always were given tickets when they were in town for a home game. They even came down one Saturday night in early December for a show.

During the show, there was an open mike for a short time. George LaPierce from Memphis went up and announced that he was old enough to remember when Ole Miss had another singing quarterback named Jim Weatherly, who went on to become a great songwriter. George asked Aeamon Lee if he would sing a Weatherly song titled "Night Train to Georgia." Aeamon Lee said he would rather sing another one of his songs titled "You're the Best Thing That's Ever Happened to Me." He performed the blues song with as much soul as Gladys Knight and the Pips. When he finished the song, a lady in the audience said to Aeamon Lee, "Honey, you could be the best thing that's ever happened to me." The audience had a good laugh.

His earthy, soulful music unleashed the suppressed emotions of patrons seeking respite from life's troubles and brought them to feel acceptance of both their sensual and spiritual selves.

One of the regular parts of Aeamon Lee's performance was a short period in which he shared some of his brand of humor. The band played "Corinna, Corinna," and in the middle of the song, they stopped; and Aeamon Lee gave a humorous story or two. On this night in early December, he gave his version of how the team reacted on getting to go to the Sugar Bowl.

"As you all know, we're going to play in the Sugar Bowl on Monday, January 2. The coaches put us in this room and said we could vote on whether we wanted to play Notre Dame. But he said, 'I think you should know that they are undefeated, ranked number one in the country, and have an offensive line consisting of Sobanski, Romanski, Sawdowski, Kosmalski, and Commiski [laughter]. They average over three hundred pounds each. They have three all-Americans on the team. They are mean devils that usually leave half of the opposition on crutches.' Everybody on our team got real silent [laughter]. The vote was close [laughter], but we voted to go play the Notre Dame Fighting Irish [clapping].

"The next thing we wanted to know was whether anybody had been to New Orleans other than when we played Tulane there. And there were several who had been on other occasions. 'What is it like?' One of them said, 'Well, there are a lot of women of the night down on Bourbon Street.' James Roy Eddings, one of our offensive linemen, had never heard of this expression and wanted to know what kind of women was that [laughter]. Several of the players offered to introduce him to one of these ladies and told him that they would read his fortune free of charge, and for him to be sure and request that he needed her services. James Roy said that he would do that [laughter].

"I've heard that New Orleans food is as delicious as the less criminal forms of sin [laughter].[100] The coaches told us that we would get to eat some of that fine Cajun food, like *cassoulet au porc a la moutarde*. One of our defensive linemen, Leron Banks, said, 'I'm not eating no food unless I know what it is' [laughter]. So we asked if anybody knew what it was. Nobody seemed to know [laughter]. So we sent one of our trainers, Billy Wayne Hollister, up to the Ole Miss library, where we keep the dictionary [huge laughter] to look that word up and come back and tell us what it was. After a while, he came back and said he couldn't find it in our dictionary [more laughter]. So we asked a fourth-string cornerback, Willard Wilder, who had made one of these all-academic teams, a white boy [laughter], if he would stand up and give us his best knowledge as to what he thought it was. And he said he thought it was some kind of pork casserole. And that seemed to satisfy Leron [laughter].

"So on January 2, in New Orleans, Louisiana, the Ole Miss Rebels will play the number one–ranked team, the Notre Dame Fighting Irish in the Sugar Bowl." And he started playing and singing:

> Corinna, Corinna,
> Way across the sea.[101]

* * *

What Aeamon Lee didn't know was that somebody was taping this little bit of contrived humor. On Monday morning, some of it was in the papers and even played on some sports talk shows. It seemed that everybody in the Mid-South was having a good laugh at the expense of Ole Miss and this exaggerated humor. The repercussions were swift.

Aeamon Lee was called out of one of his classes to see Coach Wortham in his office immediately. When he arrived, the coach was frustrated. "Aeamon Lee, I thought after that episode over that Louisiana man, you would stay out of the headlines." He explained to the coach that he had no idea he was being taped and that the whole thing was just a comedy routine that should not be taken seriously. Coach said, "I know that, but it happened and got in the news. But that's not even the worst of it. The athletic director, who was called by the head librarian, Dr. Wilma Sue Willingham, and the academic dean, Dr. Aaron B. Blakely, has notified me that they are greatly offended."

Coach continued, "They believe that what you said reflected badly on the university, and especially the Ole Miss library, because you implied we only had one dictionary and that we kept it in the library. Now, I know that you were just joking, but they are offended. And the really bad part is that they want you suspended from the team until you make a public apology to let the public know that we have more than one dictionary here.

"So here is what we are going to have to do: I will announce that you are temporarily suspended. You will need to get your college dictionary, and we will need to call a news conference where you will apologize to Dr. Willingham and Dr. Blakely. They will be present. So we need to get this over with as quickly as possible." Aeamon Lee agreed, but with some degree of resentment over what he regarded as a rather silly and childish reaction by these academicians.

The next morning in the Memphis *Commercial Appeal*, there was a column by George LaPierce in which he stated that he had heard of a lot of stupid things in sports before, but he thought the hullabaloo over the Ole Miss library took the prize. Actually, the reaction by Drs. Willingham and Blakely got more negative public press than the original story.

Some university departments were very protective of their turf and were so narrow in their scope that they could not understand the statements in their context. Aeamon Lee saw this as academic arrogance in its worst form.

At the crowded news conference, Coach Wortham simply stated that Aeamon Lee Mistral had a statement to make. Aeamon Lee walked to the microphone with dictionary in hand and began:

"I want to apologize to Dr. Wilma Sue Willingham, our fine head librarian, and to Dr. Aaron B. Blakely, our able academic dean, for my remarks in a comedy routine that were subsequently published without my knowledge. I regret any embarrassment to the university, and I assure you that was not my intent." Aeamon Lee looked over at the two several times during this statement. He continued:

"Now, I hold in my hand the *Merriam-Webster's Collegiate Dictionary*. I've been told that nearly every student on this campus has one of these in his or her dorm room. I went over to the Ole Miss bookstore, and they have a table full of these dictionaries, and I'm happy to announce that they are on sale. You can have one of these for $29.95 plus tax. I've been reading this dictionary, and I'm here to tell you that there are some mighty fine words in this book. So I decided to use some of these words in the course of my talk here today. It would not, therefore, be prudent for me to disparage such astute and sagacious professionals."

At this point, Coach Wortham rose and came to the podium and gently led Aeamon Lee, who would have continued his perverse pleasure, to one side. He said, "Now, I believe that this apology has been sincere, and on behalf of the football program, we express our regrets. We hope you"—he turned and looked at the two—"will accept our apologies, and we all hope that this matter has now been settled." Drs. Willingham and Blakely's initial smiling presence had turned into a fixed stale glare. Nevertheless, they assured Coach Wortham that they were satisfied. Evidently, they had received flack even from some of their own colleagues.

*   *   *

As had been done throughout the regular season, Aeamon Lee met with the offensive and defensive coordinators and some of the other coaches to work up the game plans against Notre Dame. They watched film and read statistics of their team. For the first time all season, there was nothing that stood out for them to use against Notre Dame. There simply were no real weaknesses that they could find. Notre Dame had talent and depth at every position. Only the University of Southern California had played them close, and that was for only three quarters. No wonder this team was ranked number 1.

The coaches kept changing things, and then they would argue for a while. Aeamon Lee mostly kept silent during these discussions. There was nothing that seemed obvious to him that could be used effectively.

He was drawing blanks in his mind. Finally, he excused himself from the meeting. He stated that he needed to keep all this information in his mind and give himself some time to think. He said, "We seem to be thinking too much alike, and if everyone is thinking alike, then someone is not thinking."[102]

He spoke with Coach Wortham and reminded him that Ole Miss would be underdogs in the game. All the media pundits would be predicting a Notre Dame victory. Almost everyone in the football world expected that this would be Notre Dame's year to win it all. Not a single player on Ole Miss's team made first team in All-SEC. There were several who made second and third team. Aeamon Lee actually made only second-team All-SEC to a quarterback from Florida, a senior who had put up big numbers in some of their games.

He lay awake at night racking his brain, and finally, it dawned on him. There had been times when he had limited his own powers by his own limited thinking and doing. There were times when he actually resisted the truth about himself. They won games when he was allowed more involvement. Granted, he had always given way to others who could get the job done rather than doing it himself and taking the credit for it. Maybe now, it was different. *No maybes*, he thought. *It's time to exert my influence like I've never done before.* But he wondered how the coaches would react.

He first approached Coach Wortham and thanked him for allowing him the unorthodox involvement in developing game plans and making suggestions on the field. He reminded the coach of the low expectations that abounded for the team against Notre Dame.

"Nobody believes we can win the game but us. There are actually some in the media salivating about the possibility of another team bringing us uppity upstarts down.

"What do you have in mind, Aeamon Lee?" Coach Wortham had been the only one who had always listened to him. "I am not really sure why I always listen to you, but you've been right all those other times, and I will listen to you now."

He began, "Our offense has already become quite variable on the field as you know. You gave me freedom to call some plays and to check off. The team has learned my signals pretty well. Webster, who receives signals from upstairs, can call formations or whatever he wants to from the sidelines. I'll look over in that direction. But I'll call just the formation in the huddle, and we'll get to the line in a hurry. This will give me time to see their adjustments, and then I'll call the play. If I need to call a wrinkle, like a man in motion or position change, then I can do that too. What I'll do coach"—Aeamon Lee looked him straight in the eye and changed his tone—"is that I will rely on the intangible, my keen intuition, to tell me what they expect, and I'll call the play that should work. We have several weeks of intense practice to get this down pat. And we'll run it over and over and over again with no mistakes. We'll change the primary receiver and ball carrier on all but about a half dozen of our plays. If they overload to one side, I'll go to the other side. If they figure this out, and try to deceive me, I'll go to the other side. Coach, they don't stand a chance against my intuition!" There, he said it! Then he added, "Provided every one of our men play at their highest level."

Aeamon Lee said, "That's why I always win at poker. Don't ever get into a game of poker with me." They laughed.

"You've placed a lot of faith in me this season, and by experience, you know I'm right. We just have to be careful enough to sell it to the offensive coordinator without him feeling that he has been left out. Coach, this can be done, and no one else will ever know the true story."

"By the way," Coach Wortham said, "Bobby Landers, our senior passing quarterback who had that severely sprained ankle has completed rehab and will be practicing with us. Don't worry about anything. I've already talked with him, and he understands why we need to continue at this stage with you as the quarterback. He'll just be available if he's needed. But you will need to spend a lot of time with him, teaching him most of this offense. He'll get a lot of snaps in practice."

*   *   *

In practice, there was a new reason for intensity and focus. There was a new atmosphere, and it gave way to a new determination. It was a chance of a lifetime. They had Notre Dame and the bowl situation just where they wanted. The team was now truly a team, and there was one goal. Every man had his part to play. It would be done regardless of the amount of time or practice or watching film or memorizing it took. The word *commitment* took on a new meaning. Even girlfriends were complaining about not getting to see their player boyfriends as often.

In the defensive game plan, the Rebels would crowd the line and attempt to limit their strong ground game. The biggest change was that Aeamon Lee persuaded the coaches to let him go in at free safety once they crossed the 45-yard line. He assured the coaches that he could handle all his roles without exhaustion. Being on the field of play would give him the advantage of being able to better use his intuitive abilities. He could use voice signals to relay where the ball was probably going.

The team was allowed Christmas Day off, but most chose to stay on campus. There were very few other students to be found anywhere on campus that day. Aeamon Lee did get some guys to do a little pass-and-catch in the afternoon. But his thoughts kept going back to Goshen Wells and Christmases past. Martha and Plea always made sure there was something special for him on that morning. This was the first

Christmas he was away from home. He recalled how every Christmas morning, he would go down to Jo-Nathan's house to see what all he got. He would never be able to do that again. He was supposed to be growing up, but growing up had its frustration of hopes that shattered the innocence of childhood. That evening, the quarterbacks were invited over to Coach Underwood's house for a Christmas dinner. The occasion was nice, with plenty of good food, but nothing could take the place of Christmases past in Goshen Wells.

*   *   *

The team would leave for New Orleans four days before the game. The first day was for travel and getting settled into the hotel. There was a jazz band to greet them, along with city and bowl dignitaries. Crowds were everywhere trying to get to talk with the players and coaches. There was a curfew for every night, but there was actually very little free time. There were banquets to attend and sites to see in this unique and historic city. The coaches stayed with the players on these outings. It was Coach Wortham's first and probably last chance to be this close to a possible national championship. He was nervous, though he didn't want anyone to notice.

Coach Wortham was from the old school in the sense that he didn't like distractions away from his work with the team. However, it was important to include the cheerleaders and the band in a lot of ceremony and extra activities that added to the pageantry of a game. He despised having to do all this, but he knew the university and tradition expected it, so he tried to do it with a smile. He complained about all the activities planned by the Sugar Bowl committee prior to the game. They wanted a lot of exposure, but the coach wanted the team to stay focused on the game at hand.

Coach Wortham selected some seniors to be the spokespersons for interviews. They were experienced in using all the old, tired, and meaningless clichés. They knew how to say "We have to stay focused and go out there and play the way we are capable of playing." Another one was "We sure had better have our game face on." And "We have to come to play and leave everything on the field." Coach actually had them practice being interviewed so they would not say anything that would give away secrets and also not say anything that might antagonize the other team. He tried to shield Aeamon Lee from the media because he sure didn't want him to be the cause of any more controversy.

However, that was impossible. The one interview the reporters wanted was with Aeamon Lee Mistral. After one event, several of them cornered him, and one of them asked him to state what the main reasons he played were. There were microphones held up in front of him and he began:

"I play on behalf of all those work hard, pray hard, and play hard people who have been left out, forgotten, exploited, and who just want a chance at opportunity. I play in honor of Elvis, B. B., Archie, and Miss America. It is a privilege to play for a great university and for coaches who help us improve. So I play for freedom, tolerance, inclusion, equality, justice, and the true American way on my personal journey to find my mission. Most of all, I play for my dear mama and daddy. And finally, I play in memory of my lifelong friend, Jo-Nathan Markum, a United States Marine who was recently killed in the line of duty. That's why I play."

This quotation was reported in all the newspapers covering the Sugar Bowl. Every part of it was analyzed and discussed. Coach Wortham didn't say anything to him about the interview, so Aeamon Lee felt that what he said must not have been too egregious.

As time passed, Aeamon Lee tended to be purifying the memory of Jo-Nathan's loss of his life in the Marine Corps. Maybe it was a more noble sacrifice than he had first thought.

At the main banquet that brought the two teams together for dinner, there were awards given out, speeches by the coaches, and a little entertainment. Fighting Irish Coach, Leon Doria, never referred to a previous Notre Dame game with Ole Miss. In 1977, Ole Miss was their only loss in a national championship year for the Irish. He may have made a mistake, however, by talking about football in the Midwest. He referred to smashmouth football as if they, and they alone, knew how to play that kind of game. The Rebel line took notice of this and decided to let them know they did know a little something about it in the South. One lineman said, "Just wait till I stick the pine to 'em."

Each team was to select someone for the entertainment part of the evening. Notre Dame went first, and they had four guys harmonize on an old ballad a capella. Aeamon Lee had been asked to sing a song representing the Rebel squad. He took a guitar and sang "Proud Mary,"[103] except he changed the word *Mary* to *Rebel*. "Proud Rebel keep on rollin'." The team had not heard this twist before, and many on the team didn't even know that he also sang and played the guitar. The Rebel side of the room stood up, cheering and clapping while polite applause coming from the other side.

*   *   *

The New Orleans Superdome was filled to capacity. The crowd was equally divided between each team's supporters. There was more than one "Hotty Toddy" yell to be heard, with the Irish fans frequently asking what that meant. Even when told, they still didn't seem to understand. It was probably the most attractive bowl game for that January 2 because both teams were undefeated. The Irish also had a national following, and they also had a lot of fans in Louisiana. After the National Anthem, one Ole Miss's fan yelled, "Go to hell, LSU," which amused the Irish fans that passed it off as some drunk who thought Ole Miss was playing LSU.

After the warm-ups, the team was in the dressing room for their final instructions before entering the field of combat. Usually, Coach Wortham had one of the seniors give a pregame speech, but today, he asked Aeamon Lee to say a few words. Judgment day had arrived, and there had been the knock on the door for the team to get on the field. Aeamon stood up and said, "I am proud to be a part of this team. We've been through the valleys of despair and the mountain peaks of success all season, and we've done well. There is one giant left to fall. And he will fall! We'll never have another opportunity like this one. When they write the history of this game, they will little note nor long remember what we say here, but they will never forget what we did here today.[104] We *will* prevail because we will pierce the heart of the enemy as you would a fellow that spit in your face, knocked down your girlfriend, burned down your house, and called your dog a skunk![105] The devils cannot defeat us, reporters cannot disillusion us, weather cannot weary us, injuries cannot stop us, penalties cannot discourage us, battles cannot beat us, money cannot buy us, governments cannot silence us, and hell cannot handle us. Even death cannot destroy us. So open that door, and let the world know that the Rebels are coming."

It was like an old-time revival message. His words sounded like the rhythmic tones of a revival preacher. The team responded to his every sentence. One player swore later that he got saved during that speech. They would have gone through the wall had the door not opened.

Ole Miss elected to receive after winning the coin toss. They started at their 25-yard line and began to drive. The play calls at the line of scrimmage worked fairly well. They mixed the pass with the run and were able to get down to the Irish 30-yard line. Acamon Lee called for a fly pattern, and he hit the receiver right over the outstretched arms of the defender for a touchdown. But wait, hold the phones—a late yellow flag had been dropped, and a player was called for holding. The lineman swore he was not holding, and Aeamon Lee asked the referee about it since he was selected also as one of the captains for the game. They recovered and drove again down to the 10-yard line but stalled and had to kick a field goal.

The drive had proven several things. First, that Notre Dame was every bit as big and tough as advertised. One Ole Miss lineman had already limped off the field. Second, they were by far the best team Ole Miss had faced, and they knew they would have a huge task in winning the game.

Notre Dame took the kickoff and started moving the ball. The defense appeared to be playing at their maximum strength, but even with that, they were hard put to stop the rampaging mass of humanity that was coming at them on every play. It seemed Notre Dame was picking up five or more yards on every play. Coach Wortham would not let Aeamon Lee go in on defense on their first drive. They scored from the five on first down and goal. The score was 7–3 in the first quarter.

Ole Miss took the ball and started another drive. It was very similar to the first one. The Irish were appearing to make adjustments, but Aeamon Lee was outguessing them on most every play. They were at the Irish 18-yard line when Aeamon Lee faked to the blocking back, then turned around and hit him over the middle with a pass that scored. In the midst of the celebration, they heard someone say, "There was a flag." The line judge had thrown a late flag for holding. This set them back to the 28-yard line.

Again, the Rebels regrouped to keep the drive going. From the twenty, Aeamon Lee completed a play action pass at the ten, but the ball was stripped, and the Irish recovered. This time, their offense ran the ball four out of every five times and was able to go down the field

and score again. This made the score 14–3. On the sidelines, Aeamon
Lee was seething mad because for the first time all season, he believed
the referees were not calling it fair on both sides of the ball. Linemen
were telling him about holding on them. Maybe the refs believed all
that hype about how strong Notre Dame was and how this was their
year. Maybe they made their minds up before the game as to how the
game would go. These were basic mistakes referees should never make.

With four minutes to go in the second quarter, Aeamon Lee was
driving the team down the field and had the ball on their 38-yard line.
He scrambled and carried the ball up the middle as a hole had opened
up. As a host of tacklers knocked him to the ground on his stomach, he
felt something sharp scrape across his back. He couldn't see what it was,
but something had cut into the lower part of his back. As he went back
to the huddle, Linnell Washington told him he was bleeding badly. He
ran the next play for some yardage, but he could feel excruciating pain.
The injury was affecting the offense, so he motioned to the sidelines that
he would have to come out. The referee told him he could not continue
on the field of play bleeding that badly.

Bobby Landers, the senior quarterback, came in to run the team.
The trainers and team doctor got Aeamon Lee to the bench and looked
at what happened. The team doctor, Dr. Phelps, immediately said, "We
need to get him off the field." So he was helped off the sidelines to the
dressing room.

He was stretched across a table and examined by the doctor.

"You've got what appears to be a deep laceration across the lower
part of your back that stretches about six inches. Evidently, the cut came
close to your spinal cord, so we can't take any chances. You don't need
to play anymore in this game, because I don't believe we can sufficiently
stop the bleeding. It's also a risk too dangerous to take."

Aeamon Lee was panicking. "How in the devil could this have happened? I felt something sharp come across my back. I'm wondering if one of those guys had something sharp on the bottom of his shoe, because I don't believe a regular football shoe could have caused this."

"Regardless of how it happened, the reality is that I can't agree for you to go back out there and play," the doctor said.

"Okay, but I'm going back out there, and I may not play again, but here is what I want you to do. I want you to pull the wound together real tight, and I want you to stitch it up as tightly as you can."

"This laceration needs to be sutured in an emergency room. If I did it, it would be a rather crude way to repair it," the doctor reminded.

"I'll go to the emergency room after the game, but right now, I want you to stitch it up and hurry up. You've got to do it, Doc. I know what I'm doing. You won't be responsible, but I do need to go back out there and support the team."

Dr. Phelps reluctantly complied and stitched the wound real tight. Aeamon Lee then said, "Now I want you to pour a lot of that stuff you put on small bleeding sores to prevent further bleeding."

"That won't work either, but I'll do it."

After the trainer and the doctor did this, he asked them to wrap him with gauze and then tape him up all the way around his waist. They taped it tight on his back, and then Aeamon Lee had them to tape a dark towel over all the taping.

In the midst of all this, the team came into the locker room for halftime and reported that the score was 21–3 in favor of Notre Dame. This was the usual pattern for the Irish all year against their opponents.

The team left for the third quarter and had to go on defense. After about five more minutes in the locker room, they were finished with Aeamon Lee, and he returned to the field, trotting down the sideline. There was a huge roar and applause from the Ole Miss faithful, not knowing the extent of his injury. They just knew he would be returning to the game.

At this point in the game, Ole Miss had held the Irish and had the ball on their own 45-yard line, first and ten. A small group of players told Aeamon Lee that they could get the Ole Miss crowd riled up against the referees when he went back into the game. He said to Coach Wortham. "Coach, I'm ready to go in. I'm wrapped good, and the bleeding has stopped." He proceeded to go in. Passing by the line judge, Aeamon Lee told him without looking at him, "Number 78 on our team will be guilty of holding." In the huddle, he told number 78 to hold his man as they ran the ball to the line of scrimmage. A flag was thrown, and ten yards was marked off. The players were motioned, and they started the crowd yelling, "Go to hell, referee, go to hell." It was a constant yell that went on and on.

Again, walking by the line judge, he said, "Now this time, number 65 is going to hit his man across the face with an elbow. And in the huddle, he ordered number 65 to flagrantly hit his man with an elbow. Again, a flag was thrown, and now the ball has been backed up to the 20-yard line. The yells had grown louder and louder. This time, Aeamon Lee went over to two referees standing together and said, again without looking at them, "This time, we will score a touchdown, and there will be no violation committed, *no violation*!"

In the huddle, he warned the offense that on the next play, there had better not be a penalty of any kind. He called a play that required the swiftest receiver to go down on a post pattern and be ready for a bullet. It was a timing route they had practiced many times. It worked perfectly, and the receiver faked the defender, got in the open, and ran to the end zone. This made the score 21–10, and it was the middle of the third quarter.

The reaction on the team was remarkable. There was a bit of momentum, and determination was at its peak. The defense held on the very next series, but the offense only got the ball back on the 15-yard line. Everybody was rejuvenated, and the next drive was a thing of beauty. Aeamon Lee exploited their weakest points as he saw them. The drive ended with Aeamon Lee faking to a running back and outrunning the defense to the pylon and a touchdown. Now the score was 21–17.

In the fourth quarter, there were several exchanges of punts. With three and a half minutes to go in the game, Ole Miss got the ball on their own twenty and started a slow but methodical drive down the field. They brought in Milo Millon, who caught two third-down passes on the top of the turf. On one of the plays, a frustrated defensive safety roughed up Milo. Aeamon Lee rushed down field to verbally rebuke the defender while picking up his receiver. No personal foul was called on the play.

From the opponent's 12-yard line, they sent the tallest possession receiver to the back of the end zone where Aeamon Lee threw a high aerial that required him to leap and catch it. He came down inbounds, and Ole Miss finally regained the lead, 24–21 with a minute and a half to go.

On the sidelines, he had the trainer that helped sew him up to raise his jersey and wipe some more blood off and to strengthen the wrap and put in another towel. They tried to do it where no one could see how bad the wound was because the bleeding had started again.

Notre Dame was really fired up now; they had the ball on the 33-yard line and, in two pass attempts, had the ball on the Ole Miss 42-yard line. The Ole Miss sideline was shouting encouragement and instructions to the defense. Aeamon Lee went to Coach Wortham and said, "This is when I get to go in." He proceeded to go in at free safety and directed the defense. The Notre Dame brute strength still resulted in some positive yards, even when the Rebels knew where the ball was going. Time ran down, and it was obvious, after the Irish got the ball down to the 5-yard line that they believed they could score. When the next play started, two Irish players blocked Aeamon Lee and flagrantly held him, but there was no called penalty. While he frantically tried to break free, they scored. The Irish had come back to go up 28–24.

The whole team looked up at the clock at the same time—three seconds left and no time-outs. The Irish fans were whooping it up so much it seemed that the whole Superdome was swaying. The Ole Miss fans were stunned in disbelief. No one believed at this point that anything could be done to change the outcome—except Aeamon Lee.

He quickly went to Coach Wortham while Notre Dame was kicking the extra point and told him that he had the play. "Just get me the best blockers and ball handlers over here, and I'll call the play." Coach again felt compelled to comply. He knew more than anyone that they were where they were because of Aeamon Lee. He owed it to him to give him this one last chance. Coach would direct traffic and act like he was in charge by conferring with his coaches, but all the while, Aeamon Lee was calling the play.

Then suddenly, as he looked again at that three seconds on the scoreboard, it felt that time began to move in slow motion. There was something beckoning him. He first thought was it was someone on the sideline or in the stands trying to get his attention. The scene came to him in the vision of his mind. It was Jo-Nathan's voice in the hollow below the house at Goshen Wells, "When the breaks are going against you and your back is against the wall, remember to run like the animals." And again, remembering that last letter from Jo-Nathan when he wrote the same thing—"Run like the animals. You know what I mean."

Almost simultaneously, he heard the voice of Maleah reminding him of the final saying, "Finishing is better than starting.[106] And you're not finished yet because the game is not over."

He quickly assembled the huddle. "I know what they will do. They will attempt to kick it short on our right side rather than kicking it away." He looked at the four guys who would be on that side and said, "Now listen, you cannot go down and recover the ball. You cannot let your knee hit the ground. You will have to *pick the ball up*, and you'll have to sling it back to me in the air around the twenty-five or thirty-yard line. If any one of you commits a penalty, I will personally kill you. You must keep on blocking, blocking, blocking—legally! I will run wherever there is an opening. Remember, the play is not over, even though the buzzer will go off, till I'm in the end zone with the ball."

As predicted, the kick went to the right side, and there was a mad scramble for the ball. One of the Rebels picked the ball up, looked around, and as he attempted to sling the ball backward, he was hit in the back. This made him throw the ball farther than intended, and it went over Aeamon Lee's head at the thirty. He quickly reversed like a cat, ran backward, and caught the ball on a perfect bounce. By this time, the buzzer had sounded. He headed up the Notre Dame sideline and reached the 42-yard line. He was able to see that there were Irish tacklers closing in on him. He saw no good coming from continuing this route. He came to a dead halt like a fox and ran in the opposite direction. Adding to the stress of the run was the fact that he saw an Irish player come onto the field of play as an illegal participant. But obviously, he couldn't stop the play to go over and tell the referee.

As he was being pursued in the opposite direction, he began to cut in and out and through the defenders like a snake. Now he was at least going across the field until he found another opening that would carry him back toward his goal. Bodies were flying in the air, ankles were being twisted, and grunts and groans were heard everywhere. He had to take flight over a would-be tackler like a chicken. Other tacklers came at him from several angles, and he had to zigzag and jump and zigzag some more while jumping like a deer. Some defenders were just swinging at him, and he had to quickly jerk his head to one side or the other like a cow. To avoid some others, he had to sway at an extreme angle like a horse, but his body never touched the ground. It seemed to Aeamon Lee like there were twenty defenders on the field. But after he swayed, he had open field before him. Now it was indeed a horse race as he sped straight ahead. Trouble lay ahead, though, because some defenders had headed toward the goal line and created another line of defense. However, they must not have been thinking because they lined up on the goal line instead of the five. Aeamon Lee cut across in front of them for a few yards and then quickly turned toward his left, lowered his head like a goat and plowed through an Irish defender into the end zone. The would-be tackler literally went up into the air after the hit, and Aeamon Lee just kept plowing on like a caterpillar across the end zone, not knowing where he was exactly.

Now the Ole Miss side of the Superdome was rollicking, but not for long as everyone began to realize that flags were all over the field. As one looked back across the field, it resembled the scene from the motion picture *Gone with the Wind* that showed all those Civil War wounded. Bodies were just lying there. Some were holding ankles or knees. Some were being helped off the field. Others were hobbling off. Pieces of equipment, helmets, and shoes were lying around on the field. Trainers and doctors were running about trying to tend to the wounded. Both head coaches were screaming at the referees.

Several players tried to help Aeamon Lee up, but he couldn't get up. He lay on his back trying to find a position to get some comfort. Also, he was telling everybody around him, "They had too many men on the field. They should have been flagged for that. Go tell the referees about the illegal participation."

The referees conferred as a silence fell over the Superdome. The outcome of the game lay in the balance. It was in the referee's hands, and Aeamon Lee didn't like those odds. After the refs had taken their time to make sure they had the call right, the referee came toward the sideline and announced, "We have illegal participation on the blue team [Notre Dame]. The penalty has been declined. The touchdown is good. The game is over." Film would show later that at one point, there were fourteen Irish players on the field. The final score was 30–28 in Ole Miss's favor.

There was a thunderous roar from the Ole Miss's side. For one glorious moment, all was well with the world. There was hugging, running about, jumping up and down, and pile-ons; and the band struck up the fight song. Coach Wortham received the traditional barrel of Gatorade. Some fans slipped by security and were on the field. There was one "Hotty Toddy" yell after another. The team doctor and trainer were tending to Aeamon Lee and suggested that he immediately leave the field and go directly to the locker room. He would miss the Sugar Bowl Championship trophy and the Most Valuable Player trophy presentation, which was awarded to him. The team went around the stadium to thank the Ole Miss fans, and all of them stood together in front of the band as they played "From Dixie with Love." If there were one not shedding a few tears, he or she could not be found. It was a moment to be savored, to be remembered, and to be cherished for a lifetime.

The television announcers stumbled around in an attempt to explain the unexpected outcome. One admitted that the runback at the end of the game was great. Another announcer corrected him by saying, "Listen, it was not only great, but it was possibly the greatest runback in bowl history and certainly the most dramatic. Now we will all have to wait until tomorrow to find out the results of the final polls to see just who the national champion is." They spent their time speculating how that might turn out. Some still gave Notre Dame a chance to win because they just barely lost, and Ole Miss would have had to win convincingly. And Ole Miss would have to jump three spots to end up at number 1.

*   *   *

Aeamon Lee was put in an ambulance and taken to the emergency room at Charity Hospital in New Orleans. The medical team removed the crude stitches, cleaned the gash, and did x-rays. The spinal column had not been affected, and the cut had missed doing severe damage only by millimeters. They completed their work in the early morning hours of Tuesday, January 3. A trainer accompanied him to the hospital. The team was leaving shortly. Not knowing when he would be released, Webster, Aeamon Lee's roommate, had volunteered to drive him back home from New Orleans.

The hospital wanted to draw some blood from Aeamon Lee's arm, but he objected. He said, "I'll cooperate with whatever you want, except I cannot approve your taking my blood, and you would not understand the reason. I must reject this particular procedure." No, they didn't understand and explained why they needed to test his blood, but he stubbornly refused. He reassured them that he had a history of healing quickly.

He was put in a treatment room for observation and to wait for the gash to stop bleeding. Once he was in the room, a nurse came in and said, "We haven't been allowing visitors, but we thought you might like to see this one.

He said, "Well, invite them in."

And in walked Coach Leon Doria, the Notre Dame head coach. He said, "I wanted to tell you in person that was one outstanding performance you gave out there last night. One of the greatest I've ever seen. You should be proud of yourself and your team. But I'm primarily here to tell you that I heard about what happened to your back. I can't imagine what could have caused that injury. But I do want to promise you that I will personally investigate until I know for sure if it was one of our players. I want you to know that we don't stand for anything like that."

"Coach, you have the best team we played all year. By the way, what about that illegal participation at the end of the game?"

"That's something else I obviously have to deal with. I thought we had more discipline than that. Well, best of luck, and I wish you well in your career."

About an hour later, the nurse came in and announced that he had another visitor. Again, this was someone they thought he would want to see. This time it was Coach Wortham. He had the sports section of the New Orleans *Times-Picayune* in one hand and the Most Valuable Player trophy in the other.

He said, "They tell me you're going to be all right. That was quite a relief, because my allowing you to play at the end of the game went against everything I'd ever practiced as a head coach. I trusted you when you said it would be all right. I'm just sorry you got hurt the way you did." Aeamon Lee related the visit of Coach Doria and what he had said about it.

"Webster is going to drive you home, and we'll see you back on campus." Then he continued, "I can't put it into the proper words, but I do want to thank you for your part in making this such a special season. Since I first met you, I had an unusual appreciation for your abilities. And I think that I'm a better coach and a better man for having been around you. Now that's hard for me to say because I don't usually pay compliments like that. Oh, you've certainly tried my patience all right, but we worked through it. And I liked all those wise sayings you had for the team. I don't know where you got them, but we needed every single one. By the way, I've never seen a runback like the one you made there at the end of the game. I know we didn't teach you all those moves."

Aeamon Lee said, "A special friend of mine taught me how to do those. I'll thank him when I see him, and I will also thank the dear friend who gave me those sayings. They weren't original with me."

Coach Wortham said, "I've always felt close to my players. In a strange way, I've especially felt close to you, like you were a son. I knew you didn't have your family nearby and that you were making a courageous effort. I just want to shake your hand and thank you again for what you did, not just for the team, but for all of us in personal ways."

By this time, Aeamon Lee could see the sports page headline, "Notre Dame wins national championship. Ole Miss second in polls." Coach Wortham could tell that Aeamon Lee had seen the headline, and he said, "I really wanted to win it for you, the team, and the university. I'm sorry that we came up a little short. This is the second time they've won the national championship, and their only loss was to Ole Miss."

Aeamon Lee could tell that Coach needed some reassurance. He said, "Coach, let me remind you of something. We were picked to finish ninth in the conference. And you took this bunch of mostly inexperienced players during a rebuilding season, a few walk-ons and pickups, and you made us into real men. We became a powerful team and a competitive force. It was because of you that we ran the table. You made decisions no other coach would have made, and they all turned out right. No matter the polls, because we will always know in our hearts that on January 2, 1984, we beat the number one–ranked team in the nation on the field of play where it really counted. Nobody can ever take that away from us, and don't you ever forget it. 'The tragedy of life is in what dies inside a man while he lives.'[107] We must not let this cause us to die a little inside. I'm not, and I don't want you to."

Coach Wortham started walking toward the door. He stopped, turned around, and said, "What I didn't want to do was to take a thoroughbred and coach him into mediocrity. I don't think I did."

CHAPTER 5

The Homecoming
JANUARY 1984

On the morning of January 3, 1984, Aeamon Lee was discharged from Charity Hospital. The nurses gave him a walking cane, which would help relieve some of the pressure on his back. Webster drove him toward Goshen Wells, Mississippi, and home.

Aeamon Lee told Webster, "You know you didn't have to do this."

"I know, but I got to thinking that I needed to let my faith cause me to do some good works." They both laughed.

Webster added, "By the way, I felt stupid over there on the sidelines acting like I was signaling in a play when you were calling them on the field. I made up all kinds of weird signals, and I know they had spotters trying to figure out what I was calling. Wouldn't it have been hilarious to see them talking about my signals and trying to make sense out of it?"

"Yeah, you did look a little stupid doing that, but I did, at least, look over in that direction once in a while."

Aeamon Lee had to lay down in the back seat to try to find a comfortable position. Finally, they got close to home. He said to Webster, "I've heard that you can never go home again.[108] What do you think?"

"Well, it's never really the same. We'll always go back as visitors knowing that it will only be for a short time. We're the ones who have changed, and we have to love our family anyway."

Aeamon Lee looked at Webster and said, "You know, I think you are right, and that's very well stated. I like that."

Webster asked, "You've had quite a year. Looking back, what made the biggest difference in your being where you are today?"

Aeamon Lee thought for a while and said, "I lived and worked in these hills and hollows in Goshen Wells for all my life. When I graduated, I had a choice, and 'two roads diverged in a wood and I—I took the one less traveled by, and that has made all the difference.'" [109]

"What about you, Webster? A lot has happened to you as well. Looking back, what has affected you the most?"

Webster said, "Even though I didn't play much in the games, I felt that what I did in practice, preparations, and on the sideline was done well. I feel good about myself. I've ridden the emotional roller coaster, too, just dealing with all of your ups and downs. Heck, 'we can't all be heroes, because someone has to sit on the curb and clap as they go by.'" [110]

Aeamon Lee looked at him and said, "I don't know about that hero part, but, man, you just scored another one."

*　*　*

They passed by Zion's Grove church, and Aeamon Lee asked Webster if he would pull in the parking lot and stop. He got out of the car and, with his cane, started limping out to the grave of Jo-Nathan Markum. There was an American flag in a flower urn on the tombstone where the inscription had been engraved.

While Webster stayed behind in the car, Aeamon Lee turned his back to the car because it was an emotional moment for him. He didn't want Webster to see him talking.

He kneeled down, trying his best to deal with the profound pathos in his soul. He said, "I told coach I would be sure and thank the one who taught me all those moves like animals. So I'm here to tell you that you were right. Our backs were against the wall, and the breaks were going against us. You made the difference. I sure wish you could have been there, Jo-Nathan Markum. I felt that in a way you were there, giving me good advice as always. You truly were semper fi.[111] You remember when I was talking about living on the ethereal plane and you said, 'I sure wish I had it'? You never knew it would become true, my friend, but it did, because these and other mighty warriors, in the earthly battle slain, by their valor and their virtue walk the bright ethereal plane.[112] I'll come by to see you every chance I get. Rest, and go peacefully into that long night. For me, 'I have promises to keep and miles to go before I sleep.'[113] Then someday, I'll see you again, and we'll sit down, and we'll talk and talk until God comes along and puts us both to work."

As they neared home, they passed by where the Ramirez family had lived. They had now moved, and he could remember that they called him Santo Tomas. Hosea was the first one, besides his mother, to tell him that he had special abilities.

*   *   *

When they came to the turnoff that went up the hill to his house, they saw Maleah Marcelles running toward the car. Aeamon Lee rolled the window down, and Maleah was beside herself with joy. She kept touching his hand and pulling on his arm. She leaned into the car window to give him a hug. Aeamon Lee got out of the car and looked at Maleah in a way he had never done before. He raised his hand to her cheek and saw beauty and strength of character he had never fully appreciated until now. She had been the solid support, the one person who had loved him so much; she would not leave him to fight Caster Nuckolls alone. It was now coming to him like a burst of revelations; she rose above all the young women he had ever known. For a while, they just looked at each other as he moved closer and closer. Finally, he passionately embraced her over and over again.

Maleah attempted to say to him, "I know you've thought that I would hold you back, but I could never do that. Wherever you go—" Aeamon Lee only wanted to hold her and love her, forgetting about his back. Maleah also whispered these words: "Whatever it is that you have, I have some of it too."

Webster couldn't help but notice the romantic display of attraction that each had for the other, though he attempted to be inconspicuous. He had never seen this side of Aeamon Lee and even wondered if he was ever going to show this kind of emotion since he had focused so strongly on his academic and football goals.

Aeamon Lee knew that at the moment, he had to move on to the house. He said to Maleah, "I now know that you would never hold me back from my mission, but that does not mean that I should ignore the feelings I have for you. You have stood with me for a long time. Right now, I want you to go and tell the others that I have come home. I'll see you tomorrow."

Maleah slowly left and faithfully carried out his wishes.

* * *

The sun was now setting as they drove up the road to the house. As Aeamon Lee looked around at familiar sites, he noticed that nothing appeared the same as he knew it when growing up. The memories were failing because the places that spawned them were now disappearing. The paths were grown over, and the way was not so clear anymore. The nostalgia became blurred by the signs of a new generation that would come along to make their own memories. He saw a perfect parable of all that fades.

Even though he wanted to hold on to the past, time was fleeting, and change and new experience came and interrupted the status quo. Accepting that things would never be the same again and adjusting to a new day with new opportunities, he guessed, were part of growing up. While in his mind he knew it was inevitable, in his heart, he wanted to see the old paths.

Webster drove him up to the front porch of the house so he wouldn't have far to walk. It was nearly dark. Martha rushed out to see her boy while Plea was not far behind, taking his time. All of them helped him inside. Webster had a newfound feeling about himself for rolling up his sleeve and showing an altruistic side. Before he left, however, Aeamon Lee looked at him and said, "'O Captain! My Captain! Our fearful trip is done. The ship has weather'd every rack, the prize we sought is won. The port is near, the bells I hear, the people all-exulting. While follow eyes the steady keel, the vessel grim and daring.'"[114] These confident, valiant conquerors nodded at each other, and Webster departed for his home.

Aeamon Lee had been given a sack full of gauze and tape at the hospital with instructions that the dressing would need to be replaced later that day. With much gentleness, Martha carefully changed the bandage on his back. She said, "Aeamon Lee, what are these other things in the sack?"

"Oh, there are a couple of things there I got for you and Dad. I'll go ahead and give them to you even though I didn't get a chance to get them wrapped. I see you still have the little Christmas tree up, waiting for me to get home." On top of the sewing machine was the little cedar tree all decorated with homemade ornaments.

"Dad, I got you a 1984 Sugar Bowl jersey with the logos of each school on it. It's size XXL, so I think it will fit."

To Aeamon Lee's surprise, Plea said, "Well, let me see that. Yeah, I think that will fit." Right there, Plea put it on, looked in the mirror, and sported it around for the rest of the evening. "I just can't wait to show this to the fellows," he said. The thought kept coming to Aeamon Lee that his dad was definitely in a mood like he had not seen since before his accident.

Aeamon Lee gave Martha a set of Cajun utensils he found in New Orleans. She said she sure could use them and that they would really come in handy.

Later, they sat down at the supper table for some of Aeamon Lee's favorite food. He and Plea repeated a ritual they had experienced for many years together. After supper, Martha poured each of them a glass of buttermilk, then came a pan of freshly baked cornbread. They crumbled the cornbread in the milk. With spoon in hand, what followed was the partaking of a Southern delicacy that only those who have been reared in the rural South could fully appreciate.

Afterward, they just sat and had light family conversation. It was obvious that Martha and Plea were thrilled beyond words to have him home. It seemed they spent a lot of time just looking at him. Aeamon Lee reminded, "I told you that if you would put a candle in the window, as long as I could see the light, I would be home soon."

Eventually, the conversation got to the game. Martha and Plea had watched on their little television set, and Martha explained how anxious she was when they said that he had been hurt. He noticed that Plea was alert and spoke with a new optimism about things. At one point, Plea chimed in, "You know, I wanted to tell those referees a thing or two."

As the evening wore on, Aeamon Lee said he was a little tired and needed to go on to bed. Martha said, "Aeamon Lee, since we didn't get to have Christmas together, I have something for you too." She brought out a carefully wrapped Christmas box with a ribbon. Inside he found two new shirts Martha had made for him. One of them was black with white dots, the design he had always wanted. They had three-quarter-length sleeves. They were cotton and had been starched and ironed.

As he was admiring the brightly colored shirts, Plea said, "Aeamon Lee, I have a little something too." His hands were shaking a bit as he handed his son a simple box tied with string. Aeamon Lee carefully opened the box and took out some paper. He reached down and brought out a perfectly contoured wooden football that had been carefully carved, complete with laces and seams. The football stood on a little pedestal, which was all part of one piece. Carved on the front of the pedestal were the initials, A. L. M. Aeamon Lee swallowed and couldn't say anything. Plea swelled with pride, and together these two grown men silently hugged each other.

When Aeamon Lee went to his room, everything was fresh and clean. He put the carved football on the nightstand. He sat on the side of the bed looking at it. It had been carved out of walnut wood. When he pulled back the covers, he noticed that the sheets and pillowcases had been clothesline dried.

LITERARY PARALLELS IN THIS NOVEL BETWEEN AEAMON LEE MISTRAL– MALEAH MARCELLES AND YESHUA–MARY MAGDALENE*

1. "He looked straight into his mother's eyes and said, 'I've got to be about the business and work of my daddy. I know how to do it'" (page 8).

    "Did you not know that I must be about my Father's business?" (Luke 2:49 NASB).

2. "Maleah Marcelles was a neighbor of the Markums and Mistrals and was often referred to as a woman who was a tower of strength" (page 26).

    "Mary, who was called Magdalene" (Luke 8:2 NASB). *Magdalene* was a title and derived from a Hebrew word *Migdal edor* and referred to a "tower of the flock" (see Micah 4:8 NASB). Thus the Magdalene was a great lady, a tower of strength.

3. "Her [Maleah Marcelles] parents had died some years before; and because her sister, Marleece, was about ten years older than she was, she and her brother, Landon, were allowed to continue to live

on their own. They had inherited their parents' place and their resources, which meant they enjoyed a more comfortable life than most of their neighbors" (page 26).

"Now a certain man was sick, Lazarus of Bethany, the village of Mary and her sister Martha" (John 11:1 NASB).

4. "When he sensed he was fighting over some kind of injustice, he was unstoppable and unbeatable. It didn't make any difference what the situation was or how many people he had to subdue; he prevailed one way or another" (page 26).

"So he made a whip out of cords and drove them all out of the temple courts" (John 2:15 NRSV).

5. "He took his big hands and, starting with the top of Joel's head, gripped and rubbed his hands all over Joel's weak body all the way to his toes. He called the family in and asked them to continue washing Joel's body with the wet cloths. Joel broke out in sweat that dampened all the bed linens. He rose up in bed and told his mother that he was thirsty and hungry. His fever had broken, and soon his strength returned" (pages 35).

"But Jesus . . . healed the boy and gave him back to his father" (Luke 9:42 NASB).

6. "Aeamon Lee stopped and just looked at the woman, having compassion on her" (page 55).

"And when the Lord saw her, He felt compassion for her, and said to her, 'do not weep'" (Luke 7:13 NASB).

7. "I never told you this, but you were the one who made a difference in my life. I was able to get rid of all those demons that seemed to be around all the time" (page 87).

"And also, some women who had been healed of evil spirits and sicknesses: Mary who was called Magdalene, from whom seven demons had gone out" (Luke 8:2 NASB).

8. "After she wiped it clean of all the dust, dirt, and blood from the wound, her long unbound hair fell on his leg. She then took a tube of what she called special ointment and put some on his wound and told him it would make the wound heal faster so he would be ready for his big day" (page 93).

"Mary therefore took a pound of very costly perfume of pure nard, and anointed the feet of Jesus, and wiped His feet with her hair; the house was filled with the fragrance of the perfume . . . Let alone, in order that she may keep it for the day of my burial" (John 12:3, 7 NASB). This was Mary of Bethany who did this anointing (John 11:2 NASB). There is much evidence that Mary of Bethany and Mary Magdalene were the same person.

9. "Aeamon Lee, I just want you to know—and I don't think I've ever said this to you, though it's been in my heart ever since you came—you were a special gift, and we had waited a long time, as equal partners, for you to come. We kept feeling that someday you would come. We had almost given up hope. We've always known, as I explained, that you would have a special mission in your life, and I know that someday you will find it. We don't know what it is exactly, but we've got to let you start out on your journey" (pages 96).

"O Hope of Israel, our Savior in times of trouble! Why are you like a stranger to us? Why are you like someone passing through the land, stopping only for the night?" (Jeremiah 14:8 NASB).

10. "He remembered the envelope that Maleah Marcelles had given him. He got it out and opened it up. There was $31.68 in it with a note that read, "I know that you will need this. I know you're just like all the rest of us in not having a lot of money. But we admire what you are doing, so some of my friends and I put a little money together to help you out" (page 98).

In Greek gematria, 3,168 is the numerical value of the most sacred name in Christianity: Lord Jesus Christ.

11. "She said, 'I know you don't get down this way often, but even if you just need to talk, here is my phone number to call, 222-153-1746'" (page 224).

The number 153 is not only the number of fishes caught in the net, nor is it merely a basic measurement of the Holy City (New Jerusalem). By gematria, the number 153 is also the sum of the letters of h Magdalhnh, "the Magdalene." The kingdom of God is like "a grain of mustard seed," a simile that has the sum of 1,746 and represents the image of fusion.

12. "He said to Maleah, 'I now know that you would never hold me back from my mission . . . I want you to go and tell the others that I have come home'" (page 259).

After the resurrection, Mary Magdalene met Jesus in the garden and He said to her, 'Stop clinging to me . . . but go to My brethren" (John 20:17 NASB).

13. Observe that Maleah Marcelles knew the Scriptures as well as Aeamon Lee. "Whatever it is that you have, I have some of it too" (page 259). Mary Magdalene knew the meaning of the crucifixion and resurrection when only a few others did.

* Hints to historical similarities in these four characters are found in the use of Greek gematria, a literary device involving the use of numerical values. A combination of behavior, sayings, and numbers indicate in subtle ways persons they symbolize.

See also Margaret Starbird, *Magdalene's Lost Legacy: Symbolic Numbers and the Sacred Union in Christianity* (Rochester, Vermont: Bear and Company, 2003).

ENDNOTES

1. Bible, James 2:16 NASB.

2. William Congreve (1670–1729), English dramatist.

3. "Midnight Special," performed by Creedence Clearwater Revival, words by Lead Belly (Huddie William Ledbetter, 1885–1949).

4. *Billy Jack*, 1971, National Student Film Corporation, words by Coven.

5. President Abraham Lincoln (1809–1865), sixteenth president of the US.

6. Henry David Thoreau (1817–1862), American author, philosopher, and transcendentalist.

7. Bible, 1 Samuel 17:1–58 NASB.

8. Bible, Mark 11:15–18 NLT.

9. "Again I looked, and behold I saw a white cloud, and sitting on the cloud One resembling a Son of Man, with a crown of gold on his head and a sharp scythe in his hand" (NASB).

10. Bible, "And another will write on his hand, 'Belonging to the Lord'" (Isaiah 44:5 NASB).

11. William Faulkner (1897–1962), American novelist, Nobel Prize for Literature winner (1950).

12. Words by Al Price, based on the Bible (Psalm 143 NASB).

13. Bible, 1 Corinthians 14:26, "The Voice."

14. President John F. Kennedy (1917–1963), thirty-fifth president of the US.

15. "Have You Ever Seen the Rain?" performed by Creedence Clearwater Revival.

16. "Who'll Stop the Rain," performed by Creedence Clearwater Revival.

17. Thomas della Peruta.

18. "I think, therefore I shoot."

19. "You can, come on, strive."

20. "Our reason for living."

21. Arnold Toynbee (1889–1975), British historian.

22. Bible, Ecclesiastes 4:11 NASB.

23. Ralph Waldo Emerson (1803–1882), American poet and essayist.

24. E. D. Nixon, Montgomery Alabama Improvement Association, American civil rights leader.

25. Myra Angelou, *I Know Why the Caged Bird Sings*, Random House, 1979.

26. Robert Lewis Stevenson (1850–1894), Scottish poet, novelist, and essayist

27. Eudora Welty (1909–2001), American Pulitzer Prize writer and photographer.

28. From the poem *"George Gray"* by Edgar Lee Masters (1869–1950), American poet, biographer, and dramatist.

29. Bible, Job 12:7 NLT.

30. Ralph Waldo Emerson (1803–1882), American poet and essayist.

31. Oliver Wendell Holmes (1809–1894), American poet and essayist.

32. Johann Wolfgang von Goethe (1749–1832), German writer.

33. Langston Hughes (1902–1967), American poet.

34. Bible, Ecclesiastes 9:10 NASB.

35. Bible, Proverbs 18:24 NLT.

36. Eleanor Roosevelt (1884–1962), America's most influential First Lady.

37. Winston Churchill (1874–1965), British statesman, soldier, and author.

38. Line from the character Tom Joad (Henry Fonda) in 20th Century Fox *Grapes of Wrath*, 1940.

39. Line from the character Martin Brody (Roy Scheider) in *Jaws*, Universal Pictures, 1975.

40. Line from Captain (Strother Martin), Road Prison 36, in *Cool Hand Luke*, 1967.

41. Lines from Billy Jack (Tom Laughlin) in *Billy Jack*, National Student Film Corporation, 1971.

42. Lisa Birnbach, *The Preppy Handbook*, 1980.

43. "Life's greatest good."

44. Dante Alighieri (1265–1321), Italian poet.

45. "Long as I Can See the Light," performed by Creedence Clearwater Revival.

46. Henry David Thoreau (1817–1862), American author, philosopher, and transcendentalist.

47. Theodore Roosevelt (1858–1919), twenty-sixth president of the US. *"Citizenship in a Republic"* speech at the Sorbonne, Paris, April 23, 1910.

48. Henry James (1843–1916), American author, known for novels and novellas based on themes of consciousness.

49. Ralph Waldo Emerson (1803–1882), American poet and essayist.

50. Bible, Ecclesiastes 10:8–9 NLT.

51. Henry Wadsworth Longfellow (1802–1882), American poet, educator, and linguist.

52. Bible, Mark 16:15 NASB.

53. Francis Butler Simkins, *The Everlasting South*, Baton Rouge: Louisiana State University, 1963

54. Winston Churchill (1874–1965), British statesman, soldier, and author

55. Ernest Hemingway (1899–1961), American novelist.

56. Bible, Ecclesiastes 5:7 NLT.

57. Søren Kierkegaard (1813-1855), Danish existentialist philosopher.

58. Bible, Matthew 6:6 NASB.

59. Bible, Ecclesiastes 9:10 NASB.

60. Bible, Ecclesiastes 10:10 NLT.

61. William Faulkner (1897–1962), American novelist. Acceptance speech for winning the Nobel Prize for Literature, Stockholm, Sweden, Dec. 10, 1950.

62. Line from Sam Spade (Humphrey Bogart) in Warner Brothers' *Maltese Falcon*, 1941.

63. Performed by Creedence Clearwater Revival, words by John Fogarty.

64. President Abraham Lincoln (1809–1865), sixteenth president of the US.

65. Shelby Foote (1917–2005), Civil War historian.

66. Frank E. Everett Jr., Graduate of the University of Mississippi, 1932.

67. In 1983, the University of Mississippi formally disassociated itself from the Confederate flag.

68. Unknown.

69. From *Othello* by William Shakespeare (1564–1616), English poet and playwright.

70. Marcus Aurelius (AD 121–180), stoic philosopher and emperor of Rome.

71. From *A Tale of Two Cities* by Charles Dickens (1812–1870), English author.

72. In World War I, the battle-tested veteran marines served a central role in the US entry into the conflict, and at the Battle of Belleau Wood, marine units were

in the front, earning the marines a reputation as the first to fight. This battle marked the creation of the marines' reputation in modern history. They rallied under the battle cry of "Retreat? Hell, we just got here!" The marines drove German forces from the area. Captured prisoners and German letters referred to the marines in the battle as *Teufelshunden*, literally, "Devil Dogs," a nickname marines proudly hold to this day.

The French government renamed Belleau Wood *Boies de la Brigade de Marine*, or "Wood of the Marine Brigade," and decorated both the Fifth and Sixth Regiments with the Crois de Guerre. Franklin Delano Roosevelt, then secretary of the navy, stated that enlisted marines would henceforth wear the Eagle, Globe, and Anchor on their uniform collar.

73. Traditional Spiritual, There is a Balm in Gilead.

74. Ernest Hemingway (1899–1961), American novelist.

75. Bible, Ecclesiastes 7:4 NLT.

76. An old spiritual song sung by Paul Robeson.

77. Bible, Psalm 23:4 KJV.

78. Bible, Psalm 121:1–2 KJV.

79. Bible, John 14:1–3 KJV.

80. Bible, John 15:13 KJV.

81. Bible, 2 Timothy 4:7 KJV.

82. Bible, Psalm 103:14 NLT.

83. Line from the song "Abraham, Martin and John," performed by Dion. Words and music by Richard Holler, 1968.

84. President Herbert L. Hoover (1874–1964), thirty-first president of the US.

85. George Bernard Shaw (1856–1950), Irish playwright, Nobel Prize for Literature winner, 1925.

86. John Donne (1572–1631), English poet and writer.

87. Herodotus (484–425 BC), Greek historian.

88. Taps began as a revision to the signal for Extinguish Lights (Lights Out) at the end of the day. Up until the Civil War, the infantry call for Extinguish lights was the one set down in Silas Casey's (1801–1882) Tactics, which had been borrowed from the French. Union General Daniel Butterfield adapted the music for Taps for his brigade (Third Brigade, First Division, Fifth Army Corps, Army of the Potomac) in July 1862.

89. Four months after the marine barracks bombing, the US Marines were ordered to start pulling out of Lebanon. It was the bloodiest day in the Marine Corps' history since WWII, when marines fought to secure Iwo Jima. The French also joined the US in this peacekeeping mission. A separate blast on the French compound killed fifty-eight French service members. There is a Beirut Memorial at Arlington National Cemetery. Some of the memorial statements are as follows:

> They did not make war. They were simply victims of war in the honorable attempt to keep the peace. The gift of these men was of the ultimate quality and we know that it was of such value that it cannot be given again.

> They came in peace, and they wanted to provide an opportunity for people to live in peace.

> No one was ever held accountable for the 1983 blasts.

> Arlington National Cemetery, Beirut Barracks Memorial.

90. Bible, Ecclesiastes 9:11 NLT.

91. Plato (327–347 BC), ancient Greek philosopher.

92. Words by Al Price.

93. Bible, 1 Corinthians 11:22 NASB.

94. Bible, Ecclesiastes 4:12 NLT.

95. "Slay them all! God will know his own."

96. "Yes, we can."

97. Number approved by the North American Numbering Plan Association.

98. Mahatma Gandhi (1869–1848), Indian political and spiritual leader.

99. Gospel of Mary Magdalene 4:27; 5:4.

100. Mark Twain (1835–1910), American humorist, novelist, short-story writer.

101. First recorded by Bo Carter, 1928.

102. General George Patton (1885–1945), US Army general in WWII.

103. Performed by Creedence Clearwater Revival.

104. President Abraham Lincoln (1809–1865), sixteenth president of the US.

105. David Crockett (1786–1836), American folk hero who died at the Alamo, warrior, and statesman from Tennessee.

106. Bible, Ecclesiastes 7:8 NLT.

107. Albert Einstein (1879–1955), American theoretical physicist and Nobel Prize in Physics winner (1921). He was born in Germany but moved to the US in 1933.
108. Thomas Wolfe (1900–1938), American writer.
109. Robert Frost (1874–1963), American poet.
110. Will Rogers (1879–1935), American humorist and entertainer.
111. "Always faithful," motto of the United States Marine Corps.
112. Alfred Russel Wallace (1823–1913), English naturalist and social critic.
113. Robert Frost (1874–1963), American poet.
114. Walt Whitman (1819–1892), American poet.

Printed in the United States
By Bookmasters